James Grieve Press

STOLEN

PJ Adams

Web and mailing list: http://www.pollyjadams.com/
Twitter: @pollyjadams
Facebook: https://www.facebook.com/pollyjadamswriter

Cover images © prometeus and ipopba
Cover design by James Grieve

Published by James Grieve Press

ISBN-10: 172460774X
ISBN-13: 978-1724607744

Also by PJ Adams

Rebound (a Section Eight novel)
Trust (a Bailey Boys novel)
Hit Me (a Bailey Boys novel)
Ruthless (a Bailey Boys novel)
Damage
Let's Make This Thing Happen
Escape
Four Temptations
The Wings of Desire
Outliers
Black Widow
The Object of His Desire
Winner Takes All

Writing as Polly J Adams:
Loaded
Bad Girls
Girl Talk
The Billionaires' Sex Club
Seduced

Writing as Ruby Fielding:
Last Alpha
Rogue Male
Snow Wolf

PROLOGUE

Why didn't Jimmy Lazenby just focus on the stripper, like any normal guy would do?

Why did he let his attention drift, his eyes skipping around the room until he saw *them?* His brother Glenn, sitting at that booth with Mel Conner, the woman Jimmy had once, long ago, briefly loved.

The stripper.

He focused on her again, if only to gather his thoughts. She hung one-handed from a pole on a small stage to one side of the long, low room, looking back over her shoulder at Jimmy as he paused in the club's entrance. Her free arm trailed gracefully out toward the half-empty room, an almost ballet-like grace to the curves and line of that arm and her body, the string of her thong cutting her bare ass in two like cheesewire on a soft brie.

She had a tattoo of angel wings across her shoulder blades, and blue eyes that fixed on him with some kind of desperation. Dancing here can't exactly have been the most sought-after gig in town.

Jimmy had been in seedier places than this – way seedier – but there was something about this girl, and the others working the room for private dances, that made his heart sink.

He was distracting himself, he knew that. Pausing. Hesitating in that brief moment when he could have turned and walked away from this dive. Walked away from this town forever, as he had done once before.

Then Glenn spotted him, and something in the way he straightened and rolled his shoulders made Mel look first at him and then follow his stare, find Jimmy, and if his heart had sunk moments before, now it plummeted.

Mel. Those eyes, the look in them – betraying something like the same emotions, the same feelings of *Sweet god, not him.*

Jimmy looked away. The stripper was still studying him, perhaps sensing that something was going on, that he wasn't the usual customer.

He gave a little shrug.

He should have stuck with the stripper. Taken her for a private dance and whatever else she had on offer in one of those curtained-off booths at the rear of the club.

Anything would have been simpler than looking up, meeting Glenn's stare again, nodding and heading across the room to join them.

In the ten years since Jimmy had last seen him, Glenn's features had rounded out, and he had a long scar over one eye that Jimmy didn't remember from before. His dark hair was slicked back, his jaw peppered with stubble, and his eyes narrowed as he watched his kid brother approach across the club's sticky wooden floor.

As he approached Jimmy noticed how one arm trailed across the back of the U-shaped leatherette bench he shared with Mel. Proprietorial.

Mel. Blonde hair cut in choppy spikes, a tiny black nose stud, a wary look. She'd been beautiful ten years ago, but now she sucked the air out of Jimmy's lungs. She was everything the girl back then had promised to become, half of the future they were supposed to share.

He had to look away.

Glenn nodded at the seat opposite, as if his brother had been waiting for permission to sit.

Jimmy remained standing.

"Surprised you came back," Glenn said, finally, his voice – always surprisingly soft – barely audible above the thump and grind of the dancer's music.

"It'd be rude not to, really, wouldn't it?" Jimmy said. "Now the old bastard's dead and all."

The old bastard. Their father. Another of the reasons Jimmy had left this town with no intention of ever coming back. He hadn't planned to return even when he heard the news, was only here now because he had to be.

Glenn's eyes briefly narrowed even more, then a grin split his face and he tipped his head back, laughing. "You cheeky fucker, Jimmy. You haven't changed a bit, have you?"

Glenn spoke with more of a London accent now, while Jimmy spoke with a carefully cultivated anonymity. Glenn liked to stand out, just as much as his brother tried to blend in. Each to his own.

Jimmy glanced at Mel, saw her studying him. She was hard to read – always had been. He hadn't expected her to be here. Was she *with* Glenn, or was her being here just coincidence?

Jimmy knew not to believe in coincidence, though: there must be a reason for her being here, just as there was a reason he hadn't been told, because if he'd known she would be here he'd never have come home.

Mel.

The old, old story. Boy meets girl. Boy fucks up and breaks girl's heart – and his own. Boy runs away and pretends he doesn't care, and eventually teaches himself how to stop… *feeling.*

"You're staring, Jimbo. Don't you know it's rude to stare?" Glenn might have changed his accent, but he hadn't lost the bullying sneer. Jimmy met his look and realized he didn't care. He really didn't care anymore.

He hadn't understood until this moment how far he'd moved on. All this, it really was long behind him. Another life, another person.

"Are we burying him or burning him?" he asked.

"Cremation," said Glenn. "Harder for you to dance on the grave, then." He laughed again. There was no humor in that laugh.

Jimmy glanced at Mel again. Testing himself, perhaps, trying to see if there was even the faintest spark remaining.

Nothing.

He sat, and Glenn signaled to someone for drinks. Three glasses of whisky were brought over, almost immediately. So like his older brother not to ask what anyone wanted, just to order. He was showing off, Jimmy knew, making sure he understood how everyone in this dive was ready to jump at the slightest hint of a command from him. It was all his now, after all.

Jimmy knew he was supposed to be impressed.

"Your father?" said Mel, glancing between the two of them. "I'm sorry. I didn't know."

"Didn't ask, did you?" said Glenn.

So maybe the two of them weren't a thing, after all.

Jimmy met her look, shrugged, and she gave a slight nod. It felt strange to be communicating so easily again – a gesture, a look, conveying so much understanding – and it felt briefly as if no time had passed.

He turned his look away, watching the dancer with the eye-watering thong.

"Friday," said Glenn. "If you're free?"

The funeral. Jimmy nodded, still watching the girl. She looked bored now, Jimmy's arrival only a brief point of interest for her. Her attention had shifted to a fiftyish guy in a suit, who sat at a table idly thumbing the screen of his cellphone with one of the other girls clinging to his arm.

Jimmy already knew the funeral was Friday, just as he knew Glenn had the majority stake in this club. He knew what car his brother drove and where he liked to eat, knew he had an office at the rear of the old family pub he liked to use as a base when he was back in their home town.

He knew a lot about his big brother.

It's what he did.

But Mel… She was a wildcard.

He didn't like surprises.

"Don't worry," said Glenn. "I've taken care of everything. You just have to turn up. If you want to, that is."

"I came back," Jimmy said, simply.

Glenn nodded, and for a time they said nothing more. Not so much an easy silence, as a *Where the fuck do we begin?* one.

"See him?" said Glenn finally, leaning closer to Mel, his arm still trailing along the back of the bench. He nodded in what he probably thought was a subtle way toward the suited guy, still thumbing his phone. "Local detective inspector."

"Watching this place?" Jimmy asked. "Watching *you*?" In his first glance around the club he'd noticed the guy, thought he had a look of the Old Bill about him, almost as world-weary as the dancer.

"You'd think, right? But no. Had him checked out when he started coming here, didn't I? Turns out our detective inspector's just here to inspect the girls, if you know what I mean."

Mel laughed, but she was faking it, wanting Glenn to think she was impressed.

"Get all sorts in here," Glenn went on. He always had liked the attention. "Football players. Showbiz types. The lot. We get one guy, he has a fleet of yachts on the Med. He can have whatever he wants, and what does he want most? A bit of rough like this. Always the way, isn't it? Even someone like that only really wants what he shouldn't have, doesn't he?"

"Is that what you do? You get it for them, just like Dad used to do?"

And so it came back to their father. Underworld fixer, the man in the middle who could provide anything for anyone and always got away with it.

"Jealous?"

Jimmy looked away. Let him think that. Let him believe whatever he liked if it stopped him digging into why his brother was really here.

The dancer finished, still wearing her thong. A girl had to have standards, even here, Jimmy supposed. Stepping off the stage, she went to join the detective and the other girl departed, following some unwritten code between the dancers.

Jimmy should have stuck with the stripper. It would have been so much less complicated.

"How was it?" Jimmy asked, surprised that he wanted to know.

Glenn understood immediately, and said, "Messy. Lung cancer, spread to lymph, liver, brain. Only three or four months ago he was right as rain, same old bastard he ever was, and then... Coughing his insides out. Literally." A shrug, an arching of eyebrows – an oddly dismissive expression for something so awful. It wasn't often you saw Glenn betraying his feelings, even if it was by a gesture of dismissal.

"He was, wasn't he?" Jimmy said. He didn't need to add: *A bastard.*

"He was. But I stood by him, didn't I, while you just walked away."

Jimmy looked around the dimly lit club. This place was only a tiny part of the network their father had built up, he knew. He could have been part of it all, had his share. The old man's legacy. He could have been a bastard, just like him. Just like Glenn.

He risked a look at Mel, and regretted it. He'd walked away from all of this, her included, and now, every time he looked at her, he couldn't help seeing what might have been.

She'd hated what he was back then. Hated that he was a Lazenby, a part of all this. He wanted to tell her he'd spent the last ten years trying to make up for it all, trying to be one of the good guys. He shut down on those feelings, then. He didn't do that shit. He didn't let anyone in. Not anymore.

A new dancer had stepped onto the stage, a black girl with silky, blue-black hair that was clearly a wig. With long fingers she teased at a gauzy top that hung open from her shoulders and did little to conceal her figure, while her other hand curled around the pole so she could swing to one side. The detective inspector was watching her, even as the previous dancer sat with him, one hand on his arm. Was he like the guy Glenn had mentioned, one of these men who was only interested in what he didn't yet have?

Mel was still watching him, still impossible to read.

And then it all fell into place. Mel, Glenn, the missing girl, Harriet Rayner.

Mel knew Harriet's family, almost certainly knew the girl herself. He hadn't made the connection until now –

he'd had no reason to, because he hadn't expected to find Mel here.

But now he saw that Mel was here for the same reason Jimmy was. Somehow she'd found out his brother was one of the last people to have been seen with Harriet before she went missing, and she was here to dig.

The only difference was, Jimmy knew what he was doing, while Mel was an amateur.

She didn't understand what she was getting into.

Didn't know just what kind of bastard Glenn Lazenby was.

And what kind of danger she was putting herself in just by being here.

The whisky burned in his throat. He'd only ever been a whisky drinker to blend in, like now. Generally, he tried not to drink. Losing control only ever exposes you. He'd learned that lesson a long time ago.

They talked a little more. Glenn told his brother who would be at the funeral, relatives Jimmy hadn't seen for years, a few names he recognized as acquaintances of the old man – he wasn't sure Trevor Lazenby had ever had anyone close enough to qualify as a friend. So many people Jimmy had never expected to see again.

When Mel made excuses, Jimmy watched Glenn's eyes tracking her across the club to the restroom, eyes fixed on the way she filled those dove-gray jeans and the way she moved.

Then Glenn turned with a lecherous smile, knowing it would wind his brother up.

"You fucked up there, didn't you, bro'? Could have had all that."

And Jimmy could have told him. Told him it wasn't *him*, it was everything around him. That the more she had found out about the family, the more she saw how impossible it was. How back then she'd seen the world as black or white, moral absolutes rather than points on a spectrum, and Jimmy hadn't yet worked out which way his murky shade of gray would go. He probably still hadn't, even now: his life was all about doing the right thing, but not always the right way, after all. Did that make him a good person, or just another shade of his old man?

He shrugged. He'd fucked up. He'd lost her, hadn't stood up for himself and defended his particular shade of gray.

"Whatever," he said.

"Yeah," said his brother. "Whatever."

Jimmy had forgotten how much that sneering tone wound him up. The look on Glenn's face.

He stood, went over to the bar and asked for tap water.

He wasn't usually so unfocused. He'd underestimated the impact of being back here, of seeing Glenn again, perhaps even of coming to fully understand that the old man was gone.

And he hadn't expected Mel.

A short time later she emerged from a dark doorway. She hadn't seen him at the bar yet, and stood hesitating, as if trying to decide whether to come back to the table or simply to walk away. Right then Jimmy willed her to take the latter option. Walk out of there. Get away from Glenn, away from *him*.

There were all kinds of reasons she shouldn't be here right now.

She spotted Jimmy, met his eye, threaded her way through the tables, the scattering of punters. Some of them watched her rather than the dancer – all that naked flesh on display and eyes were drawn to Mel, the way she moved, the toss of the blonde hair and the swing of that ass.

She'd always had that about her.

She paused before Jimmy, eyes fixed on his. A challenging look. A searching one, too. Maybe she was having as much trouble reading him, as he was her.

He wanted to tell her.

He wanted to tell her he understood what she was doing here, why she was sucking up to Glenn and why she was laughing at his jokes and pretending to be impressed. That he understood she was digging, and that she thought she was being clever and getting away with it, even when she was being way too obvious.

He wanted to tell her he was here because of her – for now he understood that as well as being sent here to look into the disappearance of Harriet Rayner, he was also here to look out for Mel and stop her from putting herself at risk. He wanted to tell her who he was, who he had become. *What* he'd become.

And yes, he'd admit that he wanted to see the look in her eye, wanted to impress her, just as Glenn clearly wanted to impress her.

Above all, he wanted to tell her she was in danger. Every second she was here, every question she asked, she was digging herself deeper into something she didn't understand, couldn't comprehend.

He wanted to tell her all that, but he couldn't, because when you're an officer in Section Eight, a branch of the security services so secret not many people even know it exists, a unit that operates on the murky fringes of the law to do whatever is necessary to get the right result… when you're someone like that, someone like Jimmy Lazenby, you can't tell people, can't even hint, not even when you desperately want to impress the girl you won and loved and almost immediately lost again and who now, when you meet her look, snatches the air from your lungs.

He looked away. He didn't do this shit. He didn't let people get to him.

He was too professional to let that happen.

"You have to get out of here," he told her. "No matter how bad you think this is, it's worse, and you're not equipped to handle it. Leave now. Stand up, slap me across the face just like I know you want to, and storm out. I'll tell Glenn I pissed you off and in the meantime you'll have a chance to get away. Run, Mel. Leave this to me. My people. Get out of here."

She understood. She knew he wouldn't say something like that lightly. She must know he was trying to protect her.

Her eyes narrowed, and he saw a tensing in the tendons at either side of her neck, a tightening of the shoulders.

She was fast. No backswing, her arm straightened, her hand flat, the palm stinging against his cheek with a sound like whiplash.

Then she turned and walked back to the booth where Glenn sat laughing.

Jimmy couldn't do anything, was powerless.

He couldn't just drag her out of there – that first glance around the club when he'd arrived had picked out two bouncers and at least three other guys almost certainly in Glenn's employ. His brother owned this place and the people in it. Jimmy wouldn't stand a chance.

And so, just then, all he could do was finish his water, stand, and walk away, hoping desperately this wouldn't be the last time he set eyes on Mel Conner, the girl he'd loved, the girl he'd lost, the girl who had changed him forever.

1. MEL, A FEW DAYS EARLIER

Voicemail, again. "Hi. You know what this is, you know what to do, so beeeeep."

She'd heard that message three times now, and this time, finally, decided to leave a response. "Hey, Harriet. Mel here. But you know that. Anyway… Call me, yeah? You're starting to make me worry, and that's not cool, okay? So… you know what to do."

Mel didn't even understand why she was worrying like this. Yes, Harriet had failed to turn up the previous afternoon when they were supposed to be going shopping, but Harriet was hardly the most reliable of people. Just turned seventeen, the trip had been a late birthday treat, not something she'd be likely to forget about, but still… Harriet could be a law unto herself sometimes.

Maybe it was the big sister, little sister thing. Mel was ten years older, and there was no actual family connection, but they'd been close for a long time now. The two had a connection, an easy understanding where they would communicate with an expression – a roll of the eyes, a subtle smirk, a wrinkling of the nose – and finish each other's sentences. Mel had lost count of how many times people had asked if they were sisters.

But now…

It was Sunday, and even if she'd forgotten the arrangements they'd made or got distracted, Harriet would have been in touch. She would, at least, have answered her phone.

"Hey, Jo. Mel. Yeah, that's right. Listen, have you heard from Harriet recently? She was supposed to meet up with me yesterday, but… No? Oh, okay, then. If you do hear anything, though, right?"

She sat back in the over-sized beanbag that occupied one corner of the little loft bedroom she had in a house-share in north London. Outside, a train rumbled past. The window set into the sloping ceiling showed a rectangle of blue bisected by a wispy contrail.

None of Harriet's friends knew anything. Nobody had seen her since Friday.

She should leave it, but she couldn't convince herself that this was just Harriet being flaky old Harriet.

There was another call she could make, but she hesitated, knowing that would be an escalation in many ways. She'd learned never to ask her father for favors, knew it always became more complicated than it should.

But… Harriet.

Even if the nagging fear gripping Mel's belly was a false alarm she knew she would hate herself if she did nothing. What kind of friend was that? What kind of faux-sister?

She had to make that call.

"Dad?"

She walked across short grass. Sun shone down from the blue sky she had glimpsed from her bedroom's dormer window. Families played ball games all around her. Dogs chased and barked.

Her ear hurt from pressing the phone too hard against the side of her head. She forced herself to relax, let the tension go from her shoulders, her jaw.

"Melissa." He never gave anything away – no expression, no intonation to give a clue as to his mood. When she'd first moved away to go to university it had taken her a long time to get used to how he was on the phone, and she'd had to learn not to take it personally. He was a far easier man in person.

Sometimes getting outside, with normal life all around, was the best way to deal with this.

"How're you doing, Dad?"

"Oh, you know."

She didn't. That was the point of asking. When had he ever given a straight answer to anything?

"Listen, I just wanted to pick your brains." Straight to the point – cut the small talk. "You remember Harriet Rayner? Penny's daughter? I've been trying to get in touch with her, but, well… nothing. It's not like her. I don't know what's happened. Nobody's seen her since Friday. What's the appropriate thing to do here? How long do I leave it? What can I do?"

"Have you asked Penny?"

"You know what she's like." Even flakier than her daughter, Penny Rayner had never found life easy. "I don't know the last time Harriet even saw her mother."

"Is that normal?"

"For them, yes." Harriet might only have just turned seventeen, but she'd lived on her own for most of the last year in an apartment funded by the trust fund her late father had left her, knowing she and her mother could never actually live together.

"Has anyone reported her missing?"

"I don't know. I haven't. That's why I'm asking. I don't know what a normal person does in these circumstances."

"Do you have any reason to suspect she's at risk? Either from other people, or…"

Mel swallowed. Looked around at all the happy little groups in the park. Her father didn't need to finish that sentence, even though it was an obvious thing to ask.

"She was doing well, Dad. Going to college. Happy. I see a lot of her. I'd know if she was… I don't know… *unstable.*" Like her mother.

Silence.

"What do you want?" It sounded blunt, but that's just how he was: he knew there was a point to this call – he'd probably already worked out what it was – and he was a direct man.

"Advice?" Mel said, tentatively. "Help?"

It was the great unspoken. What he did… who he was. The strings he could pull but never acknowledge.

"Report it, Melissa. Do the right thing. Then leave it to the professionals. That's the way to handle it. And when she turns up in a couple of days, back from the kind of bender her mother used to pull, you can be embarrassed for making a fuss but you'll know you did the right thing."

He was trying to be kind, but it was the sort of kindness that felt like a slap.

She wasn't asking him to tell her to do what everyone else does in a situation like this. She was asking him to *help*.

And she knew he was right and she should never have asked. Whatever he did in the corridors of power, it wasn't something that could – or *should* – be exploited for personal reasons.

"Sorry," she said softly. "I shouldn't have asked."

"No, you shouldn't," he said. "But I'd be disappointed if you hadn't at least tried."

Penny Rayner lived in what had been a free-standing garage in the garden of a very up-market house in north London. Mel always thought it an odd choice. On the one hand, it allowed her to continue to live in the kind of neighborhood she had when her husband had still been alive. But on the other, every time she looked out of her converted garage and saw her surroundings, it was a reminder of the life she had lost. Of the fortune she had eaten into for drugs and rehab when her husband had been alive; and then of the fact that his will had left her a carefully managed income and the wherewithal to pay for this modest home, living a life that was a quiet shadow of the one she'd had with him.

Mel wasn't quite sure what to expect when she rang on the doorbell, but she wasn't ready for–

"Melissa! Have you found her? Is she safe?"

Penny Rayner's eyes were wide, the whites showing all the way around the irises, made even more dramatic by exaggerated use of mascara and eyeshadow, the animated workings of her mouth emphasized by thick red lipstick so dark it was almost black – a shade chosen to match the dark auburn hair cut into an Eton crop.

Mel couldn't work out if the woman was high or simply alarmed.

Gently, she extricated herself from Penny Rayner's grip on both arms, so tight it must surely leave bruising.

She'd expected confusion, had been trying to work out how to broach the subject of Harriet's whereabouts without alarming a woman already prone to outbreaks of paranoia and anxiety, not to mention the various pharmaceutical ways she had of coping with those outbreaks.

Or better, she'd hoped Penny might actually know where her daughter was.

Now, Mel felt as if a lead weight had descended into her belly, a confirmation that her fears were well-founded.

"You don't know where she is?"

Penny had wrapped her arms around herself when Mel eased her hands away from that tight grip on her. Now, she shook her head. Looking closer, Mel saw faint black panda smudges around each eye from where she'd rubbed away tears.

"When did you last speak to her?"

Penny shrugged, those wide eyes turning away. "I don't know. What month is it now?"

Stupid question.

Penny and Harriet rarely spoke, barely acknowledged each other's existence, but Mel knew she kept tabs on her daughter. The woman had no concept of normal timekeeping, so on more than one occasion Mel had been woken in the early hours by a call to ask how Harriet was keeping. She suspected these calls had something to do with the peaks and troughs of Penny's emotional condition, but at least they showed she gave a shit.

"Have you spoken to anyone?" asked Mel. "Any of her friends?"

"You!" That shrug and eye-slide again, this time accompanied by a fragile smile. "I asked Jo and... what's her name? Surita. One of them, I forget who, saw her on Friday, I think. Or Thursday."

"So what makes you think she's actually missing?"

"Saturday. It's the anniversary. She always goes and lays flowers, first thing in the morning. I… I see her there. I watch."

Mel put a hand on Penny's arm and gave a gentle squeeze. Three years since her husband had passed away, the glue that had held this brittle family together. She hadn't realized Saturday was the anniversary.

"Do you think… Was she upset?" Unbalanced. Over-emotional. Mel realized she was repeating her father's questions, sounding like him, but this was a question that had to be raised. Particularly as it was the anniversary of Harriet's father's death.

For the first time, she found herself believing her young friend might have done something stupid.

Penny was shaking her head. "No, no. Harriet, she always had a… a *sensible* head, do you know what I mean?"

Mel nodded. For all her unreliability, it was hard to imagine Harriet losing control of herself as her mother had repeatedly done over the years.

"Have you reported her missing?"

Penny gave a brief nod, eyes averted again. "This morning," she said. "There's a superintendent I know, an old chum of Geoffrey's. I thought he would listen."

Mel sighed. There was so much unsaid in those last five words: squashed hopes, a sense of being let down, the implication that her husband's old friend *hadn't* listened. She reached out, squeezed the older woman's arm again.

"What did he say?"

A shrug. An eye-roll.

"He asked how I was keeping. People have a way of doing that, don't they? You wouldn't know, dear, but when you're... well... you know. When you have my history. It means something different. It means 'Are you straight?' It means 'Are you having another breakdown?' And while they ask you just know they're looking for signs, the smell of booze, the tics."

"He didn't take you seriously?"

"Oh, he did, dear. He took me very seriously, but for all the wrong reasons. I'm sure he thinks I'm undergoing some kind of major paranoid delusion. I didn't help myself. I became hysterical, and it's not as if I have anything like facts or evidence or eyewitnesses to back up a mad woman's fears, now, do I? When you banged on my door I thought it was the mental health crisis team coming to take me away again."

Mel smiled in what she hoped was a sympathetic way. She could understand why someone would read Penny Rayner in that way when she was like this. And she was reminded how she had slowly come to the understanding that Harriet wasn't estranged from her mother because they fought or didn't love each other, but because she simply didn't have any idea how to deal with her mother when she became unstable – or even when she was relatively stable. Penny Rayner was not an easy person to handle.

"She loves you, you know," she said now.

"Oh yes. Of course. I do know that."

Penny remained silent for a moment, her gaze faraway.

"What do you want me to do?" Mel asked. Again, she was aware of how she retreated into her father's responses: practical questioning, straight to the point, looking for simple answers that suggested a course of action, a difference that could be made. Until now she'd never really seen how like him she could sometimes be.

Mel's hand was still on Penny's arm, and now Harriet's mother moved a hand to cover it, to press it against her. "You're the closest she has to family," she said.

Mel opened her mouth to protest, but stopped because what Penny said was true. Arguing the point would only open wounds.

"Find out where she is, Melissa. You know who to ask. You know *how* to ask. I just mess things up." She paused, that absent look in her averted gaze once again.

"I'll do what I can. I'm already asking around. That's why I came here. Is there anything? Anything at all that might help, Mrs Rayner?"

"Give me a sec," said Penny, straightening, and easing Mel's hand away from her arm as if it were something fragile. She turned, and vanished into the house, emerging a short time later with a photograph in a wooden frame. "This," she said. "This is her. It's all I have."

For a moment Mel battled to suppress a smile. She knew what Harriet looked like! Then she realized the significance of this picture. Penny Rayner had never got to grips with technology – computers and tablets and fancy phones. She didn't do social media, so didn't have access to the hundreds of selfies and other photos Harriet had posted.

And also... The picture was of the three of them, shortly before Geoffrey Rayner had died of a heart attack. The three of them cuddled together, somewhere outdoors, arms around each other. Smiling and happy. It wasn't just a photograph, it was a talisman, a relic of another time, another set of people.

"It really is all I have," said Penny, still holding the photograph close. "I... After Geoffrey's illness, I wasn't well. I moved here, and lost a lot of my things."

'Lost' was a euphemism. In a manic phase, she'd been found one night burning most of her past life in her then back garden, Harriet clinging to her in an effort to subdue her after calling the police.

"My memories... Geoffrey. Harriet growing up. They're not what they were."

Memories lost to drugs and drink and breakdown. The remaining memories blurred and muddled. Much of a life: lost.

This small photo really was one of the pillars of her existence.

With shaking hands, Penny teased the picture out of its frame and handed it over.

Mel held it carefully, studying the smiling faces. "Are you sure?" she said. "I could just–"

"Take it," said Penny, folding a bony hand around Mel's wrist. "It means a lot to me that you have it."

And with those words, that gesture, Harriet's mother transferred a tremendous weight of responsibility onto Mel's shoulders, and they both knew it.

Mel looked at the picture again. Oddly, given that this photograph must have been at least three years old, the likeness of Harriet as she was now was uncanny. Straight golden blonde hair, a simple, very English-rose beauty to those round eyes and bud-like lips and the tiny stub nose – almost doll-like in her looks. She always had looked much younger than her years, much to her frustration. As Mel sometimes joked, Harriet had the angelic features of a twelve-year-old and the gutter humor of someone twice that age.

"Thank you," said Mel. "I'll be careful with it."

Penny hugged her then, her body feeling bony and frail, like that of someone a good two or three decades older. She smelled of Chanel and cigarettes, and Mel realized even she was doing that thing: smelling for booze, just as earlier she'd wondered if Penny was high or merely anxious.

Mel stepped back, her turn to avert her gaze. "I'll ask around," she said. "And I'll let you know as soon as I hear anything."

2. MEL

Guilt.

That was the other reason she paid so much attention to that nagging fear, why she believed something awful had happened to Harriet even before she knew for certain her friend was missing.

A couple of weeks ago, she'd been out on the town with Harriet and a couple of the other girls. Just a normal night out. Pizza, a movie, a couple of drinks in a pub near Harriet's apartment. A bad choice, as it turned out: the barmaid knew Harriet from college, and for once it wasn't only Harriet's pubescent looks that stopped her getting booze but a barmaid who knew she was most certainly underage.

Then, standing at the bar to get another round of drinks, Mel had heard a familiar soft voice.

"Hey, there, how you doin'?"

Glancing to her right, she saw a face she struggled to place at first. Thick, dark stubble on slightly rounded features, a long scar above dark eyes that fixed you to the spot.

"Glenn?" she said. "Glenn Lazenby?"

When he smiled, his whole face lit up, the same smile as his brother, Jimmy.

"Look like you just smelled something bad," he said, still grinning.

"I just did."

How did it get from that to him paying for the drinks she'd just ordered and helping her carry them back to the table? To him standing there, all wide boy charm, and insisting he wouldn't join them, explaining he was just buying them drinks for old times' sakes, then backing away, leaving the other girls to press Mel on what he'd meant by 'old times'.

Harriet, in particular, had been intrigued, drawn to that rough charm and the chance of some juicy snippet from Mel's past. "Go on, doll, spill. Is he an ex? Did you dump him, or him you? Look at him. How could you *not*…?"

"No," Mel had finally admitted. "Not an ex. An ex's brother."

After that she'd had to let them extract some of the details from her, enough to feed their curiosity. As little as she could get away with.

Yes, the brother shared those rough good looks. Yes, he had that glint in his eye, too, and the way of just looking at you and making you feel as if you were the center of everything, if only for a moment. No, there weren't any more Lazenby brothers to go around, but if there had been her friends would have been welcome to them all as far as she was concerned... and that's when she'd clammed up, didn't want to spill anything more. Didn't want to have to explain how nothing good ever came of getting close to the Lazenby family – that their father and uncle were just the same, charmers with the attitudes of men who owned the world and an underlying subtext of chilling brutality.

"You okay, Mels?"

It was Harriet, leaning in close. She'd always had the ability to be sensitive to Mel's moods, when she could be bothered.

Mel nodded, smiled.

"Good, 'cos your man's watching us, and if you don't want him I might just..."

"You're sixteen!"

"Seventeen in a couple of days, and as you always say, I have the intellect and maturity of someone much older."

"Mind of a trooper, I think I said." The two had laughed, and later, when Mel found herself at the bar with Glenn Lazenby again, she said to him, "Hands off, okay? She's only a kid. I've seen the looks you're giving her."

He played innocent, holding hands up, palms facing Mel. "Don't know what you mean, girl," he said, even though he clearly did. She'd seen him eyeing Harriet up. She knew the look. Then he added, "Anyway, I only have eyes for you, Mel. Always had. You know that."

She'd tried to be pissed off with him, not to let that roguish charm do its thing, but it wasn't easy. Damn those Lazenby boys, that had always been the way.

It should have been nothing, that evening. Just an encounter with someone from the past. A bit of flirting, a bit of a laugh. Nothing more.

Even when Harriet had asked about Glenn the next day, gently teasing out a few more snippets from Mel's past, the alarm bells didn't go off.

"So did he really just happen to be there?" Harriet had asked. "Just bump into us like that? Or was he hoping to bump into *you*, Mels?"

She'd wondered the same thing. In a city of nine million people and however many thousands of pubs and clubs, how likely was it that she'd encounter him?

There was something in Harriet's expression, just then. Something that made Mel pause, reassessing. "What is it?" she asked. "What aren't you telling me?"

That enigmatic expression broke into a smile, the cat that really had found the cream. "I think he liked me," Harriet said. "A girl can tell. Or at least, *I* can."

"What? What do you mean?"

"He spoke to me. You were off in the ladies', powdering your nose or whatever, then you went straight to the bar. He came over to introduce himself. Proper gent, he was."

"Believe me," said Mel, "there's nothing either proper or gentlemanly about Glenn Lazenby. What did he say? What did he do?"

"Oh, nothing. Just asked how I was, how I knew you. He made out he was interested in me, but I reckon he was digging about *you*."

Mel saw then that her friend had produced something from her purse, a business card. She reached across and took it, ignoring Harriet's look of mock outrage. Saw

Glenn's name, a couple of numbers, an email, a LinkedIn address. The words 'FIXER AND FACILITATOR'.

"The Lazenbies," said Mel, trying to impress on Harriet that she was being serious, "they're a bad lot. Old-school gangsters in a modern world. Glenn's father is mixed up in all kinds of things, and the sons are just the same. I learned that the hard way. I got too close, and I got burned. I just hope last night was a fluke, bumping into him like that, because I really hope I never set eyes on him or his family again."

Looking back, though, it was obvious Harriet didn't get it. Didn't get it at all. She'd smiled, raised her eyebrows, pursed those rosebud lips, and then said, "That spark's still there, isn't it, Mels? Well I never… I never knew you had a bad boy thing going on. A bit of rough."

It was only now… now that she looked back, reassessing everything, that she realized it wasn't just Mel who had a thing for bad boys. It was Harriet, too.

And so she felt guilty.

Guilty that she had inadvertently introduced Harriet to Glenn Lazenby. That the encounter had clearly made an impression on the girl. And scared that there might possibly be anything more to it than that.

She hoped desperately that Harriet – or Glenn – hadn't followed up that interest. Because, as she'd tried to convince her young friend, nothing good ever comes from getting involved with the Lazenby family.

She called him on the mobile number on the business card he'd given Harriet, and asked to meet. And even as she thumbed the number, she wondered if that had been a ploy: leaving the card with Harriet, knowing the two would talk and so Mel would at least see the card, the number…

"Don't go getting ideas," she said. "I just want a few minutes of your time."

"Even so little would make my day complete, darling," he said in that deceptively soft voice of his, and she wondered how it was that he could simultaneously make her skin crawl and make her feel a thrill of… of *something*. She didn't know what it was. Didn't like it. Didn't like any response to a Lazenby that didn't involve a healthy dose of distrust.

"Glenn, I'm serious. Just a few minutes, yeah?"

She didn't know what to expect – a seedy pub, a greasy spoon café, perhaps, but not this, an up-market wine bar in the West End, all darkened glass and chrome and tall, jagged-leafed pot plants. Or him: patent leather shoes and a gray designer suit that probably cost as much as a small house back in their home town. The shades pushed back on the top of his head, the heavy rings on three fingers of one hand – had he worn those the other night? She hadn't noticed them.

When he saw her he stood, reached for her hand, kissed the knuckles with a soft brush of lips and a rough scrape of stubble.

"Hey, good to see you again. Drink?" Without waiting for an answer he raised a hand, signaling to the bar, and as they lowered themselves into either end of a deep leather sofa a waitress in a ridiculously short black skirt came over with a glass of white wine and what looked like a whisky on ice. "Sorry, I presumed. You said you only had a few minutes so I thought we'd save time on the logistics."

Briefly Mel considered taking the whisky, then the moment was gone, Glenn taking the chunky square glass and cradling it, leaving her to reach for the elegantly shaped wine glass. In the background, anonymous jazzy music played, merging with the murmur of voices. It was funny seeing Glenn like this, all grown up and almost managing to pull off sophisticated.

He sat studying her, waiting, in no obvious hurry to open the conversation, despite his claim of making efficient use of their time.

She would have thought it was a power thing, a ploy to get her to make the first move, but, to be blunt, she didn't think Glenn Lazenby had ever had the smarts to do something like that. He'd always been direct, like her father. He didn't do psychology.

"So… serious, you said?" He kept his voice low, soft, hard to catch above the background noise.

She smiled. She'd won that round, got him to break the silence. She was better at this than him.

"Sorry, yes," she said. "I… I don't know who to turn to. And then I found your number." She didn't explain how, didn't tell him the number was on the card he'd given her then-sixteen-year-old friend. If that had been a ploy she wasn't going to give him the satisfaction of knowing it had worked.

She hated playing the ditzy blonde, but sometimes, particularly with men like Glenn Lazenby, it was the best approach.

"Yeah, darling? What is it?"

For all his lack of moves, Glenn was hard to work out. As far as she could tell he didn't appear to be hiding anything, but he lived in a world where hiding things was as automatic as breathing out after you've breathed in. For the first time, she considered the possibility maybe she was the one out of her depth here, not him.

"My friend. The girl I was with that night we bumped into you. Harriet. Have you seen anything more of her? Have you been in touch with her?"

Still, he gave nothing away. He shrugged, spread his hands, palms out, in that innocent, defensive way of his. "Been in touch with her? I wouldn't know how to. And besides, why would I do that? You said hands off, she's a kid."

She didn't say because Harriet not only had a thing for bad boys, but also she had daddy issues and Glenn Lazenby's rough, worldly charm reminded Mel of her friend's late father.

Challenging Glenn would get her nowhere. He had an ego to protect.

"I… I don't know. I'm just worried for her."

"Hey, hey there," Glenn said, reaching for her, pressing a hand to her shoulder and caressing the soft flesh above her collarbone with his thumb, a strangely intimate touch.

She pulled away, reminding herself how any response to a Lazenby other than distrust was a dangerous thing.

"What's up, darling?"

"Oh, I'm sure it's nothing. It's just… Well, Harriet's gone quiet. Not answering calls or messages. Not showing up for things we'd arranged. Her mother's worried, asked me to ask around. I guess that's freaked me out a little. I'm out of my depth, and I don't know who to turn to. I'm just talking to anyone who's run into her over the last week or so. You… well, you seemed to show an interest." You gave her your card, you bastard.

"And you wondered if she'd fallen for me?" Glenn laughed, hands up, facing out, again. "No, no, it's okay. Don't apologize. Like I say, she's a kid. I've done some bad shit in my time, but none of that. And like I say, when I'm in a room with someone like you, how could I ever look anywhere else?"

He was joking, laying it on so heavy it became a comical thing, and they both knew it. He'd always done that. It used to wind his brother Jimmy up no end.

"Maybe that's it," he continued. "Maybe I thought I'd get to you through her, so I gave her a bit of the old chat. But that's all it was."

He leaned back and took a drink. "Okay, darling. You said serious. I can do serious. I can see you're worried. So what can I do? I'm guessing the Old Bill aren't being much use, or you wouldn't be chasing this yourself, right?"

Mel shook her head. "Harriet's mother tried but, well, she has issues, and they didn't take her seriously. I don't want to leave it until they're forced to."

"Makes sense. So…?"

She looked at him, wishing she was a whole lot better at this. She'd thought as far as coming here, looking him in the eye, and trying to work out if he knew anything about where Harriet might be, but that had failed. He gave nothing away. The last few minutes had blown away her first impression that she was the one with the wiles and she could outsmart him. If she wanted to wrap Glenn Lazenby round her little finger she'd have to try another tack.

"Well, I guess… I remember how things were. You, your family. You were always the one who was in the middle of everything, the one who knew people and could make things happen. You had… *connections*." Was there any less obvious way to say he was a gangster in a family of gangsters and maybe he could help?

"You want me to put some feelers out?" He understood. He got it. And this was the first time today she'd been able to read him easily: she was asking him for a favor and right now he was busy working out the price.

Even as she understood this, she almost felt relieved: that old distrust of the Lazenby family kicking in again. That had to be healthy!

"That'd be great, if you could? As I say, I don't know who to ask."

"Tell you what. Can you get back to the old town tomorrow evening? I have family business to take care of back there, but I'll have had time to ask around by then. I'll be at the Flag and Flowers. You could meet me at seven and we'll grab dinner somewhere, take it from there. What do you say?"

The price. There was always going to be a price.

"That'd be lovely, thanks. If you're sure you don't mind?"

"Sure thing, darling. You just leave it to me, you hear?"

Outside, the street was busy with stop-starting traffic, and pedestrians rushed all around her.

She was glad she'd given herself a get-out, told him she wasn't going to be here for long. The rush of emotions was heady, the memories it brought back, the feelings. That had been a different Mel, back then. She'd been in love, briefly, with this man's brother, and she remembered the rivalry between them, the way Glenn had always encouraged her to play the two Lazenby brothers off each other.

In the intervening years she'd made herself forget the positives, the reasons why she'd got involved with the family in the first place. But now... Glenn was just the same equal mix of charming fun and irritation he'd always been.

She took a deep breath. Held it until her lungs hurt, before letting it go.

She must look a freak standing here, while everyone rushed about her.

She started to walk.

Had he been genuine? He seemed so. He really seemed to want to help, or at least to use his help as a bargaining chip to make her go to him, spend time with him, and whatever else he hoped for.

Did he really want that, after all this time, or was he just playing with her, having a laugh, as he always did with people?

She didn't know, so she didn't know whether to feel flattered or frustrated, and it was just the same as it had always been, and that was strangely reassuring.

As she walked she tried not to feel annoyed at all that the two men she'd turned to – her father, and now Glenn

Lazenby – had both, effectively, patted her on the head and told her to go away and leave it to the grown-ups.

Not annoyed at all.

She sat on the train, her bag on the seat next to her, guarding her solitude. Her phone buzzed, and when she glanced at the small screen her first reaction was to dismiss it.

Her father.

Why now? He never called, always leaving it to her to make the move to establish contact. That was just the way it was, the way *he* was.

And it was only that fact that made her slide her thumb across the screen to accept the call. The curiosity. He must have a reason to be calling now.

For a second or two, she held the phone, staring at it, before raising it to her ear. There was no-one sitting nearby, just a young woman with a small child in the seats on the other side of the carriage, and a couple of seats down a teenager with big earphones on, leaking a hiss of muffled music. Outside her window, outer London peeled itself away in a succession of shabby industrial units.

"Melissa."

"Dad. How're you doing?"

"Oh, you know." Then silence, as if he was waiting for her to strike up conversation, even though he was the one who'd called.

"So, how are you doing?" he finally asked. It wasn't a general question, the kind of thing people say: Mel knew that in this case it was specific, to the point, referring to their last conversation.

"Oh, you know." She could play that game too. She didn't want to admit she'd spent the last couple of days chasing shadows and getting nowhere. Not to her father. Not to herself, either.

She'd left Harriet another message this morning, but still no response. There had been no sign of her friend on social media, either, which was so out of character.

More silence on the line, until Mel relented. "Penny's frantic," she said. "She's tried reporting it, but the police aren't interested – they see her as just a hysterical addict screaming at them."

"I'll have a word."

She opened her mouth to speak, then stopped. That was the first offer of help. She didn't know if he meant in some kind of official capacity, or if he would step in as a friend of the family, but she didn't ask.

"Listen, Melissa," he said. "I think perhaps you've done enough for now. You've raised the alarm when no-one else took this seriously, but now... Well, if anything's happened, if Harriet has got caught up in anything, please don't expose yourself, too, Melissa. Do you understand?"

Oh yes, she understood. It was the same old thing, another pat on the head and instruction to leave it to the grown-ups. He'd obviously paid enough attention to know she was asking around. She just wished he'd invest that effort in actually bloody helping.

She understood now that she didn't know whether she could even trust her own father. Yes, he was saying the right things at last, but was he actually doing anything, or was he just fobbing her off?

Right now, the only thing she truly trusted was that she was the one person she knew for a fact was out there for Harriet.

"Harriet's missing, Dad. It's been four days. I'm scared for her and nobody else seems to be taking it seriously, so I'm not going to let go, whatever you say."

A pause, then: "I know. But I had to ask, at least. Where are you now? What are you doing?"

Just then the train went over a junction and there was a loud rumble from the track. She hoped he hadn't heard.

"Sitting outside Starbucks," she said. "Watching the traffic. Trying to work it out. Asking around."

"Don't get in too deep, Melissa, you hear? These people are far worse than you could ever imagine."

"I won't."

It was only after she hung up, and had sat staring out of the window for a time, that she started to wonder what he meant by that. What people did he mean? Did he know more than he was letting on, and if so, just how bad was it for Harriet? And did that warning imply he knew who Mel had been talking to, and she might be heading along the right lines, or was it just a generality?

Don't get in too deep, Melissa, you hear? These people are far worse than you could ever imagine.

I won't, she thought. I'll only get in as deep as I need to.

3. MEL

The Flag and Flowers was an old town-center pub, owned by the Lazenby family for as long as Mel could remember. It stood alone, a red-brick building with a parking area on one side and derelict land to the other side and the rear.

Last time she'd been here it was to tell Jimmy Lazenby it was over between them. He was too wrapped up in his family business, too much in the thrall of his villainous father. The Glenn she was coming to know now was very much the kind of man she'd feared Jimmy would become back then.

She breathed deep, suddenly anxious. Was she out of her depth? Would she even *know* when she was out of her depth, or would it sneak up on her until it was too late?

These people are far worse than you could ever imagine.

Did her father know she was here, that she'd been talking to Glenn? Had he been warning her against getting involved with the Lazenby family again?

She'd taken it too glibly before. She knew that now. Thinking she could run rings around Glenn, that she was far smarter than him.

How much of that brash persona was front, she wondered? The sharp suit and the rough, almost brutish, charm. His father was just the same: giving an impression he wasn't as smart as those around him, when in truth he had the ability to see right through people, read a situation, and always stay at least a step ahead.

She pushed the door and stepped in, determined to keep her wits about her this time.

It was like stepping back in time. She recognized Sandra behind the bar, her hair pinned up in the familiar bun, perhaps a slightly whiter shade of nicotine-yellowed gray. Game machines lined the back wall, just as they had ten years ago, and the walls were the same dull wood paneling. Even the light had a sepia tint to it, reinforcing the sense she had stepped back a decade.

People were looking at her, and she tried not to feel intimidated. She nodded at Sandra, who hadn't recognized her at first but now gave a slight nod in return, a flash of recognition in her eyes.

"Glenn around?" Mel asked. "He's expecting me."

Just then, Sandra turned, and a door behind the bar opened and Glenn stepped out.

The sharp suit he'd worn at the wine bar had gone, and now he wore blue jeans, a white shirt, and a black leather jacket.

"Come on through, darling," he said, waving a hand at the door, then stepping forward to lift the hinged part of the bar so she could step through.

As she slipped past him, she breathed leather and a heady cologne.

The door opened onto a large office, an old wooden desk arranged diagonally across one corner. A big aquarium full of jewel-colored fish stood against one wall, surrounded by tall pot plants. Another wall bore a big screen, paused partway through what looked like a shoot 'em up game.

Unnoticed at first, a tall black girl stood by the room's one window. She wore a black vest top and short skirt that did nothing to conceal ridiculously long supermodel legs.

Glenn stepped past Mel, nodded at the girl, and she slipped past them and out of the room, pulling the door shut behind her.

"Don't mind Suze," Glenn said. "She's my PA."

Mel didn't say a thing, just looked at him until he laughed, shrugged, held his hands up, palms out, a gesture that covered just about everything for him.

Even with the door shut, muffled sounds drifted through from the pub – voices, music, the jangling clatter and chimes of the games machines.

"Good to see you," said Glenn. He waved to a sofa, said, "Please," and sat at one end of it, one knee drawn up so he could twist to face her.

She sat upright at the other end, elbows on her knees, hands clasped, not wanting to give in and sink back into the sofa and inadvertently mirror his position.

"So," she said, "Have you found anything?" Too abrupt. She gave a little smile, and added, "And thanks for saying you'd ask around. I really appreciate it."

Now she worried she might be over-compensating, that her appreciation might seem too much like acknowledgment of a favor to be returned. That comment about dinner and 'taking it from there' still hung over her, unclear if he would hold her to it, or if he'd been teasing her in that way of his.

"Straight to the point, eh? No small talk? No telling me about your life and at least pretending you like me?" He was smiling – hadn't stopped since emerging from that doorway. Glenn liked it when people wanted something from him, liked the feeling of being in control. He'd always been that way.

Again, she was reminded of the paradox that was Glenn Lazenby: a man who could be charming and attractive, and simultaneously quite the opposite.

These people are far worse than you could ever imagine.

"Sorry," she said. It wasn't hard to play the pathetic girl role this evening. Four days now, with nothing from Harriet; she had run out of ideas and nobody else seemed to be doing anything. "I just…" She shrugged. "I'm not in a small talk place, right now, okay? You want to know about my life? It's not that interesting, believe me. I'm a postgrad student at UCL. I live in a tiny room in a house I share with four near-strangers. What more do you want to know? Right now the only thing that matters to me is that one of my closest friends has disappeared off the face of the Earth and nobody seems to give a shit."

"No, I'm the one who's sorry." Was that actual kindness in his voice? "You know me: no matter how bad things get I try to turn it into a joke. It's a defensive thing."

So maybe he did do psychology sometimes, after all.

Mel gave a little shake of the head. It was nothing. She just wanted to get to the point.

"I know some people," said Glenn. "Contacts in the police. Contacts… elsewhere. I've been asking questions about your friend."

"And…?"

"Nothing," he said, with a shake of the head. "Sorry. But that's maybe not so bad a result. The kind of people I know… well, let's just say, the business they're involved in – if they were able to actually tell me anything about your friend's absence then you'd have a lot more to worry about. Kid like that…"

He was trying to reassure her, in his clumsy way, but his words drove a chill deep through Mel's core, opening her mind up to possibilities she'd been shutting out.

"She's only a child," she said.

Glenn just raised an eyebrow, driving that chill even deeper.

"Like I say," he finally said, "nobody's heard anything, so we're good. And my friends in blue are aware – they haven't entirely dismissed the concerns of her mum, even though they know all about *her*."

"Thank you." She swallowed, then went on. "These… *contacts*. You trust them?"

He laughed. "On this?" he said. "Yeah, I do. They know not to fuck me around, you know what I mean?"

"If they're lying. If your friends have done anything to Harriet… I told you: she's a child, she's off limits."

"Trust me," said Glenn, "I'd know if they were lying. I'm on your side, darling. You just need to see through all my bullshit, you know?"

That hint of kindness in his tone again, another revelation in this mature version of the Glenn she'd once known.

"You just need to tread carefully," he went on. "Leave the dirty work to grafters like me. I know you've been asking around, but you don't want to get mixed up with the kind of people I deal with."

"You sound like my father."

There was a flash of something in his look then. Hostility? Wariness?

"Have you got your old man onto this too?"

She shook her head. "He's not interested," she said. "He told me I should leave it to the grown-ups – pretty much the same as you've just told me."

There was something in what he'd said that bugged her – not just the hostility to her father.

"Why have you been looking into me, too? Why does it matter to you what questions I've been asking?" She didn't like that he'd clearly been investigating Mel when he should have been focused on Harriet.

"Because I care, Mel. If you're asking help from a bastard like me, then I just worried who else you might be asking, that's all."

Why did she feel as if everyone was fending her off, trying to placate her? Was she the only one who really cared?

"I'm not going to back off," she said. "Not until I've found her."

"Okay, okay." Hands up, calming. "I'll keep digging, okay?"

"I…" Her shoulders slumped. She wasn't any good at all this.

"So…" said Glenn. "How about that dinner you promised me?"

"I… I'm sorry, but…" She didn't know what to say, what to do. "I'm tired," she said. "I wouldn't be good company. I–"

"It's fine. No worries. Look, just give me another twenty-four, okay? We can get together again tomorrow evening, take it from there, okay?"

He messaged her the name of a club the next day, and a time: *Ryders. 7.00pm.*

She'd taken an Airbnb room in a small terraced house a few minutes' walk from the town center. After retreating there from the Flag and Flowers the previous evening, she'd slept surprisingly well, and spent the next day continuing to dig. Phone calls to Penny and to Harriet's friends. Trawling through social media for any sign of activity from the missing girl. Searching the depressingly large number of sites and groups dedicated to tracing missing persons. Googling news stories for anything that might be relevant.

But… nothing.

So, drinks with Glenn.

She hadn't expected a place like this. A strip club? Really? What kind of point was he trying to make?

It must be the wrong place. Another club with the same name. Were there two Ryders clubs in town?

As soon as she set foot in the club she was aware of eyes on her. The giant of a bouncer, eyeing her up. A group of suited businessmen at a table near the bar. Another suited man sharing drinks with a near-naked dancer close to the small stage. A girl hanging from a pole, a statuesque redhead with one side of her scalp shaved close and rose and barbed wire tattoos twisting down both arms, bare breasts swinging in a way no natural breasts would ever move.

As well as the dancer on stage and the one sharing drinks with the lone guy, there were at least four other girls working the club, stopping at tables to chat and flirt, no doubt hoping to get asked for a private dance in one of the curtained-off booths at the rear of the club.

All that naked flesh on offer, and yet Mel felt exposed in pale gray jeans and a deliberately unshowy over-sized top. A lone woman in a place like this, obviously not one of the dancers – was that what it was? That she was clearly not on offer? Forbidden fruit. If she'd turned up in a basque and stilettos she'd probably barely have got a glance.

"Hey there."

That familiar soft voice. The leather-jacketed guy at the bar turning on his stool, grinning at her. Glenn.

He extended an arm, as if to welcome her into his embrace.

"Drink?" he asked.

She'd been wrong about him: he really did do psychology. He must have understood how exposed and vulnerable she would feel walking in here alone, and how, now, that grin, that territorial extended arm, offered protection, sanctuary.

She walked to the other side of him and perched on a bar stool, forcing him to drop the arm and turn. She could play mind-fuck games along with the best of them. You'd think he'd remember that about her.

"Aberlour," she said, in response to his raised eyebrows. "Thanks." It was the only decent scotch on display behind the bar.

Glenn nodded, perhaps in acknowledgment of good taste or in recognition that he'd ordered for her without asking last time they'd had drinks.

She took a sip, let the burning amber liquid slide down her throat, a good burn.

"Any news?" he asked.

She dipped her head, gave a little shake from side to side.

"The police have spoken to her mother," she told him. "They seem to be treating it as a family rift, a runaway."

Glenn nodded again, and Mel looked at him, suddenly alert. "What?" she said. "What is it?"

"Did you know she was using?"

She'd suspected as much. That look in Penny's eyes, the fidgety manner. It was hardly a surprise, given current circumstances.

Then she understood.

"Harriet? You mean Harriet?"

A sad smile.

"But… she was always so *angry* about drugs. She'd seen what it did to her mother. She–"

"You can't escape your family, can you?" said Glenn. "It's in the genes. Like mother, like…" That shrug, the spreading of the hands.

She couldn't believe it. "How? How do you know?"

"I know people," Glenn said. "That's why you came to me, isn't it, Mels? My connections. The family's never been in the drugs trade – we're old-school, we don't touch that stuff – but I know the people who do. Your friend's a wild child, just like her mum."

He put a hand on her shoulder again. She hated how he did that, what it implied and the fact that on some level that touch actually got through to her, calmed her and… did the opposite of calming her. That Lazenby connection. That annoying spark.

"Again, I know it's hard to accept," he went on, "but that's actually a good thing, right now. Chances are she's lying low at a mate's house, sleeping off the old crash and burn, you know what I mean? You just need to give her some more time, then come down on her like a ton of bricks and try to stop her following the path her old mum took, you hear me, Mels?"

A squeeze of the shoulder, and then his hand dropped away as he stood. "Come on," he said. "Let's go and sit somewhere more comfortable, and I'll tell you all I know."

It all happened in a rush, then.

They walked to a booth, a U-shaped leatherette seat around a circular table. She sat and, instead of dropping into the seat opposite, Glenn sat next to her, draping an arm along the back of the seat, and she let him because her mind was still rushing, trying to work out the implications of what he'd just said, what she'd just heard. And right now, the only thing she knew for certain was she didn't want to piss him off, didn't want to alert him to the fact that he'd let something slip.

He'd called her 'Mels'.

Nobody ever did that.

Or rather, only one person ever had. Harriet.

Her father always called her Melissa, as had her late mother. Penny Rayner called her Melissa, too. Everyone else called her Mel, except for one old college friend who called her 'M'.

She thought back to that night at the pub in north London, when Glenn had shown up out of the blue and bought them drinks. She was sure Harriet hadn't called her Mels in his presence – she'd hardly said a word.

She knew Glenn had spoken to Harriet later, when Mel had gone to the ladies' and then to the bar.

That would be the simple explanation: that the two had talked about her – Harriet had seemed convinced Glenn had only spoken to her then to get close to Mel – and Harriet must have referred to her as Mels. Glenn would have noticed that, perhaps been amused or intrigued that the girl used a different variant of her name. Maybe he had started using it deliberately because he thought that's what people called her now.

That had to be it.

A simple, innocent explanation.

As if there was ever a simple, innocent explanation where the Lazenby family was concerned.

And then, as her mind still rushed to convince her of the innocent explanation, *he* walked in. She sensed it first in Glenn's response – a tensing, a straightening – and then she followed his gaze and saw him, Jimmy Lazenby, standing just inside the club's entrance, his eyes fixed on the dancer on stage. A different one now, a blonde with angel wings tattooed across her shoulder blades.

"Always had an eye for the birds," said Glenn with a chuckle. "Particularly blondes."

She looked away, down at her empty glass. She couldn't remember draining it.

Not him. Not now. Not here.

She needed to focus. Needed to work out what, if anything, Glenn had just given away.

She didn't need distractions.

And distractions could not come much more extreme for Mel than Jimmy Fucking Lazenby.

4. MEL

He remained standing, refusing the seat opposite that Glenn had indicated with a curt nod.

"Surprised you came back," said Glenn.

"It'd be rude not to, really, wouldn't it? Now the old bastard's dead and all."

More to process, to understand. The old bastard. That could only mean their father. She hadn't known. Glenn hadn't said anything, hadn't seemed particularly upset or distracted, but then how would she tell if he was? A lot of time had passed. They'd grown up. Changed. She didn't know these people anymore.

The brothers had been talking, but she'd missed what was said. She realized she was studying Jimmy. There was a hardness to his face that hadn't been there before. Funny how Glenn's features had softened and filled out, but his younger brother's had become leaner, harder. His body, too, beneath that dark blue suit, seemed wiry, nothing wasted. Where Glenn's jaw was lined with stubble, Jimmy's was clean, and his hair was shorter, tousled.

She looked away.

"You're staring, Jimbo. Don't you know it's rude to stare?"

She glanced up again, just in time to see his eyes flitting sideward, away. Had he been appraising her, just as she had him? Seeing what the intervening ten years had done to her? The crow's feet spreading from the corners of her eyes? The extra few pounds the gym just couldn't shift?

Mels. Glenn Lazenby had called her Mels.

She couldn't be distracted now. Sidetracked by something that had never really been.

She turned to Glenn, aware of his arm along the back of the seat, almost touching her shoulders. Looked up into his eyes, and said, "Your father? I'm sorry. I didn't know." Trying for a level of sincerity he might, at least, believe.

"Didn't ask, did you?" His manner had changed since Jimmy's arrival: prickly, defensive. He'd stopped toying with her, stopped playing games.

Mel fell quiet. She couldn't afford to antagonize him now.

She should leave. The brothers clearly had things to work out between them. She should make her excuses, and pick this up another time. But… Harriet.

She felt Glenn's hand on her shoulder, a brief contact. Was that his new-found sensitivity again? He must know how hard this was for her.

She stayed. Listened as the two of them talked about funeral arrangements, and then got onto the heavy stuff, talk of their father's last months. It was clear the two hadn't spoken in a long time, that Jimmy had distanced himself, was only now catching up.

She excused herself, went to the ladies'. Found a stall and locked herself in, and only now allowed her breath to race – not quite a panic attack, but a more controlled thing, a catching up with the panic she'd felt for the last fifteen or twenty minutes in the company of the two brothers.

She could do this.

She *had* to do this.

Harriet. Harriet was the only thing that mattered right now.

Mels. He'd called her Mels.

That wasn't just a slip of the tongue, an accident. He'd picked the name up somewhere, and the only person he could have picked it up from was Harriet.

She brought her breathing back under control, flushed, unlocked the stall and went to a basin. She wanted to splash cold water on her face, but knew her eyes would smudge. Instead, she stared into the mirror, studied herself for anything that might betray her state of agitation.

She took out her Chubby stick and touched up her lips, breathed deep, and headed back out.

Jimmy had moved to the bar. Had he and Glenn argued in her absence, or was he just getting some breathing space?

He was watching her, perhaps ready to rejoin her and Glenn at their booth. Instead, she headed to the bar.

He sat with one foot on his stool's footrest, the other on the rail at the bottom of the bar.

How strange to see him now, like this. So unexpectedly. She'd kissed that mouth. Felt it work across her body, felt it close on her, that tongue flicking, sliding, pushing. She'd given herself to him, unreservedly. She knew how that mouth sagged open when he climaxed, knew the widening of the eyes. She knew his vulnerabilities and strengths. Knew what made him laugh, and knew what brought him close to tears.

And now, his eyes were fixed on hers. Intense. Unrelenting.

"You have to get out of here," he said. "No matter how bad you think this is, it's worse, and you're not equipped to handle it. Leave now. Stand up, slap me across the face just like I know you want to, and storm out. I'll tell Glenn I pissed you off and in the meantime you'll have a chance to get away. Run, Mel. Leave this to me. My people. Get out of here."

Her first thought was to wonder what he meant by leaving it to him, leaving it to his people. Leave *this*... He knew there was a *this* to leave. Knew there was something going on, that this wasn't just an innocent encounter.

But what did Jimmy have to do with it? And who were his 'people'?

Her second thought was that it was the same thing again. One of the boys patting her on the head and telling her to leave it to the grown-ups.

She glanced across at Glenn, who was watching them closely.

Mels. He'd called her Mels. She couldn't let that go.

Her third thought wasn't so much a thought as an impulse, a signal from brain to nerves to muscle. Almost before she knew it, her arm straightened, jabbing forward, palm flat.

The impact hurt so much more than she could have anticipated. Ten years' worth of pent-up slap. So hard her palm stung and her wrist jarred and her elbow cracked. So hard Jimmy almost fell off his stool even as she caught herself against the bar to stop from staggering forward on top of him with the momentum of that blow.

She walked back across the room, all eyes on her as she moved, but for a different reason this time – not mentally undressing her so much as imagining the consequences of ever daring to cross her. Maybe some of them liked that too.

Glenn was laughing as she lowered herself back into her seat, his arm still trailed across the back.

"Whisky," she said. "I think I need another whisky."

And when she looked back across the room she saw that Jimmy had left. She was on her own again, just as she had been from the start.

"So, these people," she said. "These *contacts*. What do they do? Why would they know anything about a teenaged girl missing from London?"

"You not going to tell me what that was all about?"

Her wrist still hurt from slapping Jimmy. She really hadn't meant to hit him so hard. She reached for her replenished whisky with the other hand, and took a drink.

"He had it coming," she said. Let Glenn fill in the gaps however he wanted.

Up on the stage, the statuesque redhead was dancing again, wearing only a tiny white thong and the same thoroughly bored expression.

Mel watched the blonde girl with the angel wing tattoos leading one of the suited men through between the tables, her fingers entwined in his. She'd started dancing for him even as she walked, twisting sinuously, spinning around as he moved past her into a booth and she reached for the tie that secured the gauzy curtains.

"It's all changed," said Glenn, and for a moment she wondered what he meant. Then she realized he was answering her question. "My old man, he was old-school. Like I say, we've done some bad shit, but there are things we'd never do."

Standards. He was telling her he was a gangster with principles. A gentleman thug. She looked at him. He may be many things, but he was no Robin Hood.

"And these people...?"

That now-familiar shrug. "East European gangs. The Asians. Drugs and girls. Trafficking. You don't want to know."

She didn't, but… "And you thought they might know something?"

"I hoped they wouldn't, and I was right. Like I say, that's good, isn't it?" He was doing sensitive again.

"Drugs. You said she was doing drugs."

"That's the word. She's been IDed at a few clubs. Some of her friends are known on the scene, too. Two and two isn't that hard to put together, is it?"

"You have proof?"

A shrug. "People I trust," he said. "Listen, I know it sucks. I get that. But this is good. She'll show up, tail between her legs. Just give it time."

His hand on her arm, that thumb stroking.

As hard as she'd slapped his brother, she could have hit Glenn Lazenby ten times as hard right now.

Instead, eyes wide, she said, "Thank you, Glenn. You clearly know what you're doing. I should be reassured, but I just… I want my friend back. Safe."

"I know that, Mels. I do." He squeezed her arm. It was obvious what he wanted, what price he expected to extract from her.

He'd always wanted what he couldn't have.

Was this that moment? The one where she realized she was in too deep and didn't know how to get out?

He knew something – she was certain of that. He thought he was clever, that he could play her, but he wasn't as good as he believed.

Mels. Mels, Mels, *Mels.*

Mel had never been one to let things stew. She could never leave something unsaid for long. Like a kettle boiling, she had to let the pressure out.

She had to challenge him, even though she knew confrontation was not the right way to tackle a man like Glenn Lazenby. She opened her mouth to speak, but he held a hand up to silence her, raised his eyebrows apologetically, and reached into an inside pocket in his leather jacket.

A moment later, he had a phone pressed to his ear. "Sorry, yeah? Yeah, it is. So what's happening, dude?" He raised a hand apologetically again and stood, shrugged, edged free of their booth and strolled back through the club, covering his other ear with his free hand.

Mel sat back in her seat, eyeing her empty glass. She'd drunk too much already. She needed to stay in control – all too aware that Glenn would happily ply her with as many drinks as it might take to get into her pants.

"Hey, first time here?"

The redhead, a lacy top pulled across her shoulders, doing nothing to conceal her bare breasts. Mel looked around, not sure the girl was talking to her or not. She nodded, smiled.

"Sit for a minute?" The girl said, slipping into the seat next to Mel where Glenn had been moments before. "Ooh, that's better. I'm Cass. You having a nice time?"

Mel shrugged, slowly realizing this was just the normal routine for the girls between dances. Chat with the customers, maybe get drinks bought, persuade them to go through for a private dance.

"You like girls?" asked Cass, confirming Mel's slowly reached conclusion that this was just routine. The dancer's knee was pressing casually against hers.

Mel shrugged again. "I'm not really…" she said, trailing to a stop. "I came to meet someone. A friend."

Cass nodded, and moved her knee a fraction, easing the pressure. She must have seen Mel with Glenn. Maybe that was why she was paying her attention: keep the main man happy by keeping his friends happy.

"I'm looking for someone," said Mel. "A friend. She's been missing for a few days. Glenn's helping."

The dancer looked genuinely concerned, and given her inability to look interested when she was on stage, this response seemed genuine enough. Mel reached into her bag, found Penny's old photo. "Her," she said. "The young one."

"Looks like a kid," said Cass. "That's sad."

"She's seventeen."

Cass nodded. "Looks younger," she said. "You think she's working somewhere like this? That why you're asking around? With looks like that, she'd get work easy. That barely legal look, you know?"

"I don't know where she is," said Mel. "Have you seen her? Have you heard anything about someone like her?"

Cass shook her head.

It was a long shot, Mel knew, but if Glenn was hiding anything then someone who worked for him might easily have heard something.

"You want a dance? Just me and you?"

Mel smiled, said, "Thank you, but no. But maybe you could introduce me to the girls, get them to have a look at my friend's photo? See if they recognize her?"

Up on stage, with her barbed wire and rose tattoos and the side of her head shaved to stubble, Cass had looked quite intimidating, but now her features softened as she smiled. "You're really worried, aren't you, babe?" With that, she reached across and took Mel's hand and stood. Then she led her across to a curtained-off area by the stage that concealed a door.

Pushing through, the two emerged into a cramped changing area, mirrors on the walls, bags and clothes everywhere.

A blonde dancer Mel had seen on stage earlier stood with one foot up on a stool wiping herself intimately with a wet wipe, and Mel looked away immediately, embarrassed.

"New recruit?" said the dancer, balling the wipe and dropping it in a bin, still standing there with everything on display.

Cass laughed, and said, "No. Just a friend."

Mel was suddenly very aware she was still holding the dancer's hand, and couldn't work out if it was reassuring or one of the factors that had put her suddenly on edge.

Sitting on a stool near the blonde, another dancer she'd seen earlier leaned close to a mirror, fixing her make-up. Her long wig hung on a hook, and now Mel saw it was the girl who'd been in Glenn's office at the

Flag and Flowers the previous evening – Suze, who he'd referred to as his 'PA'.

"You got that photo?" asked Cass.

Mel stepped forward, showed it to the seated Suze, and the naked blonde dancer leaned in to look too. Another girl moved over from another stool to look. "My friend's the one in the middle," said Mel. "She's been missing for a few days. She's older than she looks. I'm just asking around to see if anyone has seen her."

The dancers were all shaking their heads already.

Mel looked down, struggling with her disappointment.

"Why you asking here?" asked Suze.

Mel shrugged. "It's the kind of place girls end up, isn't it?" she said, hoping she wasn't offending anyone. This or on the street, was the subtext.

"You should be careful," said Cass softly. "There are people you don't want to cross. Digging can be dangerous."

She took it as a gentle warning, rather than a threat. She turned, and met the dancer's look. "If the Lazenbies have anything to do with my friend's disappearance they'll have a lot more than a few questions to deal with. I know the family: I could bring them down in an instant..."

She hoped Cass took that as a gentle warning too, rather than a threat. One she might pass back up the tree.

She turned back to the other dancers, gestured with the photo again to see if anyone now remembered anything, but was met with blank looks.

Was she just clutching at straws? Was it really so strange that Glenn had started calling her 'Mels' all of a sudden? Maybe he'd always called her that – she couldn't really remember. It had been years since she'd seen him, after all.

Then she saw that the dancers' attention had shifted. Mel turned, and saw Glenn standing in the doorway.

"This is a private area," he said, eyes fixed on Mel. "Nobody comes back here. Health and safety, and all that."

"I'm sorry, I was just… just asking around."

He said nothing, just took a step back and waited for her to squeeze through a gap not quite big enough. Again, she breathed his heady cologne, the smell of leather from his jacket, trying not to flinch at the proximity of their bodies.

She hadn't fooled him at all, pretending to like him, being nice to him and flashing big eyes in his direction, and now he made sure she knew it. He'd just been letting her jump through hoops. Amusing himself.

She stopped a few steps into the main room of the club. Turned to face him, chin up defiantly. "I'm going to find her," she said. "I won't let anyone stand in my way."

"I hope you do," he said, his soft voice barely rising above the swell of music. "Just tread carefully, you hear me? Don't piss off the people who might have your back. People like me."

He phrased it like advice on etiquette, but delivered it as a threat. And then he smiled – the smile he used when he wanted someone to know he was fooling with them, even though often he wasn't – and Mel was reminded of her father's warning. *These people are far worse than you could ever imagine.*

5. JIMMY

"I've got an assignment for you."

This was the day before Jimmy Lazenby found his estranged brother in a strip club with the woman who should have been the love of Jimmy's life. A day when he still thought the biggest challenges in his life were secret service bureaucracy and the dull regularity with which a current person of interest would want him dead.

London. A wide corridor in an anonymous office block on the south bank of the river. Geometrically precise interior architecture and furniture, plain gray walls with abstract art hung at regular intervals between the doorways, a slate gray carpet without a mark on it, despite the regular foot traffic.

It could have been a financial services office, or a private medical facility, flawless in its anonymity and complete lack of character, but Jimmy knew better.

People were killed from here.

Not physically, but this was where the committees met to cast their judgments, where analytics and planning teams gathered around tables, pointing at screens, monitoring operations around the world. This was where they drafted orders to send to operatives thousands of miles away, to agents and dubiously employed third parties, for operations most of which would struggle to be described as legal if they were ever known about beyond these walls and a few select offices in Westminster and Whitehall. It was all about finding the right means to achieve the desired end.

Jimmy Lazenby stopped, mid-stride. "Really?" he said. "Are you taking the piss? I've just stepped out from the latest going over and you have something else for me already?"

Perhaps that wasn't the normal way to respond to your controller in an organization that operated as a strict military hierarchy, but then Jimmy Lazenby had never been regarded as a normal Section Eight agent, and his relationship with his controller was more informal than most.

And he'd just emerged from a grueling three-hour review into his most recent assignment. That kind of thing was an increasingly common activity: to most, the

Section didn't even officially exist so could never be officially investigated, so instead they constantly found themselves under internal review to make sure everything was above board. When he joined the Section, Jimmy had never anticipated how much of his existence would revolve around audit trails and three-sixty degree monitoring of activity.

It wasn't an aspect of the job Jimmy appreciated, and he'd made that clear to everyone around him more than once.

"I never take the piss," said Douglas Conner. "You know that. Let's walk."

To the left, the iconic skyline of Parliament, marked by the scaffolding-clad towers of Westminster Abbey, Victoria Tower, and Big Ben; to the right, a gray stone wall, and then a line of nondescript blocky buildings, regularly placed leafy trees breaking up the harsh grayness of it all. The path the two men followed ran immediately by the wide river, where tourist boats and heavy industrial barges plied their trade, the boundary between path and river marked by a waist-high stone wall, and regular pillars topped by lamp-posts whose bases were dark statues of serpentine, monstrous fish.

Tourists strolled and sat on benches and the walls. Ragged pigeons and gulls strutted, squabbling over scraps. Business people and civil servants in suits walked, carrying briefcases and tablets, an opportunity to get away from their workplaces, get some air, talk about the kind of shit they couldn't discuss in their offices.

"It's sensitive," said Conner, referring to the kind of shit he wasn't willing to discuss back in the office. Conner was a square-shouldered man with a buzz-cut and a stiff, military bearing, who always had the air of a man bound to his desk who had been far more comfortable in his younger, more active, days in the field.

"When is it not sensitive?" Jimmy asked – not confrontationally, just an acknowledgment – and the two laughed. They both knew there was sensitive, and then there was the kind of sensitive best discussed out of the office.

As they walked, Jimmy was acutely aware of their surroundings: the distribution of the people around them, any glances in their direction, the phones and other devices people were using. He knew that was a false comfort, that any serious eavesdropping was just as likely to come from a carefully planted bug or a directional microphone pointed from a nearby window.

"So?"

"This one's off the books," said Conner. "Even more so than usual. And it's personal."

"Personal for you or for me?"

"It's your brother." That made it personal, but it was only the following evening when Jimmy saw Mel in the club with Glenn that he understood it was far more personal than just Glenn, that Conner had omitted a vital element: Mel. Conner's daughter, and Jimmy's lost love.

"Glenn?" said Jimmy, still blissfully unaware of the rest of it. "What's he done now?"

"Almost certainly nothing," said Conner.

"But he knows a man who has, right?"

Conner nodded.

Jimmy's controller knew the Lazenby family well. Not just because Jimmy had once dated his daughter. Not just because Douglas Conner had somehow seen something in Jimmy, the kind of character traits that might allow Conner to mold him into a good agent. Not just the traits, but the determination to turn things around, to do something good with his life rather than drift into the kind of life Glenn now led.

Douglas Conner knew plenty about the Venn diagram of gangs that overlapped on Lazenby territory, the kind of people Jimmy's brother and late father fixed things for. He knew exactly what kind of life he'd guided Jimmy away from.

"There's a girl," said Conner. "Missing. The daughter of an old friend of mine. Harriet Rayner. You'd have met her, back when... Ten years ago. She was only seven then."

Seventeen now. In any other circumstances, most likely a runaway after an argument at home, or absconded with a boy in the vain hope that love was not only an actual thing but one that might last. But those circumstances didn't require an out-of-office discussion like this.

"What makes this different?" asked Jimmy. It was clearly more than a runaway friend of the family.

"Last seen by her friends Friday evening. Everything normal. Last located on CCTV Saturday morning, climbing into the back of your brother's car. Her mobile phone went offline moments after getting into Glenn's car."

Nobody just switched their phone off these days, and the chances that the battery had died at that moment were laughable. So either she voluntarily gave up her phone, in which case Glenn must at least be helping her to disappear, or Jimmy's brother had moved quickly when the girl got into the car and so must be responsible for her disappearance. Either way, Glenn Lazenby was at the center of this.

"You've checked the clubs?" The family owned several strip clubs and thinly disguised brothels in London and the Home Counties. Glenn wouldn't normally recruit for them personally, but Jimmy knew he liked to take an interest.

Even now, though, Jimmy found it hard to believe his brother would put a seventeen-year-old on stage in a strip club. Or worse…

"Nothing," said Conner. "She first met Glenn a couple of weeks earlier, and they've been in touch by SMS and a couple of calls in the intervening period. We have transcripts of the texts, but they don't give anything away."

"So they've been chatting. What makes you suspect foul play? And why is the Section involved?"

"She was last seen getting into Glenn's car, Jimmy. And he's a Lazenby."

It wasn't meant to be an insult, just a statement of fact. The Lazenby family were trouble.

"Your brother's mixed up with some bad people," said Conner. "He's upped his game in the last year or two. Given the circumstances, if anyone knows what's happened to Harriet it's him."

Jimmy nodded. "You know the old man's dead? Last week."

Conner nodded. "I do. It's the perfect in for you." No sympathy; he knew Jimmy would not be mourning. Conner reached into a jacket pocket and then passed a pen drive to Jimmy. "The files. I'm giving you a couple of weeks' family absence. Compassionate leave, and all that shit."

"I'm touched."

"This could get messy, Jimmy."

"What am I supposed to do?"

"Do what a Section Eight operative is trained to do. You'll have the usual protection. Get into the thick of it and make the best choices on the ground. That's what we do, isn't it? I trust you, Jimmy. More than anyone. Maybe more even than I'd trust myself."

The usual protection. The Section Eight equivalent of diplomatic immunity from prosecution, in case lines were crossed, laws transgressed.

In case things got messy.

Harriet Rayner. Seventeen-year-old daughter of Geoffrey and Penelope. Geoffrey deceased three years ago, a senior civil servant, which could mean almost anything. Penelope

Rayner, variously addicted to prescribed painkillers, alcohol, and just about anything that could distract her from the real world. Mother and daughter pretty much estranged, with the mother as occasional stalker of her daughter when she was more lucid.

Add to that the rich kid lens that magnified every tiny flaw in the girl's life – not that Jimmy was prejudiced, at all – and the kid had plenty to run away from.

And it certainly was a rich kid's life. Most of her father's family wealth was held in trust funds, used to pay her way through an exclusive college where she was studying for A-levels – good grades, no complaints from teachers – and paying for the north London apartment where she nominally lived with her mother. In reality, Penny Rayner had another place a mile away, her finances governed closely by the terms of Geoff Rayner's will – a protection against her excesses and inability to cope, Jimmy presumed.

Might money be a driver, here? Harriet was a good potential target for extortion: plenty of money, and not exactly living a secure, protected life.

But anyone who researched the family would know the money was securely locked away, and would be difficult to release for any pay-out. And there had been no ransom demand, yet. Why wait, if money was the motive?

Certainly if Glenn was involved. Jimmy's brother may be many things, but patient wasn't one of them. He was ruthlessly efficient, too: if he was responsible, there would be a plan, a schedule to follow, no dithering or delay.

And kidnap?

Glenn Lazenby was no better than their dead father, but kidnap had never been a family pursuit. Extortion, prostitution, protection rackets, yes, that was all there on Glenn's file – no surprises there – but kidnap took a certain type of mind.

It didn't add up.

There was a connection, yes – the sighting of Harriet in Glenn's car on Saturday, shortly before her mobile phone went offline – but there was something missing.

He should try to put the personal aspects aside, he knew. Not assess the Glenn he'd known, but the one in the files Douglas Conner had handed over on that pen drive.

There had been diversification in the family's activities, which must be down to Glenn. The changes predated their father's illness, but perhaps there had been some handing over of operations before that. Does a bastard like Trevor

Lazenby ever retire? Maybe. He had a place in Spain, and a stake in… had the old man taken up *golf*, for God's sake?

It was hard to picture his father riding around on a golf cart with his clubs. Easier to view the golf club he owned near Estepona as a front for money laundering, though. Much more realistic.

Anyway… Diversification. The properties overseas. Drugs. The latter had always been a no-no for the old man, but Glenn had never had the same standards.

Jimmy had to keep an open mind, though. His father had been a master at slipping through the gaps, and had never done jail time, only ever convicted for a couple of minor traffic offenses, and that was one standard Glenn had maintained. But the files on the two of them were full of part-built cases that had never reached court, the result of good lawyers and even better friends in the criminal justice system, Jimmy was sure.

Pretty much any major money-related crime had been dropped into their files at some time. In addition to the extortion, protection rackets, and prostitution, there were allegations of insider trading, money laundering, involvement behind the scenes with major robberies and people trafficking rings, forgery, and drugs.

He stopped reading.

It was strange raking over all this stuff. Trying to separate out what he read in the files from all the shit in his head.

Home. Family.

He'd abandoned all that a long time ago. Walked away from it all. His family was the Section now. His home wherever they sent him. He didn't get involved.

Even now, Harriet Rayner wasn't a teenaged kid, probably cowering in some locked room somewhere or lying face-down in a ditch; she was a file, a problem to be solved.

And so, too, was Glenn Lazenby. No more than a problem to be solved.

Mel.

Of course.

Douglas Conner probably at least gave a shit about the missing daughter of an old family friend, but not enough to subvert a Section Eight agent, and associated resources, on a personal quest to find her.

But his own daughter… that was something else entirely. The kind of daughter who was so headstrong she was likely to throw herself into the thick of things just as an agent like Jimmy Lazenby would do, but without any of the training, experience, or understanding. The one whose friend was missing, but any reference to whom had been curiously absent from the files on that pen drive Conner had handed over.

That was different.

That really was personal.

And Conner had known damned well that if he'd let slip that this was really all about Mel, Jimmy wouldn't have gone anywhere near the assignment. So Conner had suppressed that element, so he could throw in an agent who, once committed, could never turn his back, not now he knew the girl he'd once loved was putting herself in danger.

Finding Harriet Rayner would be a bonus. In truth, this was all about protecting Mel Conner, and as soon as Jimmy laid eyes on her in that seedy little club the family owned, he understood completely, just as Douglas Conner had known he would.

So, the club. He really should have stuck with the stripper. Let her charm him into a private dance and whatever else was on offer in one of those curtained-off booths at the back. Pretend he hadn't seen Mel sitting there with Glenn and giving Jimmy the *Sweet god, not him* stare.

Instead… the chat. The skirting around anything he really wanted to discuss with his brother because that would mean exposing what he was doing there, and he couldn't have Mel know any of that.

And later, finally alone with her at the bar. Telling her she just had to get out of there and leave it to him, and even that was telling her too much.

The slap.

That girl sure did pack some power.

That was a slap with meaning, a slap with the weight of history behind it.

He'd suggested it. He'd told her to slap him and walk out, use it as cover to make good her escape. Instead, she'd used it to go back to Glenn. A slap that gave her new credibility in his eyes. Jimmy had to credit her with that: it was a smart move, albeit one that dug her in deeper.

But he couldn't do anything right now. He was powerless.

He couldn't just drag her out of there. Even if he was able to overpower Mel, Glenn had enough security guys around the place to easily stop him.

So all Jimmy could do was finish his water, stand, and walk out, hoping Mel hadn't just made the biggest mistake of her life.

§

Outside, it was still mid-evening, still light. It was so easy to lose track of time in clubs like Ryders, a deliberate ploy on their part to lull the punters into staying for longer than they'd intended, spending more.

Jimmy waited in a fast food place over the road from the club, the only non-takeout customer. He sat at one of the four Formica-topped tables by the windows, cradling coffee in a polystyrene cup, breathing air heavy with grease. A steady trickle of customers came in and left a minute or two later with kebabs, burgers, boxed pizzas, hot dogs.

Jimmy hadn't eaten since first thing, but he wasn't tempted to remedy that now. The weak, characterless coffee was bad enough.

He watched the street. The shops were mostly closed by now, lit from within by lights that would burn all night. Occasional traffic drifted by. Smokers stood outside a pub, and at one point jostling broke out among them before things calmed down again.

The town hadn't changed much since Jimmy had left ten years before.

Ryders was anonymous from the outside, just a doorway between two shops, opening onto a small lobby area and a staircase that led up to the club. Two bouncers stood just inside, occasionally emerging for a smoke, and once to talk to someone who pulled up in a silver Mercedes.

While Jimmy watched, eighteen customers entered and six left, the place slowly filling up for the evening. Clientele were mostly suited men, plus a group of young guys in jeans and sports shirts, and two couples who met outside with hugs and laughter and went in together.

Jimmy made mental note of all this, by force of habit as much as anything else. Building up a picture of what he must assume was a typical Wednesday night at one of the family businesses.

For a time he forced himself to imagine how things might have been.

He could have stayed. Become a part of this. And by now he would have been Glenn's junior partner.

Could he imagine a world where he would have fitted into that role?

Easily.

He wasn't that man now, though. He'd seen and done too much. Changed too much. He and Glenn had fallen down opposite sides of a great divide. But back then… It would have been so easy. Far easier than the route he'd chosen.

Mel saw him straight away. She emerged from the club, stood with her arms wrapped around herself looking briefly vulnerable and exposed, then looked up and saw him watching her from his window seat.

For a moment he thought she was going to turn and walk away. He wouldn't have blamed her. Then she straightened, checked the road, and crossed.

He stood as she entered. Said, "Coffee? I wouldn't." Then sat, as she lowered herself into the seat opposite him.

Behind the counter, the young server gave him a dirty look, clearly having overheard.

They sat in silence.

Jimmy Lazenby was always in control. He could judge a situation, assess the main players. He always had the right thing to say, the strategic way to play the people around him. He could blend in or stand out, support or challenge. He could be the wit of the party, or the straight man.

All were skills he'd assiduously learned.

He was good at what he did. One of the best.

But now he sat opposite Mel Conner, aware of an unfamiliar tension in his jaw, the fullness of words that wouldn't come.

The silence drew itself out, his mind racing.

He felt the sting of her slap again, but knew it was only in his mind – the pain had been no more than fleeting. It had only been a slap. He'd felt far worse.

"So," he finally said, "how's your life been?" It was perhaps the lamest thing he'd ever said.

She was breathtakingly beautiful. That choppy haircut suited her, complementing blue eyes that were exactly as he remembered. Had he noticed the nose stud before? A little diamond glint that occasionally snagged the attention away from those eyes.

He looked away, out of the window to where another duo of suited men had paused in the Ryders doorway.

Forced himself to focus.

"Ups and downs," she said, and it took a few seconds for him to realize she was answering his lame question. Her life: ups and downs.

"Relationship shit, you know," she went on.

Relationships. She'd had relationships. Of course she had, he just didn't think of her in those terms. Didn't think of her at all until today.

"You?"

He shrugged. Looked away again. "It's strange being back," he said. "After so long."

"Your father," she said. "I'm sorry."

"You shouldn't be. I'm not."

She looked shocked, even though she knew Jimmy's father had never been a good man. Now, Jimmy was reminded of how Mel had always been a fundamentally decent person. Of course she was shocked at such brutal disregard for how most people feel about family. But Jimmy had distanced himself from all this for so long, he didn't even think in those terms: family bonds and all that.

Again, he was lost for words. No easy, quick response. No obvious way to manage this encounter.

"You walked away," she said. He'd forgotten how Mel didn't do easy either, how she had never been one to turn away from the harder things.

"You told me to go," he said. Those blue eyes… He couldn't look away from them.

"And you believed me."

He had, but only because she'd meant it. He'd seen it in her eyes, the loathing of who he was, and who he would inevitably become. He didn't say that, though. Not now.

Especially now.

That look, back then, that moment of true connection, had changed his life. Had made him the man he now was.

That was the moment when he'd fallen on the other side of the great divide from his brother.

"You made me see some truths," he said, instead. "About who I was. About who I was becoming. You deserved much better than that. I wanted to be that kind of better, but I didn't know how."

"And do you now?" That stopped him in his tracks. What did she mean by such a question? What would she do if she knew he *had* become, if not that kind of better, than at least *some* kind of better?

He looked away. He couldn't remember ever feeling so out of his depth.

"I'm a different person now," he told her, the best he could do.

"So am I."

Vulnerable. That's how she made him feel. Not for any of the stupid old emotional reasons, but for the uncertainty she created, for his sudden loss of the ability to read another person, to even begin to know what might be in their head.

He took a deep breath, stared out across the road again, away from those eyes, the glint of the diamond nose-stud.

"You should go," he said, turning back to her, seeing that she was studying him closely and had probably been doing so all the time he'd looked away. "Get out of here. You're not safe here." Again, the dilemma of how to convince her to go without giving anything more away, information that might simply dig her in deeper.

This kind of thing was so much easier with complete strangers. To them he was just the anonymous agent, the guy who was making them safe; they didn't have a history with him, and they wouldn't have a future where their understanding of him was different.

They didn't complicate things.

"You said that before," Mel said. "Inside the club. You said I was in danger and should run away. You said I should just leave finding my best friend to you and your people. What did you mean by that? Who are your people? What are you doing here?"

He should know never to underestimate Mel Conner.

"I know what you've come here for, Mel," he said. "I know about Harriet Rayner. That's why I'm here too. This is what I do. This kind of thing. If she can be found I'll find her, and I'll bring her back."

Again, he couldn't tell what she was thinking from the way she looked at him now.

"I made choices," he told her. "Back then. I turned my back on the family, all the things they represented, the things you hated."

"You did this, whatever this is, for *me?*"

He shook his head. "No. I did it for me. I chose to become one of the good guys. And now I'm going to find out what's happened to your friend and get her back."

"Why should I believe that?"

That stung. Not just the words, but the weight of history they carried: why should she ever believe something he told her?

"It's what I do."

Why was she shaking her head now? Looking away, clearly frustrated…

"You can't do this, Jimmy. You can't just stroll back into my life and expect me to trust you. To believe in you. You walked out ten years ago. You can't go claiming the noble high ground now, expecting me to believe you walked out on me so you could be – what was the term you used? – one of the good guys. You were running away."

Without a thought, he reached across the table and covered her hand with his, and they looked at each other, startled by the contact.

"You don't have to believe me," he said. "You don't have to trust me. You just need to not get in the way and complicate things. Can you at least do that?"

As soon as the words came out, he understood how cruel they sounded. Perhaps he'd even meant them to sound that way, a shock to break through her defenses, the verbal equivalent of that slap.

Fending her off.

He couldn't do this. The emotions she stirred. The feelings and responses. All of them, vulnerabilities.

The shock on her face turned to… to something else. Eyes wider, glazing with unspilled tears. A tremble of the lower lip.

"Let me do this," he said, more gently now. "And then I'll be gone again, forever." And he would make damned sure Doug Conner never sent him on a babysitting expedition again.

She stood. Straightened with an angry roll of the shoulders.

Looked down at him, and said, "Fuck you, Jimmy Lazenby. You and your family, you're all the same, and you always will be. Fuck the lot of you."

He had time to see he'd been wrong about that look on her face. She wasn't upset: that look was a flash of frustration and defiance, of biting back a response

And then she turned and walked out.

6. MEL

Once a Lazenby, always a Lazenby.

She should have known.

Should never have given in to that fatal moment of hesitation when she emerged from the doorway of Ryders, head still fizzing with… with anger at Glenn for turning on her, but also some kind of sense of justification: he'd let the mask slip, let her see beyond that veneer of charming rogue he liked to wear. He'd reminded her of why she would always regret the few times she'd trusted that family.

It was always a mistake.

And so she'd emerged into daylight, blinking as her eyes adjusted. Looked up, across the street, and seen Jimmy sitting there in that window seat. He'd looked away immediately, pretending he wasn't watching for her, waiting.

And she'd hesitated.

Just allowed that pause to go a moment beyond the point where she could turn to one side or the other and walk, pretending she hadn't seen him. Now, if she walked, they would both know she'd seen him and *then* made that choice.

It would have saved time, at least, because now, only a short time later, she was walking away from him anyway. She'd stood and marched out of that fast food joint, leaving Jimmy sitting there, just looked down at her feet and kept on going – any direction as long as it was away.

She looked up now. She'd been walking for a few minutes, along Queen's Street where Ryders was, and then left onto Commercial Road. Heading back to her room on autopilot, she knew these streets so well.

She didn't know what she'd expected, but she certainly hadn't anticipated Jimmy's mysterious claims about why he was here. She still didn't know what he was actually claiming he was. Some kind of undercover police officer? Some kind of lone vigilante, out to bring his family down?

I'm a different person now… I chose to become one of the good guys.

Whatever it was, he knew about Harriet, and the fact he was here now, staking out his brother, confirmed she was onto something.

Glenn's response, too, confirmed that. The slipping of his mask. She'd touched a raw nerve there. Asking around the club, showing the dancers Harriet's photograph. Was it just a pride thing – Glenn getting pissed with her for going behind his back on his home territory – or had she touched on something more?

He knew something. She was sure of that, at least.

He'd taken to calling her Mels.

He *knew* something.

Jubilee Park. Lines of lime trees marked the paths across open green areas. To one side she saw the trees marking where the lake was tucked away in a fold of the landscape, where she'd fed the ducks with bread when she was little.

The light was closing in now, that twilight grayness that sucked color from the surroundings.

She'd reacted too strongly to Jimmy. Too strongly in many ways.

She shouldn't have told him to fuck off. Shouldn't have told him he was just like the rest of the family. Even though that hard man, leave it all to me, attitude had pissed her off, she knew he was different to his brother, his father, knew that telling him he was just a chip off the old block would hurt him far more than any slap.

She felt her wrist automatically at that thought, imagined it was still hurting from the blow.

She'd hit him hard, and now she couldn't help a little smile at the recollection. The look on his face. The utter disbelief.

He'd been surprisingly awkward in that fast food place. The way his look kept slipping away. Him, trying to be the hard man and yet so vulnerable.

She'd got him wrong in the strip club, on that one, at least. The way he'd kept staring at the girls roaming the place in their underwear and the near-naked dancers. He hadn't been looking at *them* – he'd been avoiding looking at *her*. He did exactly the same in that smelly takeaway, only instead of looking at bouncing breasts and perfect legs he was watching the traffic passing outside, the people walking by. Looking at anything but Mel.

She stopped, out of breath for no reason. Heart thumping for no reason. She wasn't that unfit.

It had been ten years. Since then she'd been to university, had a succession of shitty jobs and even shittier relationships. She'd gone back to university as a postgrad, and finally started to find her feet. She'd grown up. Taken control.

It wasn't Jimmy getting under her skin, she realized. Making her react like this. It was the situation. Her fears for Harriet. The adrenaline rush of standing up to Glenn. The sense of empowerment of actually doing something about it, and the anger at the men around her who kept trying to put her off.

Jimmy was just a symbol – of the way she was being treated, the barriers in her way, a flash from the past she'd long since left behind, the girl she'd once been.

So when she felt her heart thumping in her chest and her breath sucking raggedly in her lungs as it was right now, it wasn't for Jimmy, it was because of all the other stuff – anything but him.

"Fuck it," she hissed under her breath. And again: "Fuck *you*, Jimmy Lazenby."

Mel wasn't the kind of person who swore much, not that she objected to cursing. She just didn't do it. Until now.

She made herself focus, reminding herself that none of this was about her, or about Jimmy Lazenby. *Harriet.*

She took the photo from her purse and studied her friend's innocent features. It was a sobering moment. A time of happiness captured, however long it had actually lasted.

She straightened, forced a long, deep breath. Started to walk again.

The footsteps behind her came up suddenly.

She had time to register the sound, sense that the approach was fast; time to curse Jimmy, first for waiting for her at that place across the road from Ryders and now for following her, for not giving up and just letting her *go*.

Then she felt a heavy impact between her shoulder blades, so hard it knocked the air from her lungs. Her head snapped back as her body was abruptly propelled forward, and bolts of pain stabbed through her – from the impact, from that sharp snap of the head jerking at her neck so hard she feared something must have broken, from her arms flying out and snapping straight.

She landed face down in the dirt, taking the impact on her chest, her chin, her nose. Her vision blackened briefly and then she was only aware of the pains in her chest as she gasped for breath, the ache in her chin and jaw, the copper taste of blood.

Her nose. That was where the blood came from, a sudden gush of blood. Was it broken? That was her main thought: would she spend the rest of her life with a crooked nose? And then she was appalled that she should be so vain, when–

A boot struck her in the side. Not a full-blown kick aimed to break ribs, but a dull impact, then a continued pressure turning her onto her side, onto her back until she sprawled there helpless, so easily incapacitated.

It wasn't Jimmy.

Of course it wasn't Jimmy!

Her mind was doing crazy right now, panic bubbling under, threatening to swamp her.

She sat, pushing herself up with hands on the hard dirt. A small stone dug into one palm, a jolt of new pain that brought her senses into sharp focus.

She rubbed at her nose with a swipe of one arm, a vivid smear of blood leaving a broad trail along the forearm of her suede jacket. Her nose was throbbing, and she breathed rapidly through her mouth.

She scrambled backward, away.

The guy just stood there, staring.

Had she seen him before? Tall, carrying plenty of weight, but clearly well-muscled. Thick, dark beard and shaved head. A silver ring through his nose and a bar through one eyebrow. Leather jacket, black jeans, Doc Marten boots.

Had he been at Ryders? At the Flag and Flowers the day before?

Her back came up against a tree trunk, and she used it to lever herself up to her feet, wiping at her pounding nose again. She wasn't going to sit there peering helplessly up at this thug. Even now, she had to look up to confront him, but at least she was on her feet.

He took a step toward her. Another.

He came to stand looming over her, so close that even through the blood she could smell the stink of tobacco and something else on his breath.

Her eyes flitted from side to side, desperately assessing options.

How could she ever hope to out-run him when she could still barely breathe?

What was this? She was thinking Ryders, Flag and Flowers, thinking Glenn Lazenby and his villainous friends, but…

The man's hand went to her neck, pushed up against her jaw so her throat burned and her head ground against the tree.

His body pressed against her, a physical presence so abruptly terrifying she almost blacked out, and maybe that would have been best.

What if he was just some random psycho preying on a lone woman? Would that be better or worse than Glenn sending someone after her?

"Right now," he said, his voice a low rumble in her ear, "you're more scared than you've ever been in your entire life."

The look in his eyes... He was enjoying this, drawing out her terror. His hand on her throat pushed up even harder, briefly tightening before relaxing enough to let her breathe.

"Your mind is racing through possibilities. Am I right? Imagining scenarios you'd never have thought you'd have to imagine. Scenarios with you, and with me."

He didn't blink. How did he do that? And why did she fix on that one detail, when she was close to choking to death? When his body was pressing against her and he was making her think... *scenarios...*?

"You're wondering how this is going to end, and what particular sequence of events will take you from right now to that end. What you will have to endure. What you might *choose* to endure, just to get to the end."

She'd never felt so powerless. So controlled by another person.

He fell silent for a moment, and then finally his gaze moved away from hers. He nodded at the hand she held out to one side and she realized that even through all of this she had clung on to the photograph of Harriet.

"'Scare her.' That's what I was told. 'Stop her making a pain of herself.'"

So he wasn't a random psycho.

Fast as a striking snake, he reached out and snatched the photo from Mel's grip, one hand still on her throat. Now he waved the picture close to her face, and said, "You're wasting your time. You hear me? You should be looking elsewhere for Harriet Rayner, not stirring things up here, making idle threats about bringing people down. You should be careful which boats you rock."

Then he laughed, and added, "And remember: unlike you, I don't make idle threats. I'll be watching you. I'll always be there. In the shadows. In your nightmares. And if you fuck off the wrong people, next time I won't be so nice."

He pushed his face into hers, his spit on her cheek, the stink of his breath in her swollen nostrils. "Do you get that? Or do I need to make myself even clearer?"

"Where?" she gasped. The blood flowed more slowly now, but still she had to swallow to allow herself to breathe, to speak. "Where should I look for my friend?" Even now, she wouldn't let go.

"How much of a shit do you think I give?" said the man. "I just know you're wasting your time here."

He squeezed her throat again, so tight she thought he'd decided to kill her after all. She felt that blackness creeping into her vision again, the kind of heat in her face that told her she was about to faint, and then he relented and she gasped for breath again.

"Do you understand?"

Suddenly, the guy tensed against her.

She couldn't work out what had changed, what this might signal, and then the grip on her throat eased again, the hand fell away, and as the guy stepped back both his hands stayed in the air at shoulder height.

"That's better," said a familiar voice.

She hadn't seen him creep up, hadn't heard him, and neither had her assailant.

Now, her assailant turned slowly, coming to stand facing Jimmy Lazenby who was casually pointing a handgun at the guy's chest – the handgun that must have been the first indication of Jimmy's presence when he pressed it into the man's back.

Mel thought her legs were going to give way, and hated that weakness. Hated the rush of emotions, the sheer relief. Hated feeling grateful to Jimmy Fucking Lazenby.

She leaned back against the tree, hands on its rough bark. Felt the tightness of blood crusting on her lips and chin, and resisted the urge to rub at it, hated that vain part of her psyche that reminded her she looked like shit and her nose was probably broken and she'd look like a rugby player or a boxer for the rest of her life and…

She closed her eyes, forced her breathing to slow.

Opened them and saw that the tableau had not changed: the big bearded guy standing with his hands partly raised, Jimmy with a gun leveled at his chest, the two eyeing each other warily.

"I think that belongs to the lady," said Jimmy, nodding toward something in the guy's left hand.

The photograph. Penny Rayner's photograph of her daughter and late husband. Penny had described it as all she had of them – she couldn't lose that!

Mel stepped forward and plucked the picture from the guy's hand, then retreated to the solidity of her tree again. She couldn't work out if breathing was so difficult because of the drying blood, any damage to her nose and throat, or the simple fact of coming down – albeit only marginally – from being so damned terrified.

She swallowed, didn't know if she'd be able to speak, but nonetheless tried. "Right now..." Another swallow against the dry ache of her throat. "Right now, your mind is racing through possibilities," she said to her attacker. "Imagining scenarios... Is that how it goes, your little spiel? You're wondering how this is going to end."

She was shaking, and fought to bring the tremors under control.

"Well it ends like this," she said, finding strength for her voice at least. "You walk away. Go back to Glenn and tell him that if he's got anything to do with my friend's disappearance he's going to pay. We're going to bring him down. Tell him to be careful which boats *he* rocks."

There was a moment when she didn't know which way this was going to go, the bearded guy's look switching between her and Jimmy as he weighed up his options. Then the man's shoulders slumped, he shrugged as if all this was nothing, and he said, "Whatever." He took a step back, then added, "But remember. I'm watching. Both of you."

"That's good," said Jimmy. "I like an audience."

And then it was over, and the bearded guy turned and walked away, as if he was merely out for a stroll.

Jimmy lowered the gun, then tucked it into his jacket.

He turned to Mel, and said, "You okay?" Then added, "I'm sorry. I wasn't following you. I just wanted to be sure you were okay."

Really? He was *apologizing?*

And then she'd taken one step, two, and almost fell into his arms.

His arms, his embrace, the feel of his body against hers. Such a strange mix of the nostalgically familiar – something that had always been and would always be – and rawness, newness.

They fit together in subtly different ways now. His body was harder, stronger, neither of them allowing themselves to relax into the embrace as they once would have done. His stubble was coarser on the crown of her head, and then against her cheek as he adjusted, arching his back so she could mold herself into that embrace.

But more than those tangible similarities and differences, it was the subtle things that threw her, the ways they moved and adjusted, the scents, even the *sounds*, that were both the same and different in indefinable ways.

Perhaps these things, the similarities and differences, were just an artifact of memory, and this was how they had always been.

She didn't know how long they stayed like that, probably only a few seconds, and then he leaned back, holding her at arms' length now.

She peered up at him, saw him studying her, wondered what this signaled and then almost immediately realized it was probably nothing more than concern for his suit and shirt – blood could be a bugger to get out.

Did he care about such things? Did they even occur to him? And those thoughts alone reminded her that she didn't know this man, that there were dangers in assuming she did simply because she had once known the youngster who had *become* this man.

"Sorry. Sorry, I…" She pulled away, made a feeble effort to brush at the red stain she'd left on his shirt, then shrugged, smiled helplessly, apologized again.

"Breathe," he said. His voice was strong, and surprisingly calming, given that everything else about him in these last few seconds had been anything *but* calming. "Breathe in and hold it, then, slowly, out."

What had he detected in her? Why was he talking like this? Was the mad rush of her thoughts manifesting itself visibly, somehow? Was she that easy to read? Was…? Was…? Was…?

She breathed.

Held.

Breathed out.

Understood what he'd seen, the panic emerging now that the peak of crisis and danger had passed.

He reached for her, fingertips gently exploring the bridge of her nose and yet, despite the softness of his touch, sending bolts of pain stabbing into her head.

When she flinched he moved his hand to cup her jaw, allowed her to press cat-like against his palm, and then withdrew.

"Is there somewhere we can go?" he said, business-like now. "I need better light."

"For…?"

"Your injuries. I need to clean you up, see if you need medical attention. I've done stitches in the field before, but if you need anyone to fix up your face you might want someone with a defter touch than me." He was trying to make light of it, but that only made her wonder just how messed up her face was. And that 'in the field' – who *was* he?

"And… I need to be sure you're safe."

She hadn't thought of that. Hadn't considered the possibility that rather than seeing that bastard off, they'd merely delayed him and he might be back, even though he'd said as much.

"What was he going to do to me?" she said. "What if you hadn't shown up when you did?"

Jimmy looked away, which was answer enough, perhaps. "He wanted to scare you."

"He did that."

"There's scared, and then there's *scared*," he said, and something in his phrasing reminded her of her father's warning that these people were far worse than she could imagine.

The house where she was staying wasn't far, just across the park and a couple more streets away. The place was in darkness, the owner either out or already in bed. Mel unlocked the front door and turned to Jimmy.

"I'll be okay from here," she said. "I'm fine. Thank you."

"No."

For a moment she didn't know how to respond. There was no room for negotiation in that response. She just stared, until he went on.

"Sorry, but no. I need to at least be sure your room is secure. And someone needs to have a look at that." He nodded at her, and she wondered again how bad her broken face must look.

She bit back on her response, her default rejection of help. She knew he cared, and she shouldn't turn that away.

She led him up the stairs, unlocked the bedroom door, and stood back to let him through.

Inside, pushing the door shut, she found all of a sudden she couldn't meet his look.

Perhaps sensing her discomfort, he stepped aside, gestured at the bed, all business-like, and said, "If you could just sit down here under the light?"

He went through to the bathroom, came back moments later with a damp cloth, a box of tissues.

She sat looking up at him as he leaned over her, gently tilting her face back and to one side to catch the light.

"So tell me," he said, as he scrutinized her damaged features, "did you black out at all when you hit your head back there?"

She thought hard, even though all she wanted to do was forget. "I don't know," she told him. "I don't think so. I felt like I was going to, but I don't think I actually did."

"Do you feel sick? Dizzy? Any blurred vision, or double vision?"

She shook her head, and winced immediately.

"What hurts?"

She reached up to touch her neck. "My neck. My nose and chin. My pride."

He moved his hand down, traced fingertips over her neck where her assailant had squeezed.

She flinched at his touch, said, "Sorry."

He said nothing. Reached for the damp cloth and pressed it gently just below her nose, where blood had dried.

"You're bruised," he said. "Your neck. Your chin and nose. There's swelling, but it'll go down. I don't think you've broken anything. You were lucky."

The pressure of the cloth was strangely soothing, warm against her sore skin. Even when he moved up to clean the blood from her nose, she was aware of the dull ache, but his ministrations felt good, comforting.

"Any damage inside your mouth? Any other pains when you move?"

She remembered not to shake her head this time, and said, "No, nothing else. I landed hard, jarred a few bones, is all."

"Adrenaline's a great painkiller. It's going to hurt a lot worse before it starts to feel better."

"You always did know how to reassure a girl." She looked away, immediately, not sure she was ready to joke about their past.

He straightened, stepped back, and she realized she hadn't wanted him to stop. Whatever else it meant, his touch was reassuring, and she wasn't quite ready to let it go.

"That's looking a little better," he said. "I'll get you a drink of water. You should rehydrate. Have you got any painkillers anywhere? You should double up on paracetamol and ibuprofen for a couple of days."

She wondered again about this new Jimmy Lazenby, a man at ease with injury. At ease with a gun, for god's sake!

When she'd sat with him in that fast food place his first awkward question had been to ask how her life had been. Now she wondered where exactly his had taken him. What he had seen and done to reach this point.

One of the good guys. That was what he'd claimed.

He came back from the bathroom again with a glass of water. For a moment she thought he was going to sit with her after he'd handed it over, but instead he moved away, busying himself with checking the door, the catches on the windows.

Peering outside into the deepening gloom, he said, "So why now? Why go after you now? Can you think of any reason? Anything you said or did at the club that might have set the alarm bells off?"

She kicked her boots off and moved up the bed so she could sit with her back against the headboard, her knees drawn up so she could hug her legs to her chest. "No," she told him. "Not really. Glenn got pissy, though. He dropped the Mr Nice Guy act."

"He can do Mr Nice Guy?"

She could tell he was trying to make a joke, but it didn't work.

"I asked around among the dancers," she said. "He didn't like that. I showed them Harriet's picture."

"And…?" He turned, stood with his arms folded, leaning back against the wall by the window.

"Nothing."

"But it was enough to stir things up," he said, his voice low, as if thinking aloud. "What else have you found out?"

She looked at him more closely now. The way he studied her, the relentless digging of his questions. Was he here to make sure she was okay, or was this some kind of interrogation?

For a moment she debated how much to tell him, then caught herself in a spiral, her mind rushing round, not knowing what was right or wrong.

She shook her head, despite the pain. Was he really just here so he could pump her for information? "I don't know what to tell you," she said. "Who to trust."

She tried to read him then, to see if that last comment had made any impression, but his face was a blank.

"Tell me everything," he said. "You've nothing to gain by keeping secrets. Right now, if your friend is in any kind of trouble I might just be her best hope."

That good guy bullshit again. Knight in shining armor. Just who was he trying to impress?

But he was right.

She had nothing to gain by hiding what little she knew.

She shrugged. "Not much," she said. "I've just been asking around. I know Harriet met Glenn a couple of weeks ago – I was with her, and there was something… I don't know… A spark? A connection? She asked about him afterward. And when I tracked Glenn down in London and asked him about it he was evasive. That's all I had to go on. Nobody else had any suggestions, so I came up here. And…"

"What?"

"It's stupid. It's nothing." Jimmy just stood there, watching, waiting. "He's started calling me 'Mels'. Harriet's the only person who ever calls me that."

"But you were with her when she met Glenn. Surely she called you Mels then?"

"I know."

"But you don't think she did."

She shook her head. "I don't know. And then tonight, that guy… He told me I was wasting my time looking for Harriet Rayner here, and I should look elsewhere. But I've only called her 'Harriet'. I haven't used her surname when I've been asking about her."

"Are you sure?"

"No! That's what's so frustrating. Is my mind playing games? I don't know." She pressed her face against a forearm where it rested across her knees, despite the pain.

When she finally looked up, he was watching her, still. "You should soak that," she said. "When you get back to wherever you're staying." The front of his white shirt was smeared a vivid crimson.

He shrugged, said, "Cheap shirt. I have plenty more."

It didn't look like a cheap shirt.

She nodded at the window, and said, "How secure is it?"

He shook his head. "Standard locks, the windows are fitted well. The door lock is okay for an internal guesthouse door. It'd take me about thirty seconds to break in. Probably long enough for you to call the police, if you hear something and realize what's happening."

"That's not reassuring."

"It's normal."

She sensed a lull, a feeling of business having just about been wound up. All of a sudden, she didn't care that he had been drilling her for information, didn't care why he was here, just that he was.

"Stay a bit?"

7. JIMMY

Mixed signals, her body language was all over the place. First she was doing all but showing him the door, telling him he needed to get back to wherever the fuck he was staying to soak his damned shirt, and then: *Stay a bit?*

It was normal, he knew. He'd seen it a hundred times before, the emotional swings from one extreme to another. Her body's fight or flight mechanisms were all over the place right now. She'd been attacked, she'd been threatened and terrified, found herself confronting possibilities he hoped she'd never had to encounter before, and never would again.

Right now, her body was coming down from that adrenaline peak, but couldn't come down fully: she wouldn't feel safe again for a long time.

Even when you're properly trained, and when you've been in far worse positions than this, your body's response is likely to be all over the place.

Mel had none of that.

All she had was him.

Talk about getting the shitty end of the stick.

"I'm not going anywhere," he said.

She nodded, but said nothing more.

He remained standing by the window, arms folded.

It broke his heart to see her like this – what heart he still had, at least. Hugging her legs to her chest, rocking a little. She was clearly in shock. Her nose was swollen, particularly across the bridge. There was a scrape on her chin. Probably bruising elsewhere, but no breaks.

When he'd examined her he'd done his best to be cold, distant, even as his fingers pressed – her nose, her eye sockets, her spine, her ribcage. Done his best to ignore the look in her eyes as he'd gazed into them, checking for any odd dilation or responses that might indicate concussion.

He'd had to bite down, turn away, make a show of checking the room. Anything but look into those eyes again. Anything to blot the sensations of touching her, the recollection of holding her earlier in the park, how she'd fit so well into his arms, as if ten years hadn't turned them into different people.

He focused on the girl. Harriet Rayner.

It was hard to tell how much weight to put on the things that were playing most prominently on Mel's mind. The use of names – that her attacker knew Harriet's full name, and that Glenn had called Mel what her friend had. *Mels*.

The first could easily be explained. Glenn had sent the guy to scare Mel, and Glenn clearly knew more about Harriet than he was giving away. Using her full name meant nothing.

And the latter was easily explained by the fact that Glenn and Harriet had been in contact before her disappearance. Jimmy knew about the calls and text messages, but Mel didn't. Harriet could easily have referred to her as Mels at some point, and Glenn latched onto it. All it proved was what Jimmy already knew: Glenn and Harriet had communicated.

What did seem significant was that someone – presumably Glenn or someone close to him – had wanted to scare Mel off. Maybe she'd stumbled onto something, or it could simply be that someone like Glenn never liked people digging around his activities, regardless of whether they involved the missing girl or not. Of course he'd want to stop her asking questions of the dancers and anyone else she might be able to approach.

It was hardly news that Glenn had things to hide.

Frustrated, Jimmy turned and peered out of the window again.

Right now he hated Doug Conner for dumping him into this, for deliberately concealing key information for fear he wouldn't want to get involved.

Whatever his controller's reasons had been, it meant Jimmy was operating at least partly blind.

He bit back on his frustration, compartmentalized it for now because it would gain him nothing. At this moment, it was all about Mel: make sure she's okay, make sure she's safe, get her away from all this so it doesn't get any more complicated than it already is.

She was watching him, and he hated what that did inside his chest – the leap of the heart, the catch of the breath. All that shit he didn't do anymore.

"Sit with me?"

Bitch.

She couldn't do this to him. The eyes. The voice. The being *her*.

She wasn't doing it deliberately, he knew.

She was just scared. Out of her depth.

He sat, and the resulting sag of the mattress tipped her toward him, momentarily, before they adjusted, straightened, re-establishing a small space between them.

He kicked his shoes off, moved so his back was against the headboard too, his legs stretched out, the space between them carefully maintained.

"You okay?" he asked.

In his peripheral vision he saw the nod, but wouldn't look. He had to keep his distance.

"You?"

Of course he fucking was. He nodded too. Was aware of his arms folded tightly, knew how defensive a posture that was.

She leaned in, rested her head on his shoulder. It couldn't have been comfortable, but it was the contact that mattered, he knew.

Awkward, he unfolded his arms, raised one so she could settle in more comfortably, her cheek against his pecs and trapezius, his arm across her shoulders, the hand resting lightly on her upper arm. At least she wasn't still bleeding, not that the shirt was going to survive this anyway.

He reached down, and felt her tense for a moment as she must have wondered what he was doing, then he eased his hand inside his jacket, freed his SIG Sauer from its concealed holster, and placed it on the bedside cabinet.

"What *are* you?" she asked. Then: "No. Don't tell me. I'm not sure I want to know."

"I'm still me," he said, then stopped, realizing that might not be the most reassuring thing he could say. Still Jimmy Lazenby, the man she'd told to get out of her life all that time ago.

They'd only been kids, nineteen and twenty. It would have ended anyway.

As if she'd been thinking along the same lines, she said to him now, "I don't think that's true. You've changed. Since then."

He couldn't help feeling intensely aware of the physicality of this situation, of sitting here, holding her, of the way she pressed against him. He could smell her hair and a hint of perfume. Could feel every tiny movement as she breathed, and as she adjusted position.

He thought then of what she'd said earlier when she'd joined him in that greasy café across the road from the strip club.

You walked away. His reply, his defense, that she'd told him to go, and then: *And you believed me.*

What had she meant? What had he missed?

Again, as if she'd been following the same track of thought, she said, "I didn't expect you to just go like that."

"You told me to."

"No resistance. No attempt to fight for me. You just went."

It was true. That night she'd found him in the Flag and Flowers, come looking for another fight with him. He'd been sitting there with Glenn and their father and a couple of other regulars, he couldn't recall who. She'd asked to talk with him and, confrontationally, he'd said okay, and waited, making it clear she could talk right there, not boss him about.

And so she had. She'd told him it was over. That she couldn't take all this – a gesture, a sweep of the chin to indicate the pub, the people in it, and all that implied. The whole Lazenby thing.

"You hated me by then," he said, not wanting that fight even now. "You hated what I was becoming."

Even now, he remembered it so vividly. The look in her eye. That gesture, the *all this* of it.

He couldn't do it, back then. Put her through it. He was a Lazenby and there was no changing that.

She'd hated that.

And so had he. He'd hated it all, and he'd hated himself, and he'd hated the slippery, inevitable path he was on, and he'd hated what he could see it doing to her.

So he'd got up and walked out. Didn't take a thing – just left.

He was a Lazenby, and he set about changing it.

But now… he couldn't tell her that. Couldn't tell her the hatred he'd seen in her eyes was only a dim reflection for what he'd felt himself.

Now, she didn't deny it. She'd hated him by then.

"I've changed, you're right," he said. "I'm not like them anymore."

She shifted, pressed her cheek against him a little more firmly, and one hand came to lie flat against his chest. It was natural to press his own cheek down on the crown of her head, even if only briefly – a reassuring contact, a comforting one.

Again, he was intensely aware of every point of contact between them – the press of her face and head, that hand on his chest, her thigh against his; the way his hand rested so comfortably on her arm; the way she fit so perfectly beneath his arm.

He hoped to god she wasn't looking down at the way his pants stretched tight, his physical response to her painfully obvious. He moved his other arm so it lay across his belly, cutting the line of sight, and simultaneously making sure his hand didn't brush against her.

He didn't need this.

Hadn't come here for this. There genuinely had been no ulterior motive to insisting on coming to her room with her. He was being professional. Doing his job, the duty of care and all that shit.

He swallowed, controlling his breathing and cursing biology.

Her hand moved down, closed around his forearm, and he tensed. He'd never understood how so delicate a touch as her fingertips against the inside of his forearm could be so intimate.

"Thank you," she said.

He didn't know how to interpret anything right now. That touch. The words. Didn't know if there were layers of meaning or if there was nothing below face value.

She shifted against him, and again he was so incredibly aware of all those points of contact, but also of her body, the softnesses, the firmness, the hardness of bone.

He should get up. Move. Check the perimeter, or some such shit.

Not just sit here, every muscle in his body tensed, battling to work out if his interpretation was…

She lifted her head, turned, pressed against him again, kissing his chest through the thin fabric of his shirt.

The soft heat of her lips was so intense. The tightening grip of her hand on his forearm. The pressing of her body.

Biology. The damned biology of his responses. The thump of his heart, the snatched breath, the hardening of his erection.

She pushed against him, with a languorous roll of the pelvis, clawed her fingers and slid that hand up his arm to his neck, his jaw.

Kissed harder, so he could feel the wetness of her mouth through his shirt.

Pulled at his head, turning him as her mouth moved up to find his.

8. MEL

It crept up on her. On them.

She hadn't planned this. Hadn't expected it or even wanted it.

But there was something about that precise moment. The security in his arms. Nestling in against him, and feeling his strength and solidity.

Jimmy Lazenby had changed in many ways, but physically he had changed, too. No puppy fat overlying that wiry, bony frame, now his body was hard and lean, her head resting on firm pads of muscle as she tucked into his embrace on that bed.

This was madness, she knew. A thing she would certainly regret. But her mind wasn't on tomorrow or the day after, it was lost in the moment. In her physical response to him, that shift from finding comfort in contact to something else, something more.

She couldn't even say precisely what triggered the shift. Just something in the way they pressed and touched, a movement, a pressure of his hip against her, the way her breasts squashed against his side. That brief press of his cheek against the crown of her head. The way his whole body tensed every time they moved.

It came as an awareness of her body's responses. The racing of her heart, the new tension in the pit of her abdomen, a heat to her skin.

There came a moment when he moved. A hand dropping so that for a moment she wondered if he was reaching for her, if that hand would come to rest on her hip, drawing her harder against him.

Her eyes followed the movement, and saw the bulge in his trousers, the fabric stretched tight. She was a little shocked to see such an obvious physical response. She wondered what was in his head, if he'd been angling for this all along, then realized that movement of his arm had been to disguise his response – a movement of awkwardness, of trying to find a way to be discreet about a response he'd clearly been unable to avoid.

She moved her hand to his forearm and squeezed reassuringly, said, "Thank you."

Wondered what he would do if she moved her hand lower, found that hardness of his response.

Was that bad? To seek physical comfort right now, in these circumstances?

Maybe that was when it happened, when she realized she wanted that, when she understood that whatever happened in this moment must be what was right for the moment, and they could deal with any complications later.

She shifted position a little, felt his hip pressing against her, a tightening of that tension in her belly.

She kissed him. Pressed her lips against his chest, the white fabric of his shirt marked garishly with dark patches of red.

Clawed her hand and dragged sharp fingernails up his arm. Found his jaw and cupped it, turning his head as her mouth moved up. Found his chin with her lips, found his mouth.

His hands, strong on her arm, turned her, pushed her back, held her away.

His eyes on hers.

She had to look away. Couldn't meet those eyes. She'd crossed a line, committed herself. Exposed herself.

And he had turned her down.

"It's okay," he said, so much damned sensitivity in his tone, the bastard. "It's okay."

He drew her into his arms again now, but things had changed, shifted again.

He held her, stroking her hair.

She tried to kiss him again, even so, but he held her firm, almost too firm, for the pains in her ribs and face.

"It's your body's response," he said. "Fight or flight. Adrenaline. It clouds things."

Clouding things right now was exactly what she wanted!

"It affects your judgment."

She knew that. She understood what was happening. Couldn't he see that?

"You're still in shock."

Holding her. Stroking her hair. His breathing was slow, deep, and as he held her so close her own breathing slowed to match his. Was that a deliberate thing, or just a normal reaction?

"It's okay," he said, his voice almost hypnotically calming.

She didn't know when the tears had started to flow, only noticed the saltiness when they reached her lips. She hoped he hadn't noticed, didn't want him to see how right he was.

He said he'd changed, yes, but she'd never have believed Jimmy Lazenby had it in him to become a fucking gentleman.

"Stay," she said softly, and she felt him nod in response.

"I wasn't going anywhere," he said, as they settled down on the bed, his arms around her, her face resting on his pecs and trapezius, her hand resting flat on his chest.

She woke, so she must have slept.

The room was dark, the air cool. The house quiet.

She was still tucked into Jimmy's side. At some point the two of them must have shuffled down the bed so they could lie, but he'd kept his arm around her, her head resting in the hollow of his shoulder.

Now, she extricated herself carefully, swung her legs clear, and sat. Jimmy didn't move.

Her body ached as if it had been trampled by a herd of cattle. Her nose throbbed, and she wasn't quite sure whether to believe that it hadn't been broken when she hit the ground.

She went through to the en suite bathroom, closing the door before turning on the light.

She looked a mess. Her nose was swollen, but as far as she could tell still straight; her chin was grazed and scabbed, her eyes tiny, as if she hadn't slept for a week. Dark bruises smudged either side of her throat.

She eased herself out of her gray jeans, wincing at pains in her side as she did so. Took her top off, and then her bra, savoring that delicious release like a sigh. In only her panties, she leaned over the basin to splash cold water on her face, removing the remaining smudges of dried blood.

Stepping back, she twisted to examine her body in the mirror. There were no obvious signs of damage – no swellings or emerging bruises. She'd landed on the ground hard, been turned roughly by a heavy boot, but that was all. That and the hand around her throat, forcing her back against the tree.

She stopped that line of thought. Couldn't let herself think about what might have happened.

She was here. Safe. With Jimmy Lazenby lying on her bed.

Such a strange situation.

Not just the Harriet thing, the terror that bunched in her throat whenever she thought of her missing friend. Or Glenn, the raking over of the past.

This.

Standing in her room's en suite in only her panties, studying herself in the mirror while Jimmy Lazenby lay on her bed.

And her response to him, the power of that need that had swept over her.

He was right. Of course the bastard was right. The adrenaline rush, the relief of getting through that awful situation in the park, the pathetic girly response to the big strong man who had saved her… She knew these were fundamental biological things, survival mechanisms.

But god, she had wanted him so badly!

She'd needed that skin on skin thing. Wanted to be held by those strong arms, to be *had* by him. Wanted to feel him in her and see the look on his face, the widening of his eyes as he came deep inside her.

Release. Escape. Call it what you will.

It had been one of the most powerful things she had ever felt.

And just because it was a thing of primitive biology, that didn't mean it was not real, a genuine need.

More cold water. A gentle dabbing with a towel coarse from too many washings.

She peed, washed her hands, breathed deep, taking her time to gather herself.

She pulled on the t-shirt she'd picked up on her way in here, tugging the hem down when she realized it wasn't quite as long as she'd thought, because of course clothes just stretched like that, in response to a tug and wishful thinking.

When she stepped back into the room he hadn't moved, but she saw his eyes were slit open, watching her.

Did he even sleep? Was that something he'd had trained out of him by the same people who taught him how to handle a gun and how to do sensitive when the situation demanded?

She fought the reflex urge to tug at the hem of her t-shirt again. He'd seen it all before, and anyway, the bastard was doing his gentleman act.

But do gentlemen watch you like that, though, as you walk across the room, your t-shirt riding up with every step? She wondered if he was getting hard again, watching her, then made herself stop.

She climbed into bed, under the covers this time. Turned so her back was to him, and tried not to get frustrated when she tried to pull the covers around her but they wouldn't move because he still lay on top, still in that damned suit, the blood-stained shirt.

Seconds later she felt pressure through the covers, on her arm. His hand, pressing down, squeezing and then withdrawing, and she hated that right now Jimmy Lazenby was the one who made her feel so safe and secure.

Morning. Bright sunlight angling in through the gap in the curtains and across the room, the angle low, so it must still be early.

Everything felt wrong.

The aches and pains in her body. The rasp of her breathing through a nose that was swollen but not quite broken. The aches in her bruised neck.

The man. Next to her. On top of the covers, still in his clothes, his blood-stained shirt.

So wrong, but so right, too.

Was he sleeping? Had he slept at all? Or did he have some ninja-like ability to stay alert through the hours of darkness?

She'd turned in the night, and now lay on her side facing him, her legs drawn up. He'd moved to make room for her, still lying on his back in the narrow space that remained.

They'd never slept together until now.

How odd was that?

Back then, ten years before, they'd been together for a few months, but she'd still lived at home with her parents. She couldn't bring boys back for the night, and she'd felt uncomfortable about the inevitable questions that would follow staying out overnight. She and Jimmy had taken their moments wherever they could, but never for a whole night.

And now, she lay there in underwear and t-shirt, the bed covers forming a barrier between her and him, lying there in his suit.

He'd taken the jacket off at some point in the night. Maybe that was when she'd turned over, taking advantage in her sleep, claiming more of the bed for her drawn-up legs.

He'd been right.

Of course he had.

How would she feel now if he'd succumbed to her advances? She'd hate herself for being so reckless, for opening up old wounds in the heat of the moment. She'd hate him for taking advantage, for coming up here with her and putting them both in that position.

It had been an adrenaline thing, a biological thing, last night.

But now…

Was it nostalgia? A curiosity for a life not lived? Some strange post-traumatic tenderness?

She moved against him. Pressed her cheek against his arm, and as if automatically he raised the arm, made room for her to snuggle in.

Was there an ounce of spare flesh on his body now? She didn't think so.

She drew an arm out from the covers so she could loop it across his chest, the hand resting easily on the ribs, just below the bulge of his pecs.

Felt him tensing in response.

She knew he must be doing that thing again, fighting the natural responses, trying to be sensitive.

All that shit.

She moved her hand down in one smooth, slow sweep, fingers dragging across ribs, across the ripples of his abdomen, the muscles tensing one by one to match the path of her hand.

She didn't give him a chance, pushing her fingers inside the waistband of his pants, and swiftly down.

Fingertips, pushing through coarse hair. The broad base of his manhood – soft, caught by surprise. Filling out.

Fingers, following that fleshy course, pushing down his length, pressing against his shaft as it filled, hardened, pushed up against her hand in the tight confines of his pants.

His hand moved across, closed on her wrist. Still the gentleman.

Almost, at least.

Gentleman enough to try to stop her, but not enough to actually pull her hand clear, so that he ended up just gripping her wrist, as if holding her there, her fingers still pressing down against his shaft, his erection still growing.

"Mel..."

His face, turned to her, as he tried still to do the right thing.

She kissed him, a soft pressing of her lips to his. Felt the scrape of his stubble against her and tensed involuntarily – so many raw, tender parts of her face.

Instantly, his hand went to her jaw, a gentle touch.

She kissed him again, her mouth molding to his, their tongues pressing tentatively.

Such a strange mixture of the familiar and the new! Back then they'd kissed so much her face had hurt for altogether different reasons. Young love, and all that.

It was a kiss she knew so well, but no, one she didn't know at all, as the initial hesitancy fell away and now he kissed her deep.

Her whole body was alive to that kiss, and for a moment she even forgot her hand, where it was.

Then she pushed deeper, managed to fold her fingers around him, squeeze and pull. His shaft still pointed downward, forced by his pants and her hand, everything restricted by lack of space in his clothing.

She needed more. She pulled away from his kiss and twisted, despite the pains in her body. Ended up leaning across him, her weight partly on his ribs and belly, her hands free, fumbling with button, hook, zipper, opening and parting, pushing the tight waistband of his shorts down.

For a moment his manhood still stretched downward, pinned into place by that waistband, and then she'd pushed farther and it sprang free, flipped up, hard and long against his belly.

She pushed down, pressed her lips against the swollen head, the tip of her tongue against the narrow slit opening.

Her left hand moved down, flat against his balls, then curling under, cupping. Her other hand pressed against his shaft, folding around, lifting his length clear of his body so she could take the head fully into her mouth, pressing and sliding her tongue against him.

Only now did she dare twist, moving her body, turning her head so she could look up and into his wide-open eyes.

That look. That moment. The *oh my god!* in his eyes.

It was as if he'd finally come to life, snapped out of a reverie, as if he'd finally accepted this was happening.

His hands moved across her. One hand on her shoulder, squeezing, the thumb caressing. The other hand, running down the curve of her back, the swell of her ass, straining to reach for her, finding firm muscle, squeezing and stroking, pulling at her as if he could drag her closer by his grip on her ass. Then moving farther down, pressing at the crack of her ass through the thin, lacy fabric of her panties.

Stretching… pressing against her softness and making her breath snatch in her lungs.

She shifted a little so he could reach more easily, so his fingers could press at the folds of her sex from behind, only prevented from entering her by those panties.

She wanted to suck him deeper but couldn't… her neck, her throat, the ache in her jaw. She started to pump with the fist wrapped around the base of his shaft, and his fingers, pressed, caressed, stretched until…

Now it was Mel's turn, that *oh my god!* look plastered over her face, she was sure, as she felt firm, delicious pressure against the folds of flesh covering her clit, and bolts of pleasure coursed through her body.

He hadn't had these moves ten years ago, this precision of touch. Hadn't had the strength and control to just twist, turn, and suddenly she was being lifted clear, laid back on the bed, repositioned like a rag doll.

He kissed her again, soft and tender, always sensitive to her injuries, reading her responses and knowing when to draw back and when to give in to passion.

His mouth moved to her jaw, down over the bruises of her neck, his touch an almost disturbingly intense mixture of pain and pleasure. Down to her chest, his turn to kiss through fabric, so she could feel the firm shape of his mouth, the wet heat of his breath, working down across the swell of a breast, finding the nipple.

He moved over her, kneeling with one leg between her thighs so he could arch his back, find her breast again when he'd eased her t-shirt up, lips closing around the nipple, tongue gliding, swirling. And if she arched her back and rolled her hips she could push against him, the hardness of his knee, his thigh, against her sex, making her so wet, so desperate for more.

Hands moving down her body, fingers hooking into the waist of her panties, pulling, so that when he straightened, rocked back on his heels, she could push up and he was free to pull her panties down, disentangle them from her legs, one at a time, cast them off to one side.

For a moment he stayed there, eyes devouring her nakedness.

And for that brief, self-conscious moment, she wondered if his mind was rushing to comparison, measuring and mapping the toll ten years had taken on her body.

Then she saw the look in his eyes, that same *oh my god!* The sheer disbelief and wonder that this was happening.

He dipped his head, pressed his mouth to her belly and worked down. Wetness, the rasp of stubble, the sharp drag of teeth.

Closing on her mound. Pressing. That pressure alone almost enough to tip her over the precipice into climax.

He started to move, pressing with his mouth, pushing his lower lip up against her, gliding across the folds that covered her clit, the wet heat of his mouth engulfing her sex.

She pushed against him, reached down and buried fingers in his tousled hair.

She was so turned on…

So ready to… just…

He paused. Held her there, right at the edge.

Looked up the length of her body and met her gaze.

And then, perhaps reading the slight sag of her body as she drew back briefly from the edge of climax, he pressed again, his tongue parting her labia, pushing up against her clit with a delicate, gliding sensation.

Her fingers tensed in his hair, her whole body tightened so that she felt as if she was about to explode, and then release erupted from the pit of her abdomen, a rippling of muscles deep within.

She cried out. Turned her head as if she might bury her face in the pillow, stifle the sounds of her climax, but that movement only served to push her harder against him, intensifying the ebbing throbs of her orgasm.

He kept his mouth against her, enclosing her sex, just the right pressure to prolong those last pulses, drawing the peak out. Then he moved, pushed lower, found her opening and drove his tongue deep.

For a moment she thought he'd somehow missed what had just happened. Wondered why he was still going. Surely he remembered she was an all or nothing kind of girl? One big O, and that was all until she'd had time to recover. That had always been the way.

She never…

Never…

His tongue, deep inside her. The pressure of his mouth against her, his upper lip now the one that pressed and slid against her clit as his tongue moved inside her. Somehow… somehow transforming those last dying pulses of orgasm into something else, a renewed arousal, a need…

This never happened.

It wasn't happening now.

She didn't believe it. Must still be sleeping, dreaming fevered dreams inspired by her trauma and the adrenaline rush of the previous evening.

She didn't…

Her fingers in his hair… reaching, changing so her hands cupped his skull, pulled at him, drew him up so that his mouth dragged across her sex, her mound, her belly. Up, until she could kiss him, taste her sex on his mouth, their eyes locked, barely even blinking.

He must have seen something in her expression, just then, the slight wince at his weight on her from the pains in her ribs and neck.

Instantly, he took his weight on his arms and knees – an act that inadvertently made one leg bear down, his thigh against her wet sex again, reminding her, as if she needed any reminding, of how he'd managed to raise her to new levels of arousal almost immediately after she'd come so damned hard against his face.

She reached down for him, needed him inside her. Now.

Instead, though, he rocked back on his heels, moved to lie at her side, and then drew her nearest leg up so it looped over his hips. Now, the head of his dick pushed against the folds of her sex. She reached down again, found him, guided him, sliding the swollen head of his manhood through her labia, against her opening.

She looked into his eyes, and all she wanted to do was kiss him, and then… he pushed, opening her, entering her from the side.

His jaw sagged, his lips parting a fraction, as he entered her, kept pushing, sliding deeper, and she felt the hardness of his shaft sliding against her fingertips as he pushed into her.

She reached for his face now, her hand wet from their sex. Pressed her palm to his jaw, craned to kiss him, as he filled her.

He started to move, small thrusts that were little more than a roll of the hips, the position limiting them but also intensifying every sensation.

She kissed him. A hungry kiss, as if it might be their last.

His body against her felt so right. Inside her… so right.

He moved a hand down to where hers had been, the pressure of his palm on her mound moving against her with every thrust, every sensation combining, building to a new level of intensity. His fingers pushed down, coming to lie along the lines of her sex, parting around the place where he entered her.

She didn't think she could take much more of this, had never known such intensity. Madly, his questions from the previous evening churned up in her brain. *Did you black out?* Not yet… not yet. *Do you feel dizzy?* Dizzy, yes. Head spinning. *Any blurred vision, or double vision?* Oh yes.

He dipped his head, kissed her shoulder, the side of her breast. Everything, so alive to his touch, his kiss. The scrape of his stubble and teeth. The wet heat of his mouth enclosing her nipple. The flick of his tongue.

She reached down. Said, "I… I…"

"I know."

He drew back, then, pulled out of her, and she felt emptied, cheated of that delicious sensation of being so filled. Then when he thrust again, his length slid up through her folds, sliding against her clit, against his enfolding hand. Her hand on his felt that wet sliding, and pressed down, grinding him against her.

His whole body tensed and he thrust again, hard and fast. That realignment must have done something, that change of sensations, the slide between pussy and hands.

She felt a throbbing sensation, a pulsing against her, and then wet heat exploded over her mound, her belly, her arm.

And that shift in sensations, the throbbing of his shaft, the pressure of their hands, the slight softening of him and the way that molded his manhood against her even more perfectly…

She cried out, twisted her head away again, as if she could somehow stifle the sounds of her climax. Felt herself pulsing against his dick, his hand, her hand.

Felt dizzy, felt her eyesight blurring, doubling, felt darkness creeping in from the sides of her vision with the intensity of her response.

Met his mouth as he raised his head. Kissed him, slow and tender, long, never wanting to stop.

9. JIMMY

He could never win, whatever spin he tried to put on the situation, on what had happened. On what he'd let happen.

He couldn't claim Mel had taken him by surprise with her wily seductress skills, her move so swift he'd been unable to stop her. Nobody ever took Jimmy Lazenby by surprise. He was too good to ever be caught off guard.

Okay, so the transition had been abrupt – from tender snuggling, from seeking and taking comfort in their embrace, to that hand dragging down over his ribs, his abdomen, to slipping inside his waistband. To the point where there was no denying, no turning back.

He could have stopped her, though. Easily. Nobody ever moved too fast for him.

But that left the other version of events, where he had known exactly what was happening and he'd let it. He'd known she was vulnerable, her head not in a good place to make choices that would have… repercussions. And still he hadn't stopped her.

What kind of a person did that make him?

He was being hard on himself, he knew. He'd stopped her last night. Stopped *himself.*

He'd wanted her so badly. That almost overpowering rush of… of what? Of nostalgia? A petty, egotistical sense of simply knowing he could? Of simple lust?

Of what might have been. A decade's worth of what might have been, if he'd only been a better person ten years ago.

She was beautiful. Always a looker back then, now she had a knowing beauty, a grown-up beauty. Something he couldn't even begin to define, but simply *was.*

They lay together for some time after she'd stretched for a towel to wipe herself clean. Ragged breathing drawing itself out, calming. No doubt both minds racing, not just his.

He was on his back, still mostly in his clothes. His shirt pulled up, his trousers and shorts pushed down. Her leg drawn across his middle, pressing down against him.

He couldn't stay like that for long. It was morning, the world coming to life again. Time wasn't going to wait. The urge to get up had nothing to do with being unable to deal with the sudden intimacy.

He went downstairs while she got ready, avoiding the awkwardness of everyday things.

A man was in the kitchen. Of Asian heritage, his skin was almost as dark as his glossy hair and beard.

Jimmy raised his hands apologetically, the man's look hostile – understandably so.

"I thought so," the man said, stirring his cup in an agitated manner. "That was a single booking. No extra guests without notification. She–"

"I'm sorry," said Jimmy, in his best diplomatic tone. He could do nice when he had to. "I'll pay any extra. It was late and there was no-one around. I only stayed to make sure she was okay – she was assaulted on her way back here last night."

Only now did the man pause, take in the vivid red smears on the front of Jimmy's shirt. Odd that he hadn't registered that straight away – a complete stranger in his kitchen with blood on his clothes – but the human mind behaved strangely sometimes.

"Aw, man," said the guy. "She okay? That's bad. Too much of it these days."

"A few bruises," said Jimmy. "A bloody nose."

"Police?"

"The authorities know. It's being dealt with. She was in shock. I'm an old friend, that's all. I really would have asked if there had been anyone around last night."

"Man, that sucks. Listen, you want a shirt? Let me get you a shirt."

A minute or two later, he came back with a white t-shirt. Jimmy removed his jacket, his shoulder holster, and laid them on the kitchen table. Undid his shirt and removed it, then reversed the process: t-shirt, holster, jacket.

"Thank you," he said. "I appreciate it."

The guy nodded. Said nothing more. Guns had that effect sometimes. Guns and blood and strangers in your house… Only now did it seem the guy's brain was really catching up, starting to wonder what, exactly, he was in the middle of. Perhaps started to reconsider the consequences of opening his house up to strangers.

"It's fine," said Jimmy. "Really. Mel will be down in a minute. She's just getting ready."

The guy relaxed a little, perhaps reassured by sounds of running water coming from upstairs. "Coffee?" he said, and Jimmy shook his head.

He sat at the kitchen table. He should have said yes to the coffee.

Last night he'd barely slept. It was a skill he'd learned long ago, to get by without sleep whenever necessary. To grab a few minutes' power nap here or there and then wake himself. He could go days on end like that.

Last night had been long, though. Always aware of Mel when she lay there motionless, but equally aware of every little move, every little sound. Aware of where she pressed against him. The touch of a hand, the press of a breast or a leg. Aware of when she was dreaming and when she was not, all those little sighs and twitches and flutters of the eyes beneath the lids.

When she got up in the middle of the night, he'd closed his eyes, not wanting her to know he was awake, but when she emerged from the bathroom sometime later she caught him looking. She hesitated, then seemed to think *What the hell?* That t-shirt did nothing to cover her legs, the white lace of her underwear, and after an initial tug at the hem she did nothing to stop it riding up as she walked.

She had such a powerful effect on him. Always had.

He'd shifted position as she slipped under the covers. Was intensely aware of where all his blood was rushing.

He lay there like that for some time. Hard and aching. Glad of the bed covers separating them, aware that his willpower was a thin layer of brittle ice by now.

He got up, went to the window and looked out into the darkness. Let it pass.

When he went back to the bed she'd turned onto her side and drawn her knees up, leaving only a narrow space for him. He shrugged out of his jacket and holster and dumped them on a chair, considering his options. Then he eased the covers so they wouldn't pull tight on her when he lay on top of them again, and settled down at her side.

All night, that tension had been there. He'd battled it. He'd won. He'd done the right thing.

And then this morning…

He couldn't win, couldn't come out of this looking good. Either she had taken him by surprise, or he'd let her. He'd given in. Whether that ice had finally shattered or melted didn't really matter.

And he understood the significance.

If he'd given in last night to a passion driven by adrenaline and instinct it would have been just that. An animal thing, a fight or flight thing. A lapse in judgment and willpower. She could have hated him forever for it and that would have been just fine. He'd have deserved it.

But this… What had happened this morning was a considered thing. Deliberate. And because of that, it had meaning. Feelings were involved. Intent. Rather than a one-off thing, this was the start of a story yet to unfold, and he didn't know if he was ready for that.

If he ever would be.

He wasn't a relationships kind of person. He had come to understand that. He'd learned long ago never to trust anyone. That was natural, given his upbringing, his family and the people around them. In his world you only ever trusted people on the way to pain and an early grave.

That was a fine philosophy for his work, for the man he'd become. But not for relationships.

He was okay with that.

It was who he was.

He knew not to let anyone close.

Not to trust.

Not to start a story with them.

She came down. Blue jeans, black t-shirt, gray suede jacket. Swollen nose, grazed chin, and something new in her eyes.

Her landlord took one look at her and left the room. This was shit he didn't want to be involved with – not so much the gun, the bruises, the blood on the shirt, but the look on her face.

"I can't do this," she told Jimmy. She spread her hands as if to indicate the scale of this thing she couldn't do.

"*This*. Us. Whatever it is. I can't fall. Not again. I won't let myself."

Jimmy looked at her, only now understanding the levels of denial under which he'd submerged himself.

"Fall?" he said. "Me neither. I have nowhere left to fall. I fell ten years ago and I never climbed out."

He shrugged, looked away, looked back at her, at the understanding in her eyes, the knowledge that, deny it all she liked, this thing between them had a momentum she couldn't divert. It always had.

How could he fall, when he'd never stopped loving her in the first place?

"Breakfast?" he said.

She nodded. Breakfast.

Breakfast was simple. Not falling, less so. You can't stop that happening. You can deny it, and not act on it, but that's different.

They found a greasy spoon café just off the High Street, a place that had been there for as long as either could recall and didn't appear to have changed at all in that time.

Jimmy ordered full English, the first proper meal he'd had in nearly two days. Mel had fried egg sandwich, brown sauce.

They'd barely spoken as they walked here, Jimmy, at least, because he didn't know what might be a safe topic of conversation but he did know enough to realize he was out of his depth.

Why had he said that? The falling, already fallen, shit. His life was measured in doing things because they were likely to achieve a desired outcome. He didn't just do or say things for the sake of it. He didn't blurt.

He didn't let people in.

And he couldn't read Mel this morning. Of course he couldn't. He couldn't tell if her assertion that she wouldn't let herself fall again was because she'd already fallen – or was falling – or if it was her mentally and emotionally running a mile from what they had done.

It was easier to say nothing. To walk side by side, mind racing. To close up, as he always did.

Food was good. Peppery sausages, beans, hash browns, thick bacon, eggs that were crispy and caramelized around the edges, fried bread that dripped when he raised it from the plate.

He looked at her. Still he couldn't read her, and he understood that was a part of it all – the hidden layers, the mysteries.

He told himself to stop with the bullshit.

"I don't know how to do this," she said.

"Me neither."

They carried on eating for a time.

"Last night," he said, finally. Immediately, he saw the question in her eyes: Which part of last night was he referring to? "That guy," he added hurriedly. "In the park. That escalated everything. You're right, it meant you'd touched a raw nerve, but that could be anything, not necessarily Harriet. Glenn doesn't like people sniffing around his activities."

"So what do you suggest?" Both of them, businesslike now – kidnapping and violence far safer ground than what was happening between the two of them.

"I need to get to the bottom of that, at least," said Jimmy. "I'll go and see Glenn, put some pressure on. One way or another he's going to tell me why he sent that ugly bastard out to scare you last night."

"You think he'll tell you?"

He had to look away from those eyes. He hated these feelings. Couldn't handle them. It wasn't part of who he was anymore. His life was all about finding ways to have the upper hand in any situation, to always be in control of what was controllable, and at least stack the odds for what wasn't.

This stuff, this *thing*, didn't fall into either category. There was nothing to control, there *were* no odds, it just *was*.

She was still waiting for an answer.

"He'll talk," he said. Glenn, at least, fell into one of those more familiar categories: not someone he could control, but certainly someone where Jimmy could play the odds: he knew how his brother's mind worked, knew the buttons to press.

"You've heard nothing more?" he asked now. "From any of your friends? From Harriet's friends?"

She shook her head, but still glanced at her phone as if she might have missed something.

Seconds later, her phone whistled to signify a call, and the two of them flinched at the unlikeliness of the timing.

"Penny," said Mel, looking apologetic, eyebrows raised in question.

Jimmy nodded, turning his attention to what was left of his breakfast. For a moment he thought she was going to take the call outside, but he shrugged in answer to another questioning look and she remained at the table.

"Hi, Penny. Yes, I knew it was you. How are you? I mean… Never mind. No, no. Not at all. No, nothing new, I'm afraid. I've been asking around, showing people the photo you gave me, but no luck. Have you…? No? No, I promise I will. Really. Of course I don't mind you calling."

She put the phone back down on the table and sat back. "Sorry about that," she said.

"No, it's fine. Really. The mother, right?" He knew who Penny Rayner was – he'd memorized the file.

Mel nodded. "She calls at all kinds of times. Uses me to check on Harriet."

"Because they don't speak?"

Another nod.

"There's nothing more there? Between the two of them? Nothing that might explain all this?" He couldn't help speculating. If chasing Glenn turned out to be a false trail – that connection was pretty flimsy and circumstantial, after all – then where else to look? In missing persons cases the answer nearly always lay close to home…

Mel looked shocked. "No!" she said. "They don't talk, but there's no animosity there. Penny wouldn't have anything to do with Harriet's disappearance."

"She wouldn't be putting her up, then? Giving her somewhere to lie low, if she had to for any reason?"

"No. They don't have that kind of relationship. That's why Penny calls me. It makes her feel like there's a link there. There's no animosity, they just can't handle each other. They can both be quite challenging, in their own way."

"That photo you were showing around. What's the significance?"

"None really. It's just what Penny gave me. I think she felt she had to give me something tangible. Something that meant something. I've got access to hundreds of pictures of Harriet on my phone, after all."

"These things matter."

Mel nodded, looking down at her empty plate. "Funny how an old photo like that feels more real than anything else, right now. I think Penny understood that. Thank you for rescuing it last night."

There was a lull, then, a sense of things unsaid.

Finally, Mel said, "Before we were interrupted by Penny's call… There was a lot of 'I'll do this' and 'I'll do that'… Not 'we'. I'm not a passenger. I'm here for a reason, Jimmy. You can't sideline me."

This is what it did. The unknowables. The way something like this *thing* opened up vulnerabilities. Expectations and assumptions.

Difficult questions and even more difficult answers.

"This is what I do," he said, trying to keep it simple, no room for discussion or negotiation.

"I know. You're one of the good guys. You've already told me that."

He couldn't tell if she was cross with him or taking the piss. Or somewhere in between the two. Was that how relationships went, always somewhere on a sliding scale between love and frustration? He couldn't remember, it had been so long.

"I am," he said. This whole thing had been made so much more complicated by Mel's involvement. More messy. Things needed simplifying now.

"I know how to handle people like Glenn," he said. "Like that guy last night."

That silenced her. He could see she was reliving that. You don't easily forget the feel of hands around your throat, of not knowing what you might have to endure before maybe dying – and even if her life had never been at risk, the fear was the same, the not knowing.

He felt bad for putting those thoughts back into her head, but he needed her to understand the seriousness of all this.

"You have a gun," she said. "Why? What are you, Jimmy? What have you become?"

"Maybe I'm exactly what I always was. I've just found a place to be me." He wasn't quite sure what he meant by that. Perhaps wanting her to work out he was referring to ten years ago, to him not being good enough for then, so how could he be now?

She still studied him. He wished he knew what was in her head, but simultaneously was glad he didn't. Put him in a hostile country, in a city run by rebels or ganglords, surround him by people who wanted him dead or worse… he could handle that. He was equipped. He'd been in some grim situations in his time with Section Eight, but he'd come through them all.

But this. Nothing could prepare him for all this shit.

"Is it even legal?" She nodded toward his concealed holster, and he knew she meant more than just the gun. Is what he does legal? Is *he* legal?

"It depends who's asking the question," he said. He hated sounding so evasive. It made him sound as if he was bigging himself up with layers of mysterious glamour. She deserved more of an answer than that, even though he knew he was crossing lines that shouldn't be crossed. "I make things happen," he said. "Or I stop them from happening. I'm on the right side. Legal and illegal aren't always clear-cut – people like me operate in the space in between, if that makes sense?"

She nodded. "Kind of. I can't work out if you don't want to tell me about it, or you can't."

"I can't answer that," he said, and they laughed awkwardly.

"You need to go back to London and leave this to me," he told her again. "What do you want? You want your friend back. If so, then I'm your best chance. Your old man wouldn't have sent me here if he didn't think I was the best person for the job."

He reached for her then, covered her hand on the table with his. "Last night… this morning… I don't know what that was. I don't know what this is. But we need to put it on hold for now. Let me do this thing. And then maybe we can meet up. Have a drink. Talk. Whatever."

He could have put it so much better. He should have. But she did this to him. Always had.

She drew her hand away, and he hated the way his mind raced, trying to work out why.

"It's hard," she said, finally.

Frustration. That was what it was. Having to accept the logic of his arguments, that she should be the one to step back, leaving it all to him. Having to accept her own powerlessness in a situation where so much was at stake.

He unlocked his phone with his thumbprint, tapped for the keypad, and turned it to face her. “Give me your number,” he said. “I’ll let you know as soon as there’s any news.”

It was a cynical move on his part, he knew. The simple act of tapping in her number and pressing ‘call’ so they each had the other’s number, was like a psychological act of signing off, an acceptance of how things would be. By doing so, she was stepping back, and yet how could she refuse the simple act of exchanging numbers?

Outside, they paused, suddenly self-conscious. How to do the most simple things? Every choice a measure of where they’d reached, what this was between them.

“I’ll call,” he said, knowing it sounded like such a damned platitude.

“You’d fucking better,” she said, and the curse cut through, the little smile.

She tipped her head up then, one hand flat on his chest. Pressed her mouth to his.

Everything else, then – the awkwardness, the uncertainty, the unspoken and unanswered questions – it all fell away.

He wanted to keep kissing her, hated it when she pulled away.

Hated the awful, sinking feeling that this might actually be the last time he felt those lips against his, because he genuinely had no idea how all this was going to turn out.

10. JIMMY

He called the office for an update. Officially he was on compassionate leave, but working for Section Eight had never been a nine to five thing. An agent like Jimmy Lazenby always had something on the go, and it would be no surprise to anyone that he would call in. The desk-based case-workers were accustomed to getting all kinds of questions from agents and Jimmy had cultivated them carefully over the years, knowing just how invaluable their services were. Any one of them would be keen to help him, even if Douglas Conner hadn't made sure a few extra resources were attached to this off-the-books investigation.

There had been no more activity from Harriet's phone – no calls or messages, and the device had not even been switched on since Saturday. The girl had made no appearances on facial recognition systems at stations, malls, airports, or other public areas, and her various online presences had remained mute. That absence in itself was confirmation enough that something was amiss. Nowadays, people didn't simply vanish. They left digital footmarks from transactions and devices, they showed up on CCTV, they appeared as bit-part players in other people's digital landscapes. Nowadays, absence was very much a warning sign.

"And the police?"

At the other end of the line, Mamta Patil paused and Jimmy heard the tap of long fingernails on her keyboard. "Are going through the motions, sir," she told him. "Filed as a missing or absent persons. The senior investigating officer is a detective constable, they're treating it that seriously."

That didn't surprise him. He'd done his research. He knew there were something like 400 people reported missing every day across the UK, and of these around a fifth were girls in their mid to late teens. More than 95 per cent of these girls returned home safely, and if the DC assigned to the case couldn't find any warning indicators they would do little more than carry out a few perfunctory inquiries at this stage.

The flip side of that was that if they *had* been able to allocate more than one over-worked junior officer to the case they might have noticed just how thoroughly Harriet

Rayner had disappeared, and realized this should be taken more seriously.

"Has the DC seen Harriet's phone records?"

"He has. He's interviewed a Glenn Lazenby…" A pause, presumably as the name registered, then: "Flagged for no further action."

Interesting. So the police had, at least, followed up Harriet's interaction with Glenn, although they'd seen no cause for alarm in that. No surprise again, though: the police and Section Eight operated to different levels of proof, and while the police were bound by procedures and other constraints, Jimmy had been given full authority to pursue even the flimsiest of leads.

It looked as if this was down to him, for now.

Lunchtime at the Flag and Flowers. The same old faces, the same scowl from Sandra behind the bar as she stood there pointlessly polishing a pint glass with the corner of a cloth. The same wood paneling stained dark by nicotine from the decades before pubs had become smoke-free zones. Games machines flashed lights and played random chimes and ditties where they lined up along one wall. The last ten years could easily not have passed.

He passed through a wide archway into the back bar, and there, at the family table right at the gloomy rear, was Glenn. He sat with a guy Jimmy didn't recognize, but who equally could have filled that seat at any time in the past thirty or more years: broad shoulders, crooked nose, tatts, and a *Don't mess with me* look in his eye.

To Glenn's other side was one of the dancers from last night at Ryders: long legs crossed so she twisted to face Glenn; a little black skirt and vest top; tattoos almost invisible on her dark skin. Her hand rested on Glenn's arm in that way the girls did at the strip club – the physical contact an encouragement to persuade punters to take them for a private dance. Here, away from the club, it had the same neediness, a simple ever-present touch to remind the man she existed. She looked like a model, or something out of a dream.

Jimmy came to stand at the table, all eyes on him. He fixed his stare on Glenn.

"So what do you know about Mel's friend?" he said. No preamble, no niceties. His brother knew exactly what Jimmy was talking about.

Glenn held his look for a moment, then shrugged and spread his hands, palms out, as if he had nothing to hide.

Then with a brief flick of a finger he dismissed his two companions.

Jimmy sat opposite him and waited.

"Harriet Rayner," Glenn said. "Seventeen, and a real looker, you know?" Glenn had always known that sleazy grin wound Jimmy up, and had always used it to do just that. "Coke habit, keeps questionable company. Took a shine to me a couple of weeks ago. Understandable, I know. And so now she's missing it looks bad for me."

"The police think so."

A shrug. "I spoke to them, yes. DC Moreton was very sympathetic. He had to ask the question, I know. And now he doesn't have to. And neither do you. You know when I'm bullshitting, Jimbo. That's why you're here."

He was right, much as Jimmy hated to acknowledge it. Glenn had always been an accomplished liar, but Jimmy knew his tells.

Also, he made a mental note of the fact Glenn clearly knew he was investigating this and didn't seem surprised. His brother appeared to be making a none-too-subtle point that he'd kept tabs on Jimmy in the intervening years, and knew exactly what he did.

"So where is she?"

"I don't know. But my guess is she's doing exactly what her mum has repeatedly done all her miserable life. Disappear for a few days, sleep it off, and then find some way to deal with the embarrassment of having to re-emerge and explain where she's been. She's on a friend's sofa, or shagging dealers for a fix. You know how it goes."

"She got into your car. Saturday morning. Nothing since."

"She had a thing for me. Maybe she thought she could screw me and I'd fix her up with a connection, you know?"

"And did you?"

Glenn's head and neck sunk back into his shoulders, his eyebrows arching – a look that combined disappointment at being asked and a proclamation of innocence.

"I don't do kids," he said. "Why would I, when I have all this?"

The stripper was over by the bar, leaning forward with her elbows on the counter to talk with Sandra, a position that emphasized those long legs and drew the eye to the first bulge of ass, just below the skirt. Jimmy knew exactly what Glenn meant when he said 'all this'.

"You like?" said Glenn now. "I could fix you up, you know. Any of the girls. Pussy's pussy, after all. Close your eyes and any one of them could be Mel – that's what I do."

That smile again. The look in the eye.

Jimmy felt the muscles tightening, and wondered if Glenn knew how close he was to being knocked cold.

Then Glenn raised an eyebrow, paused, and suddenly the two were laughing.

"Bastard," said Jimmy, a few seconds later.

"As much a bastard as you."

Jimmy nodded, surprised to have made that connection with his brother after so long – the laughter, the bastard reference that turned thoughts to their father. "We all good for tomorrow?" he asked now.

Glenn nodded. "Looks like a good turn-out," he said.

"Making sure he's really gone."

They laughed again.

This was strange. Nothing had got to him for years. Not really got under his skin. But now, in the space of twenty-four hours, first Mel and now... Jimmy had forgotten the good times. Forgotten being part of this. When you step back it's so much easier to see things as black or white, but close up...

He'd grown up with Glenn. Seen him cry, seen him scared. Seen him putting on a tough face when the old man had been screaming in his face, often taking the brunt of it to shield his kid brother. The two of them had learned to man up together, to walk the walk, to at least play the part of being the kind of men their father expected of them.

He hadn't expected to have thoughts like this. The old man's death had got to him more than he would have believed possible.

Maybe Glenn was feeling the same way. More so, perhaps, because now he had to step into those shoes – no more playing the part.

"You scared her," said Jimmy. "Last night. That bastard hurt her. Scared the crap out of her."

Glenn shrugged. "Who? Mel?" he said. "What happened? She okay?"

"You know she is. And you know what happened."

Glenn looked evasive now, even though he tried not to. He knew.

"I know why you did it," said Jimmy. "You're a businessman. You don't like people digging around in your business. Making waves. I get that. It's cool."

He paused, made sure Glenn was actually looking at him, then said, "But if you ever send anyone to scare or hurt Mel again, I'll break every bone in your body."

He didn't shout. Didn't make a show of aggression. Just spoke softly, evenly. You don't need show when the person on the receiving end of a threat knows damned well it will be carried out if necessary.

And Glenn knew. He nodded, made that hand-spreading gesture of his again. Nothing to hide.

Jimmy had never done this before, never faced his older brother down. When he'd still been part of the family set-up, he'd mastered the art of deflection and avoidance, even when it meant he found himself drawn ever deeper into the family's activities.

But he'd learned. If anything proved to him he was a different person now, this was it.

"How long's it been?" said Glenn now, leaning back in his seat and patting the table with one hand. This seat, the family table. All those times they'd sat here with the old man. Kids with fizzy drinks and crisps, the packets split open lengthways and spread out on the table. Barely understanding what was going on, the conversations and instructions – people's fates being decided and punishments meted out while they sat here eating their snacks.

And when they were older and understood more. Understood that Uncle Frank's absence for the past year and sudden reappearance was because he'd been staying somewhere that didn't allow trips to the pub. Understood that 'fixing' someone meant pretty much the opposite, and fixing someone the previous year was why Uncle Frank had been put away.

"Ten years," said Jimmy.

"Really? That long? Bitch carries it well."

Again, that muscle twitch, the hair's breadth between holding back and laying Glenn out cold – and Glenn knew it, was grinning.

Did he know? Had he picked up the signs, guessed what had happened between Jimmy and Mel? Just as Jimmy knew Glenn's tells, he was sure his older brother could read him, too.

"Ten years," said Glenn. "I was sitting right here with the old man and Uncle Frank. You remember?"

Of course he remembered.

"Having a few drinks," Glenn went on. "Celebrating a job well done."

A 'job'. A 'fixing'.

Simon Naismith. A flash young property developer only a year or two older than Glenn. Thought the kind of protection the Lazenby family offered was old-fashioned, said business didn't have to be like that anymore.

In some ways Naismith had reminded Jimmy of Mel, the way she plunged into the thick of things, carried by a pure belief that the world just couldn't be that bad. Naismith had simply wanted to get on with his business, buying, developing and selling, wheeling and dealing. Even when Jimmy's father had leaned on him he hadn't buckled. He'd even hired extra security – that innocent belief in doing things the right way.

That night, the night Jimmy had walked out of here for good, they'd been on a job. Jimmy, Glenn and Uncle Frank. A 'quiet word' with Simon Naismith. 'Fixing' the problems he was causing. All these words, these euphemisms that had sailed over the boys' heads when they were younger and even now made hospitalizing a man and two of his security guys seem somehow like a normal business transaction.

Frank and Glenn had been like madmen in the thick of it, and at one point Jimmy had realized Frank and the old man had planned this between them, cherry-picked a 'job' for Jimmy, a blooding to get him more involved in the kind of things Glenn had already been doing for a few years.

"And then your bird walks in," said Glenn now. "Mel."

Walked into the Flag and Flowers shortly after they'd got back from the job and seen them, heard them. That adrenaline thing again, the euphoria after the fight. Drinks all round – even then, Glenn with one of the girls from Ryders in his lap.

The surge of feelings Jimmy hadn't understood at the time, and had taken years to work out: that rush of excitement, the way events still fizzed in your mind, relived and enhanced and, if you're in a group, talked up and embellished. He'd done plenty of jobs for his father before, of course, but this had been the first time he'd been thrown into something like this, the first time they'd gathered like this afterward. It had marked a new phase, a fuller inclusion in the family business.

He'd been buzzing. Wired. The adrenaline rush swamping all those doubts festering at the back of his mind. The awful guilt at the first blow he'd delivered, the meaty thud of boot in midriff, the cracking of ribs. All that swamped at the time by the need to prove himself, and later by the high spirits of the others, by the look of respect in his father's eye… Had he ever seen that before?

And then, as Glenn put it, his bird had walked in. Mel.

The look on her face. Not so much the disgust as the acceptance of defeat: that this was who he was, that in the space of this one evening she had lost him to this.

"She starts screaming and shouting at you," said Glenn. "Telling you you're better than all this. Better than *us*.

Telling you she can't take it anymore. Giving you a proper pussy-whipping." Glenn laughed, seemed to find it all amusing, but that might simply have been for effect.

Was that how it had been?

It's not how Jimmy painted it in his head, how events went whenever he replayed them.

She hadn't screamed and ranted. Hadn't delivered any ultimatums.

It had been unspoken. In her look. In the slump of her body.

She'd seen him as he was, as he was becoming, and that only served to emphasize his own… disgust? Fear?

Not physical fear. He could handle himself, even then. No, a deeper fear than that. A sense of control lost, of being drawn ever deeper.

He'd clutched at that glimmer of realization like a lifeline. Gasped for air.

Walked out.

Not forever. Not then.

At first it was that he simply couldn't face Mel. Not when she looked at him like that. And not when he still felt the visceral thrill of what he'd done.

It was only later. After he'd walked. After he'd had time to gather his thoughts, work out what had happened. Only then that he'd realized he'd already crossed a line, already walked, and could not go back until he was something other than what he was becoming.

"All this," said Glenn. He'd been talking, but Jimmy had filtered him out. "Don't you miss it? We could have been something, couldn't we? You and me, bro'. You could have had yourself some of this."

He could. Maybe he should.

"It's not too late. Not for family. Not for you and me, Jimbo."

Jimmy shook his head. He knew Glenn was toying with him. That familiar thing with him: you never knew quite where you stood, whether he was being serious or winding you up.

For a moment, though, he allowed his brain to play through the fantasy, to imagine never having to walk into those anonymous offices on the South Bank ever again, never having to spend three hours in a meeting that didn't officially exist to review a mission that had never officially taken place to make sure he'd followed all the rules that had never been written.

To imagine the simplicity of living this life, of being an old-school bastard like Glenn, and their father before them. A villain with principles, if that could ever, really, be a thing.

Was that even so far from what he was?

"Fuck off, Glenn," he finally said, and his brother laughed.

Then Glenn leaned forward, forearms resting on his knees. "What if you're wrong, Jimbo?" he said. "What if I'm just doing my best here? Mel comes to me, needs help, so I try to help her. What's so strange in that? She asks me to sniff around after her little girlfriend, so that's what I do. You and me, we're cut from the same cloth. We just have different ways of asking, right?"

"So you're just being nice?"

The shrug, the spreading of hands. "What can I say? I was brought up good."

"And last night?"

"What if you're wrong about that too? Do you really think I'd send someone after *Mel?* What are you missing, Jimbo? What hasn't Doug Conner told you, eh?"

Jimmy didn't react. Glenn never had grasped subtlety, and now he was telling Jimmy not only that he knew he was involved in law enforcement, but that he worked for Mel's father. That was a serious level of inside information.

"Maybe you should ask him why he might send his daughter here, playing the innocent with her questions, stirring things up. Don't tell me you haven't wondered about that?"

Glenn sat back. Job done. That irritating smile teasing at his features. A glance across to the bar was all it took to tell his dancer friend to bring her long legs back over to the family table and join them. To sit in that way of hers, legs crossed so her body twisted toward him attentively, one needy hand on his arm.

"Remember," he said. "You'll always have a welcome here. We're family, right?"

Outside, the sun was bright, painting the street in extremes of light and shade.

Jimmy's head spun, raced.

He was surprised Glenn knew so much, but perhaps shouldn't have been. Jimmy had kept tabs on Glenn and their father over the years, after all. Partly that family thing, the connection, a sense of wanting to know what they were up to even if he didn't want anything to do with them. And partly a pragmatic thing, wanting to be sure he'd never be wrong-footed by either of them.

It made sense Glenn would do the same.

But to know he worked for Conner? And, by implication, to at least have some idea that the kind of work they did didn't fit the remit of any of the normal agencies – the police, MI5, MI6…

The suggestion Conner had actually sent Mel here was ludicrous, though. He would never use her in that way. There was no sense to it.

And even as Jimmy convinced himself there was no rationale there, a part of his mind constructed a narrative where Conner had perhaps fed Mel a few snippets, knowing she would dive in and stir things up with the Lazenby family. A narrative where, when he realized she'd dug deeper than he'd expected, he might have sent Jimmy in to protect her. Perhaps even a scenario where, when Jimmy didn't extract her immediately, Conner might have sent in someone to track Mel down on a dark night and scare her into getting the hell out. To…

He stopped himself.

Remembered that little smile playing on Glenn's features as Jimmy had got up to leave.

You know when I'm bullshitting, Jimbo. That's why you're here.

He always had. He'd always known Glenn's tells.

But did he still have that ability?

Ten years was a long time.

And now, as his head raced and jumped from one possibility to another, the one thing he knew for sure was that Glenn had always liked to toy with him, and he always would.

With Glenn it had never been a question of whether he was telling the truth or not, it was all about the spectrum in between.

11. JIMMY

"Someone went after Mel last night."

The look on Douglas Conner's face was enough for Jimmy. The shock and fear, the concern – on a face that never normally showed any kind of reaction at all. Then the rapid leap from those reactions to the screens snapping back into place as he realized that if anything truly bad had happened he wouldn't be finding out like this.

"I intervened," said Jimmy. "I dealt with it. That's why I'm there, isn't it? To look out for her. That's why you didn't tell me she was involved. You didn't think I'd take it on if you'd told me she was there."

A nod, eyes averted again – another rare chink in his armor.

It was evening, the South Bank. The scaffolding-clad towers of the Houses of Parliament loomed across the river, the anonymous gray offices lined up along the bank on this side. The lamp posts with twined iron serpents at their bases, along the riverside wall. The usual mix of tourists and commuters, and late-working civil servants grabbing a few minutes out of the office on another beautiful evening.

Jimmy had come here just for this. To see the reaction on Conner's face. To ground himself again. Right now he hated his brother more than ever, for getting under his skin so easily.

"She okay?"

Jimmy nodded. Conner trusted him to give as much detail as necessary, but also no more. Did everyone in the service learn to shut themselves down like this, or was it simply that this was how Conner handled things and Jimmy had used the older man as a role model?

"You could have told me Mel was involved. I don't like surprises."

"Would you have gone?"

Now it was Jimmy's turn to avert his gaze, avoid answering.

"You were the best man for the job," said Conner.

"I'm not a babysitter."

Now Conner fixed him with those gray eyes. "That wasn't the job," he said. "There's a seventeen-year-old girl missing. At risk. *That* was the job. It still is, if you think you're up to it."

Jimmy was surprised. He didn't think Conner was lying to him now. Yes, looking out for Mel had been part of it, but Conner seemed genuinely concerned for Harriet Rayner. This was clearly more than just a missing persons case to him.

Glenn's mind games had really got to Jimmy, made him question everything, when he should have kept it simple. He'd been sent to find a missing girl. That was the job. Nothing more than that.

For a short time the two stood leaning on the balustrade, looking out across the river at the passing boats.

"You okay?" Conner asked.

Jimmy was surprised at the question, immediately wondering what Conner had seen in him this evening. Had he picked up on the turmoil in his mind?

Then Conner added: "The funeral's tomorrow, isn't it?"

He nodded. It was a normal question, the kind of thing you would ask someone who gave a shit, who hadn't walked out on their family and all it entailed ten years before.

"I'm good," he said. "You were right. It was the perfect in for me – nobody's surprised to see me back there."

Conner nodded. "Find her, Jimmy. Get that kid home safe, okay? Pursue every lead, no matter how flimsy. Break the rules if you have to."

Again, Jimmy was reminded of what was at stake.

"Rules?" he said now. "We have *rules?*"

He spent the night at his apartment by Battersea Park. He'd stayed here perhaps three nights in the last forty, and the place had an unloved and unoccupied feel to it.

Tonight he was newly aware of how anonymous these four rooms were. Furnished from Ikea and Homebase, right down to the blandly generic prints on the walls. No books, DVDs or CDs; no photographs in frames. Nothing that might betray either the identity or personality of whoever lived here. The clothes in the wardrobes and drawers were a simple selection of jeans, dark suits, white shirts, all in multiples so he could dress fresh and still look the same. He could walk away from this place with what mattered to him in his pockets and a pen drive, and never look back.

He'd done that more than once before. Different apartments, different cities around the world.

Attachments and complications were for real people.

He felt guilty, returning to apparent domesticity when the girl was still missing, but he needed to get some sleep at some point, and he knew he'd achieve nothing by rushing back into the thick of things tonight.

He ate with chopsticks straight from foil trays that night, rereading the case files on a tablet then using various specialist search tools to hunt down Harriet Rayner again, but with no success. He logged in to the Section's system to see if Mamta Patil had flagged anything new for him, but nothing, again.

It had been almost a week now. He wondered how long it would be before the police accepted that this was more than just the case of a troubled girl with a neurotic, paranoid mother.

Because Jimmy was in no doubt now. Harriet's disappearance was not simply a domestic thing.

Even though it was late, he called Mel, his thumb pausing briefly over the Dial icon as he recalled persuading her to exchange numbers, and thereby to accept that she would step back and let him investigate. He owed it to her to at least check in, even with nothing to report.

No reply.

When it went to voicemail, he said, "Hi. No real developments, I'm afraid. Chances are still good that she's just lying low somewhere."

He was beginning to sound like Glenn. What was it he'd said? Sleeping it off or shagging a dealer…

"The police have dug around, too." Neither deeply nor thoroughly, but hey, he wasn't going to tell her that right now. It was important she knew Harriet hadn't been forgotten, but he knew he was treading a delicate line between keeping spirits up and offering false hope. "Call me, okay? It's good to talk in times like this."

Times when you should be preparing for bad news, and when even talking to the guy who'd failed you all that time ago might be better than nothing because at least he understands the situation and you can talk openly.

He didn't know how to sign off, so just cut the connection.

Where was she right now? He didn't know where she lived, although she'd said something about London. For all he knew she could be sitting in a room within a street or two of his apartment.

He resisted the urge to run her through the system.

Last night… this morning. That had been a mistake.

He was making too many mistakes right now. Letting Glenn get under his skin. Allowing himself to be distracted by all the family stuff, the funeral. Allowing his mind to fill with speculations and doubts.

This wasn't who he was.

It was late. He gathered the remains of his meal, the trays picked clean. Dumped them in the recycling and rinsed off the chopsticks, before drying them and putting them away.

Tonight he would sleep well, because he had the opportunity of a straight eight hours and that was what he was trained to do. And in the morning he had one call to make before heading back for his father's funeral.

The place was nothing more than a double garage that had been converted into a tiny two-level home with skylights set into the shallow A-frame roof. It occupied one corner of the garden of an old red-brick Victorian house.

Jimmy knocked, then took a step back, aware of how intimidating an early morning call from a stranger could be for anyone living alone, let alone someone as emotionally fragile as Penny Rayner.

She opened the door, peering out at him from round eyes, her make-up full and exaggerated even for this early, the mascara forming little clumps on her lashes. Rather than appearing intimidated by his sudden appearance, she puckered her lips into a rosebud smile, and widened her eyes farther.

It was a look he recognized. One that measured him up, assessing what he might have to offer and what she might be able to take. The look of a woman who had navigated her way through life by making exactly that kind of assessment.

He'd met many junkies over the years, and every single time he hated to see what it did to a person.

"Ms Rayner," he said, with a dip of the head. "I'm sorry to disturb you so early in the day."

"Oh please," she said. She'd already clearly worked out he wasn't just a random caller.

"Your daughter," he said. "Have you heard from Harriet recently?"

"You're with the police?" she said. "They said they would send someone."

He didn't deny it. She hadn't answered his question, but it was clear from her manner that she had heard nothing.

"I just wondered if I might take a look at her room?" he said now. "Sometimes a trained eye sees something that others might miss."

He didn't give a shit about her room. He just wanted to see inside the house.

It was one of the likeliest scenarios, after all. Girl goes missing, she's either done a runner for any one of a number of predictable reasons, or she's got herself into some kind of trouble, or there's a domestic explanation. And in this case, the only domestic part of her life she had was Penny Rayner.

As Penny still hesitated he smiled, and that was enough for her to smile in return, step back, and let him into her home.

The place was tidy to the extent of obsessive. Nothing out of place, no dust or cobwebs. He tried to imagine this woman's life, but couldn't, the excessive control and order periodically shattered by lapses into chaos.

Right now he couldn't tell whether she was on top of things, or obsessively clinging on, about to plummet.

"Her room?" he prompted.

Penny looked away, and said, "She doesn't have one. She's never stayed."

He'd read of their domestic arrangements in the files, of course, but somehow he'd assumed the girl would at least have something here. He smiled, wondering why

Penny Rayner had even let him in if that were the case, and as he did so, his gaze flitted about the interior of her home.

They stood in a small lobby area, a dark wood sideboard below a horizontal rectangular mirror that took up most of one wall. Open doorways led into kitchen and living room, and slatted wooden stairs led up to the bedroom and bathroom – he'd already checked the building's floorplan before coming here.

He didn't need to look any farther. If Harriet was lying low here, there would have been something to betray that fact. Shoes by the door, a plate or a cup left out, at least something that interrupted this place's immaculate orderliness.

"Her apartment?" he said. "Are you sure she hasn't been back?"

Penny shook her head. He knew the police had checked the place, and there had been no sign of occupation since last week.

He left a pause. Enough to unsettle Penny, expose any vulnerabilities. Could she act this well if she was trying to mislead him, or cover something up?

Perhaps. She was an addict, after all, so she was accustomed to the ways of clever deceit.

But the girl clearly wasn't hiding out here, and if something more sinister had happened between the two of them he found it hard to believe this frail and brittle woman would have come out on top.

Minutes later, Jimmy was walking away, heading to where he'd left his car out of sight around the corner.

He'd been clutching at straws, he knew.

Perhaps that was why he'd come back to the city in the first place yesterday – not to confront Conner, but in the vain hope he'd find some trace of Harriet here and so not have to head back today for his father's funeral.

He climbed into the driving seat of his black Audi. A pool car, provided by the Section; another disposable part of his life like the apartment.

He checked his phone. No messages. No updates from Patil.

No answer to the voicemail he'd left for Mel last night. She didn't have to respond, of course. He'd merely reported on progress – or lack of it – and hadn't asked any questions that might require an answer. It would have been perfectly legitimate for her to listen to the message and do nothing.

Now, he thought back to the previous morning, standing awkwardly with her in the street after breakfast.

He'd told her he'd call, knowing it sounded like such a damned platitude.

You'd fucking better.

She'd given a little smile, but there had been a spark in her look, a flash of something.

At the time he'd taken it for frustration at her own powerlessness, an acknowledgment that the time had come to step back, leave this to the professionals.

But had it been something else? A frustration directed at him, rather than her own helpless position?

Anger at him for being right, perhaps? She'd hate that. Maybe she'd gone silent now to punish him.

Or maybe she was simply leaving him to get on with what he claimed to be good at. Now, that thought only reinforced his own frustration that all he'd managed in the last twelve hours was to pursue a few dead ends and get some sleep for the first time in several days.

He stared at his phone for far longer than necessary. Telling himself, all the time, that it was only that he wanted to know she was okay, and not at all that he wanted to hear her voice, even just to read something she had written... anything. He'd gone ten years with nothing from her, and now he struggled even to go twenty-four hours.

12. MEL

Jimmy. The bastard. He was just as bad as the rest of them.

She should never have let him in, let her guard down. Never have succumbed to a nostalgia fuck.

Jimmy Fucking Lazenby.

The bastard.

It had been fine. Really.

She'd almost believed him. Believed *in* him.

He seemed genuine. There was a new raw honesty about this Jimmy. None of the Lazenby bullshit. The front and bravado. None of the denial that the Lazenbies were what they were. None of the need to fit in with the family and prove his worth.

Or rather, maybe that was it. He still labored under the same need to prove his own value, when he should have known he never had to do that for her. Ten years ago, she'd seen who he really was, beneath the Lazenby layers.

Seen who he could be. The only problem was she could see what he was becoming, too.

But whereas back then the need to prove himself had led him partway down a slippery slope, the same need appeared to have driven this new Jimmy along a different route.

He'd become one of the good guys.

In many ways, this Jimmy scared her more than the old version. He seemed to have shed so much baggage, stripped himself down. How could he do that? Was he really so cold inside?

But then last night… this morning… she'd managed to get beneath his skin, see that perhaps he had not so much shed those layers of the Jimmy she'd once loved, but submerged them.

And she'd started to fall again.

That glimmer of the old Jimmy she had loved. The new Jimmy she was discovering.

The Jimmy who could look her in the eye and say something like *I have nowhere left to fall. I fell ten years ago and I never climbed out.*

The bastard.

Making her feel that way. Letting her fall.

And then he'd let slip the minor detail that he hadn't come here for any noble reasons, hadn't come here because he was the good guy, come to save the day.

He'd come here because her father had sent him.

It was a job.

And not only a job, but one her father had dished out, no doubt pulling shady strings in that shady role in London he was always so cloak and dagger about.

She'd had no idea Jimmy and her father had any kind of connection these days, let alone one that had, presumably, survived the ten years since she and Jimmy had parted.

Had her father swept in when they'd split up? Seen that he could make use of Jimmy in some way?

Or had Jimmy turned to him, found some kind of Lazenby angle – because the Lazenbies always found an angle – to lean on him, and secure some kind of role?

Either way, she didn't like it.

It felt as if the two men who had figured the largest in her life had conspired against her.

She knew she should be grateful.

She should thank her father for actually responding to her plea for help, and sending someone in to look for Harriet.

She shouldn't feel misled.

Shouldn't feel that she could trust no-one. Neither her father nor the man she had, briefly, fallen for, all over again.

And so she'd tried. She'd meekly sat in that shabby little breakfast café, nodding wide-eyed as the brave good knight assured her he'd take care of everything and she should just go home and wait for him to get in touch.

"I'll call," Jimmy had told her, as they paused awkwardly outside in the street. She could tell from the look on his face he knew he'd won. Placated her. Fobbed her off.

"You'd fucking better," she told him.

She'd intended to leave it at that. To turn and walk away, knowing his eyes were on her and she was absolutely not going to look back. Keep it simple.

She'd had no intention of tipping her head up, meeting his look.

Of putting a hand flat on his chest, so she could feel the thump of his heart through her palm.

Of pushing up on the balls of her feet so her mouth could find his.

Treating herself to a moment where the complications fell away and there was just this kiss. A moment where she fell again, albeit briefly.

And then, at last, stepping back, turning, walking away without even a glance back to see him watching her.

She did it though. Went home. It was the sensible thing. She'd seen how ill-equipped she was to deal with this kind of shit when it got serious.

She had hand-shaped bruises on her throat, for goodness' sake! Not to mention an ache in her ribs that reminded her every time she breathed of how close she'd come. And a swollen, sore nose.

She wasn't vain at all, but right now she was very aware of how she must look. She'd done her best with foundation and a pale concealer from Superdrug to cover the marks, but she was acutely aware of what people must be thinking every time they glanced in her direction.

She hated to think how far that guy might have gone if Jimmy hadn't stuck a gun between his shoulder blades.

Not to mention hating that these memories reminded her minute by minute of how right Jimmy was, of how she'd totally misjudged the consequences of throwing herself into something like this.

She was out of her depth.

And so, today, her body both sore from the night before and strangely invigorated by events of the morning

– such a peculiar mix of sensations! – she sat on the train heading back into London and hoped desperately that one day Harriet might forgive her for walking away. Forgive her that, when it came down to it, all she could really do for her friend was hope.

She would go to her father, she decided, as the suburbs stacked up on either side. Swallow her foolish pride and thank him, and use whatever daughterly influence she could muster to persuade him to prioritize this. If he'd been able to pull strings enough to send Jimmy in, then surely he could throw more resources at the investigation now?

She stared out of the window at graffitied walls, at ramshackle industrial units, at rows of terraced houses that looked as if a giant had pushed them together from either end to try to squeeze in just one more. At shopping streets and parks, playing fields and cemeteries.

So many hundreds of people – thousands – just going about their normal lives, unaware of quite how close they might be to tragedy. To losing someone, or worse, to not knowing if that someone is lost, or damaged, or might simply walk back in one day as if nothing had happened.

Harriet always tried so hard to be nothing like her mother, but she was just as volatile and strong-headed, with a lot of the same erratic traits. And if Glenn could be believed, she had been using drugs and hiding it from people like Mel. It was odd that this, above anything, should be cause for hope: that she might be more like her mother than anyone had suspected, that this whole episode could just be an epic crash and burn, just as her mother had done so many times before.

That was what Mel found herself hoping. Crash, burn, and then the bitter taste of regret, an opportunity to learn from the experience and choose a path that would not lead to a bitter, lonely existence where even your memories are no longer your own and all you have is a tattered photograph to remind you of what you had enjoyed and lost.

The woman opposite was looking at her. Mel couldn't tell if she'd seen through the concealer to the bruises beneath, or if it was simply the tears sliding down her cheeks that drew the attention.

She dabbed at her face with a tissue, so as not to smudge her camouflage, gave a small smile, and returned her gaze to the passing buildings.

She didn't seek out her father. Didn't meekly thank him for his intervention and then wheedle for more.

He didn't need that. He'd made a judgment call and was doing what he could. Further interference from Mel would simply complicate things.

She'd only get in the way.

That's what everyone told her, wasn't it?

She tidied her room, not that it was a mess to start with.

She stared at the pages of a book, alternating that with staring up through the skylight at blue sky.

She walked in the park and was reminded again of all the people, all around, living their normal lives, untouched by tragedy. Was reminded of the last time she'd walked here, when she'd needed this normality all around to ground her when she called her father to ask for help.

And later, she stepped onto another train.

She couldn't do this.

Just as everyone seemed to be telling her, she might be crap at solving a mess like this, but she was so much worse at not even trying to.

He took her for dinner, finally extracting his price for help. Or at least part of the price – she knew he saw dinner as no more than a down payment.

Glenn Lazenby. The man who, last time they'd met, had snarled a threat at her about the importance of not pissing off the people who might just have her back. His mask had slipped then, no more Mr Nice Guy, no more Mr Smooth.

She'd called him from the train, but only got through to Suze. Perhaps she actually was his PA, at least when she wasn't dancing. Or maybe she and Glenn were a thing, and it was normal for her to answer his phone when he was unavailable. Apparently he was in a meeting, but Suze said she'd made a note for him to call back when he was free.

There was nothing subtle about the brush-off. Her last encounter with Glenn had been hostile – he'd practically kicked her out of Ryders after he'd caught her in the dressing room, showing the girls Harriet's photograph.

And then later he'd sent that bastard to scare her out of her skin. She knew this was stupid, coming back out here and trying to shake something out of him, after all that. But… Harriet.

It hadn't worked, though. He'd got his assistant to fob her off. End of.

She should have called him before getting onto the train. If he wasn't even going to grant her an audience, her big-eyed ditzy blonde thing didn't stand a chance.

Her phone buzzed ten minutes later, and a glance at the screen told her it was him. For a moment she considered playing hard to get, too. After all, he'd called back, so he still thought he could get something out of this – she knew that's how his mind worked, and didn't kid herself he was interested in her intellect or jokes.

She answered. Save the mind games for when it really mattered.

"Hey, darling," he said, as if nothing had happened between them. "How you doing? What can I do for you?"

She hesitated, for effect, then said, "I... Thanks for calling back, Glenn. I couldn't leave things like that. I was stressed. I still am. I just thought... well, you said something about dinner?"

She felt sick.

Sick that he might say no, might laugh at her for even suggesting it, or just see straight through her flimsy pretext.

Sick that he might say yes. That he might see through her flimsy pretext but still want to extract the price for his pretense of help.

Sick that she didn't know where her own boundaries lay. What she might be willing to do to get her friend back.

He laughed, although there didn't appear to be anything cruel in the laughter. "You chicks," he said. "I'm fighting you all off, I tell you!" He was joking, trying to wind her up in that way he had that could sometimes be funny but often was used as a way to intimidate, and this time she wasn't sure where that balance lay. He did this to Jimmy all the time, wrapped him around his little finger with digs and barbs, each carefully selected to not only get under his kid brother's skin but to embed and twist.

"It's not that," she said perhaps too hurriedly. "I just... well, I thought we could talk."

"I know, I know," he said. "You still want help. No, don't deny it, it's fine. I get it, darling. You're desperate, and even though sometimes you love me and sometimes you hate me you know I'm the kind of dude who can make things happen, right? It's fine. I get it. Listen, how about this evening? There's a do I have to be at, but you could be my plus one?"

"Thank you. That sounds perfect."

"But hey, just one thing, right? All this me being nice, and us being up front that you just want me for my smarts, right? All that, well, it doesn't mean I'm not going to try to get into your pants, okay?"

He laughed, cutting off any reply, and Mel tensed her jaw, clamping her mouth shut. Playing his game.

"Seven?" he said. "Flag and Flowers. We'll go from there. And scrub up, darling, okay? This is a classy do."

§

Scrub up. From anyone else she'd have been offended, but from Glenn she'd have expected nothing less.

She hadn't brought anything fancy with her, just a shoulder bag with a change of clothes and the essentials. She had time before seven, though, and after dumping her few things at Mr Singh's, where she'd taken a room again, she spent a couple of hours touring the town's many charity shops. She ended up with a smart little black cocktail dress, slingbacks with heels she could just about manage, and a matching purse, all on a budget that was only a little too much for a postgrad student trying to get by at London rates.

To use Glenn's terms, she scrubbed up well. The dress, the heels – which she took a while to get accustomed to, given that her normal footwear decisions revolved around which color Converse to go with today's jeans.

The bruising seemed to be fading too, and the swelling on her nose had gone down. She did a better job with the concealer, this time – paler than her usual shade to cover the dark marks, blending it carefully for a more natural effect.

She felt guilty, to feel so glam while her friend was still missing, but it was for a reason. All this was for Harriet.

She walked to the Flag and Flowers, avoiding the route across Jubilee Park, not because she thought it likely she'd be attacked again but simply for the memories the park stirred, the gut-level fears. The bruises might fade, but it'd be a lot longer before the psychological harm had receded.

When she walked into the pub, long-time barmaid Sandra and the others turned to stare. Mel wondered how she looked to them, if they could see through the mask. Then Glenn stepped out from the office behind the bar, straightened with a slight backward roll of the shoulders, and said, "Wow, Mels. Just wow."

He seemed genuine, and for a moment she reflected on his reactions to her, the jokey flirting which had always, perhaps, been used to deflect attention from his true feelings.

She smiled, dismissing the thought. 'Genuine' was not a word that could ever be applied to Glenn Lazenby, unless you were making the point that he faked genuine well.

She let him kiss her on the cheek. It was always disturbing to be reminded of the very physical similarities he shared with his brother – the way he rested hands on her arms when he leaned in to kiss, the ways he moved and held himself, the subtle natural scent that underlay the cologne.

"So are you going to tell me what all this is?" she asked.

"An associate of mine," he said, straightening and adjusting the hang of his jacket. "Thom Sullivan. He's in the country for a few days."

He said it as if she should recognize the name, but she just smiled and raised her eyebrows questioningly.

"Thom Sullivan of TSI," he said. "They're behind some of the biggest software developments in social media of the past few years."

Mel did her best *oh gosh* look. Guys with money clearly didn't impress her as much as they did Glenn.

"You and Thom, you're close?" she asked, trying to play his game.

"We go back some," said Glenn. "Sometimes a guy like Thom needs a wheeler and dealer, you know? He knows I'm a safe pair of hands."

They were driven there, even though the event was only a couple of streets away from the Flag and Flowers. The venue was unprepossessing from the outside, just a blank wooden door to a redbrick building that looked like an old industrial unit of some kind. Bizarrely Mel was reminded of the entrance to Ryders, and she wondered if this was something similar, a bit of sleazy chic so the big guy could think he was roughing it. The two suited security guys on the door only reinforced the idea they were entering one of the Lazenby family's clubs and dives.

Inside was not what she'd anticipated. They entered via a lobby area, with glass doors onto a restaurant naturally lit by windows and wide skylights. A five-piece jazz band played softly in one corner, something smooth and slow. You could tell from the wide spaces between the tables alone that this place was seriously up-market, and quite unlike anything Mel had either experienced or anticipated in her home town.

People had gathered around the bar, the men in suits and the women in a selection of stylish dresses. Mel could not have felt more self-conscious if she'd tried. Not just the injuries she'd struggled to conceal, but her outfit, her hair. The clothes she'd bought this afternoon almost certainly cost less than a single drink in this place.

She reminded herself of Glenn's reaction to her when she'd arrived at the Flag and Flowers. The *wow*.

"What?" he asked now, turning to look at her.

She'd taken his arm when they'd stepped inside, faithfully playing her 'plus one' role, and she realized now she'd unconsciously squeezed just a little, leaned in a little closer.

"All this," she said, filling the silence, hoping to distract from that moment of weakness when she'd only wanted reassurance. "He's taken over the whole restaurant, hasn't he?"

It was clearly all a single gathering, no casual diners. She'd been registering just how expensive a place this was, and Thom Sullivan had taken the entire place over for the evening. That must take serious money.

Glenn nodded. "Oh yeah," he said. "People like Thom, they can't be too careful. Everyone's after a piece, you know what I mean? This is his world: he regularly takes over places if he wants to use them. Goes with the territory, doesn't it? He's a man who gets what he wants."

That was the real measure of success for Glenn, she realized. He'd mentioned before men who got what they wanted, used that reference point as if it was something that would impress, as if it was what everyone must aspire to.

"Stop it," she said now, digging him playfully in the side. "You sound like you've got a man crush."

She'd turned it on him, had a little poke that she could see had momentarily wound him up, doing exactly what he liked to do to everyone else. He saw it too, and laughed.

He put a hand on hers, holding it in place in the crook of his arm. A protective gesture, and perhaps a possessive one, too.

She was reminded now of his comment that he wouldn't stop trying to get into her pants.

"It's not going to work," she said, and she saw in his eyes that he understood.

"A man can dream," he said, that same mischievous smile that Jimmy had breaking out over his face.

She looked away.

She hated that about him. The way he could transform any moment, undermining tension with a smile, animosity with a wink. Just as she hated all the little things – that hand on hers in the crook of his elbow, the solicitous way he checked on her, made sure she was okay, the way he stepped back to let her through, held doors, was always on hand.

All these things, the bits she liked about Glenn, were the ones that reminded her of Jimmy. And now she realized that all the bits she didn't like about him were the ones that reminded her he was not his brother. How screwed up was that?

And just how far had she fallen this morning?

It unsettled her, that now she measured other people – measured the world, for goodness' sake – in terms of Jimmy Lazenby.

"You scared me," she said. "Sending that man after me." She tilted her head, knowing his eyes would be drawn to her neck, the barely concealed bruises.

For a moment she thought he was going to lie to her, but then he paused, his eyes fixed on hers. Maybe he read something there, knew he could be straight with her right now.

"I'm sorry," he said. "You picked a bad time to be asking questions. My business… it's sensitive. I can't have anyone rattling the bars. Wayne went too far, and I made sure he knows that."

There was something chilling in the way he said that. Everyday words had different meaning for people like Glenn Lazenby, different depths. *I made sure he knows that* meant more than simply sending a memo.

She broke the moment, looked away, down. Let her hand tighten on Glenn's arm again, as if to support herself.

Looking back up at him from a tilted face, she said in a small voice, "I really was scared."

She didn't have to try hard to achieve the frightened little girl thing. She was telling the truth, after all.

"I don't know what's worse," she said. "You treating me like that, or the fact that Jimmy got to step in and save the day."

Glenn laughed. "He being a pain, is he? He always did expect a bit of quid pro quo, if you know what I mean."

She smiled, hating herself for doing so, for not pointing out the hypocrisy of Glenn accusing his brother of being the one who always expected to extract a price.

"He doesn't even seem to be finding anything out," she said. "He walks the walk, but… Harriet's still out there somewhere. I…"

Glenn's hand covered hers again. They'd moved across to the bar now, and paused as Glenn ordered two eighteen-year-old Highland Parks. He still didn't ask her what she wanted, but at least this time he'd remembered she had good taste.

"And you?" he asked. "Are you getting anywhere? I've been asking around still, but I haven't found anything more. Just silence."

She shook her head. "Nothing. But silence is good, right? Isn't that what you said?"

He nodded. "She'll just waltz back in some time soon, you mark my words."

"I just make a mess of it," she said. "Blunder in. Get myself in trouble." She fell silent, reminding herself not to lay it on too thick. He already thought she was out of her depth after all.

"Listen, Mels, I really am sorry."

Every time he said that – *Mels* – her breath caught and her heart pounded.

"Like I say, bad time and all that. You know what I mean? Juggling too many balls and then you walk in and start asking questions and, well, I know your connections. I know your old man, and maybe I put two and two together and thought he'd sent you to sniff around."

He was smiling. Everything about his body language said relaxed. But his eyes were fixed on her like those of a predator.

Was he serious?

Did he really think she might be here on behalf of her father for some reason?

Her mind raced.

She'd thought she was a bumbling amateur, making a mess and getting nowhere, and here was Glenn Lazenby actually digging to see if her father had sent her here.

And by implication, he was telling her he knew something about her father's work – a hell of a lot more than *she* did!

More than anything, though, it made her angry. She'd been straight throughout this. Honest. All she wanted was to find her friend.

She wasn't part of any conspiracy against Glenn, wasn't part of her father's maneuverings, and she hated anything that might complicate why she was here.

And she didn't know how to answer, to protest innocence or tell him to mind his own business, or even to pretend that she actually *was* some kind of undercover agent and he had every reason to fear her. How had she ever got herself into this position?

She laughed. A sudden, snort of laughter, then a fist pressing against her mouth, trying to stifle it.

It broke the moment.

He hesitated, then laughed, too. Then his hands were on her arms and, briefly, he hugged her before stepping back, still holding her arms.

"I know, right?" he said. "I'm not usually so paranoid. I just…"

"Juggling too many balls," she finished for him. "All I want is to find Harriet. Will you keep asking around?"

"Of course I will," he said. "I'm not going to stop. That kid..." He shook his head, was momentarily lost to his thoughts.

She'd seen that look a lot recently, people taking in the meaning of her questions: not just someone missing, but a teenaged girl, a kid.

They mingled. Glenn introduced her to a property developer and the coach of a Premiership football team. She accepted another Highland Park, and picked at a few canapés as they came round so she'd at least have something other than whisky in her stomach.

At one point she found herself standing off to one side on her own while Glenn spoke with a white-haired guy in a perfectly tailored suit. She could see the way Glenn puffed himself up, the way his mannerisms and gestures became just a fraction more exaggerated as he tried to fit in and impress. She wondered if the older guy was the man himself, this Thom Sullivan who Glenn had been so in awe of.

She looked around the gathering, wondering what she was still doing here. She'd renewed contact with Glenn, continued to gently dig to see if he knew anything more. Unanswered questions remained, hints that he was hiding something from her, but she knew Glenn was the kind of person who would always have secrets and this might all be a big distraction.

Again, she was struck by how slow this was, and couldn't work out whether that was because she was incredibly clumsy in her investigations or if this was the reality of how these things worked, that in the real world progress was always so painfully slow, with lots of dead ends and backtracking.

She should slip away. Glenn had said he'd keep looking, and she believed him, and she wasn't achieving anything more here. She could hardly circulate with Penny's photograph of her daughter, asking these people if they happened to know anything, could she?

She became aware of a presence at her shoulder, a guy standing there with a champagne flute.

"These things," he said, and she sensed how awkward he felt, too.

She turned, smiled, detecting something of a kindred spirit, or at least another outsider.

He was tall and thin, perhaps around fifty, although his athletic frame, sandy hair and smooth skin made it hard to put an age on him.

"I know, right?" she said, as if she attended this kind of gathering all the time. "All these people. I was just looking around."

"Hard to resist a spot of the old people-watching, isn't it?" he laughed.

Mel nodded. "It feels like we're on a movie set, doesn't it? People playing roles. Stage managed, you know?" That's exactly what it was: as if Thom Sullivan's people had stocked this event up so the man would feel he was mixing with real people, but in reality it was a carefully designed glamorous party scene. She knew she was emotionally stepping back from it all, reinforcing her feeling that she didn't belong.

"I read something once," she said. "One of the Russian tsars, I think. Everywhere he went his people had the edifices of buildings set up so it looked to him as if he was traveling through normal towns and villages, but in reality it was little more than a stage set, an airbrushed reality. That's what this feels like, isn't it?"

He was smiling at her, studying her closely.

"That," he said, "is perhaps the harshest review I've had."

It was him. Thom Sullivan.

Shit.

"True, though?" she said. It was interesting how he didn't appear to like to put himself center stage. She recalled his comment about people-watching, and sensed he was more comfortable giving other people the space they desired.

He laughed. "Perhaps, in a way, although we don't need to stage manage these events to the extent you suggest. People would line up to get into something like this. That doesn't mean they're any less fake, though."

Her first reaction had been to warm to him, to sense a connection there, but now she wondered. It almost felt as if he was mirroring her, repeating her somewhat disparaging observations back to her with only minor twists. A social chameleon.

He was smiling still, but she wasn't convinced it reached his eyes.

She looked away.

The strain of the last few days was getting to her. Coming here this evening had been a mistake. Coming back to her home town again. All of it.

She wasn't cut out for this, and now she hated the way the strain was coloring her view of the world.

"I'm sorry," she said. "I..."

She was apologizing for her brief rush of confusion, but he took it as an apology for her harsh judgment of his party. "It's fine," he said. "Really. I don't do these things for fun, believe me. It's business. Fun's something very different." He leaned in then, touched her elbow briefly.

She didn't like him. That touch. The sense that he owned not only this event but everyone here.

Again, she knew this was partly her viewing the world harshly right now, but…

She still felt that touch on her elbow, even when he took his hand away.

"You," he said. "Tell me. Who you are. What you do. What you do for fun."

She didn't need this. She cursed Glenn for bringing her here, for abandoning her to this while he schmoozed his way around the gathering.

She didn't need to be hit on right now.

She smiled, doing her best. "I'm nothing," she said. "Nobody. I'm just here with a friend."

That brief touch on her elbow again, that smile. "Oh, please. I'd believe many things, but not that. You're most definitely *somebody*."

She was a plaything. A toy. A minor distraction for him right now.

She didn't like this. This wasn't her world.

She smiled again. Glanced across at Glenn, who was at the far end of the bar, center of attention in a small group. He met her look, briefly, and smiled, and that gave her pause. Jimmy's brother was many things – ruthless bastard, charming rogue, occasionally even surprisingly sensitive, and now she realized, some strange kind of friend – but whatever he was, she owed him; at the very least she owed not messing this evening up for him.

"My name is Mel. I'm a postgrad at UCL. I'm an old friend of Glenn Lazenby. I bought this entire outfit this afternoon for little more than loose change. That's about it, really." It felt as if she was being interviewed, being subjected to some kind of test.

At the mention of her clothes, his eyes roamed – her fault, she knew. She'd drawn attention to the dress, if not specifically to the way it hung, the way it clung, but once the eyes moved down... well, she knew how well the clothes fit. Again, she felt as if she was being assessed.

"So not only beauty, but brains and financial acumen," Sullivan said, taking his time to meet her look again, finally. "And if you're a friend of Glenn's, you have the street smarts, too. I should hire you on the spot."

This was crazy. Someone like Thom Sullivan hitting on her, or at least toying with her.

She shook her head. "I'm not available, sorry," she told him.

"Oh, I doubt that. You think it was easy for a place like this to cancel long-standing reservations at a moment's notice?"

His subtext was clear: *Everything's available. Everyone's available.* She hated that flash of arrogance, and it reinforced the fact she didn't really like Thom Sullivan at all.

She stayed quiet, biting back on any number of sarcastic responses bubbling just below the surface. Where Glenn might be impressed by all this, it pressed the wrong buttons for her: privilege, and all the assumptions that went with it.

"Forgive me," said Sullivan now. "I was indulging myself. Enjoying myself. It's good to get away from... from all this." A gesture of the hand, indicating the restaurant, the people.

She waited for him to explain.

"I know who you are," he went on. "Glenn told me about you. He said you were..." A shrug. "He didn't do you justice, even though he tried. Let's leave it at that."

Earlier she'd thought Glenn was exaggerating his relationship with Sullivan to impress her, but clearly the two were close. Close enough to talk about her.

Should she feel flattered that they'd discussed her? Or just creeped out?

And what did that tell her about Glenn? That he was talking about her with people like Sullivan? She didn't like to think she was on his mind enough for that.

"I need to go, I think," she said, glancing across at Glenn again.

"We won't meet again," Sullivan said.

His peculiar choice of words made her pause, and only later did she wonder how many times he'd used a line like that.

"We mix in different circles," he went on. "And yours are so much more real." A reference to her comment about that Russian tsar earlier. "I'll always wonder how it might have been."

He really was hitting on her.

His eyes were the palest blue, fixed on her intently.

"I don't know," he said, doing that thing again, leaving an enigmatic statement dangling so she had to wait for it to unravel. Finally, he continued: "I don't know if under other circumstances we would ever have chosen to meet again, but… living this life…" That gesture of the hand again, indicating the rest of the gathering, his world… "I rarely get the opportunity to even reach the point where I might get to know."

She thought she understood. That stage managed thing. A life scheduled and constrained. His whole existence pretty much stripped of the kind of casual encounters where you meet someone, meet them again, get to know them. Briefly, she felt sympathy for him, then she reminded herself of her earlier judgment, that he was a man who said whatever suited his audience, a chameleon.

"This may seem presumptuous," he said, "but let me make you an offer. No strings. Let me buy a week of your time. I'll have you flown to my place in Monaco. It would be a chance to get acquainted. Nothing more than that. Consider it a job, an internship, whatever. What do you say?"

He really did live on a different planet. You can't just buy spontaneity. You can't buy casual acquaintance.

Well… you could, but they didn't usually call it internship.

"No," she said. "Just no. I'm not for hire. Or for… whatever."

"Oh, I doubt that," he said, smiling. *Everyone's available.* "Think about it. Talk to your friend Glenn. He can arrange everything."

She backed away, still shaking her head. Turned, momentarily disoriented, trying to see where Glenn was now and simultaneously cursing him for bringing her here and abandoning her.

She didn't need this. Any of it. Didn't need to be hit on. Didn't need spoilt wealthy megalomaniacs trying to sweep her away.

What *was* that? A game? A whim?

She didn't even know what she'd just turned down. He'd said no strings, but she was smart enough to know there were never no strings, particularly with a man like Thom Sullivan.

So what did he think she was? Or was it simply that this was how his world worked? One transaction after another, an investment in possibility – perhaps that's how he would term it.

"Look, I'm sorry," she said. "I don't know you. I shouldn't have come here. I just…" She looked at him more closely. He was a man of influence. A man of money.

"I'm not myself right now," she said. "If Glenn talked about me, well, he'd have told you why I'm back in my old home town, why I've been bugging the hell out of him for the past few days."

"Your friend."

He knew. Glenn had said he'd been asking around among his contacts, but this was the first confirmation he was telling the truth.

"I'm scared for her. I just want to find her safe and sound."

Sullivan was nodding. "Understandable."

She reached into her purse for the photo, which he studied closely. "So young," he said. "I wish I could help."

She didn't know what she was asking, just that he was clearly a man of both means and influence. He might know who to lean on, a contact in police or government who might have the pull to get the search stepped up. Money for a reward, for publicity… Anything.

Those pale blue eyes met hers again. "And my offer?" he said.

The moment was snatched from her, the sense that he might actually want to help. He couldn't have been more crude in his leap to the price he might extract for any help – so like Glenn, but without any of the roguish charm.

Earlier, she'd asked herself the question of just how far she would go to get Harriet back, what price she might be willing to pay. And now she knew the answer: not far enough for a man like Thom Sullivan.

"I have to go," she said. Then: "Right now, I'm only focused on one thing, finding Harriet. Nothing else."

He shrugged, didn't seem too bothered at the rebuff. He'd thrown his dice.

She wondered what was really behind those eyes. If he had any grasp on what was at stake here, or if it was all just a game, a series of moves, of dice being thrown.

This really was a different world.

She found Glenn, stood by him as he talked, waiting for him to acknowledge her. This whole thing had been a mistake. How many times had she thought that since getting here?

And now she just stood in Glenn's shadow, all so she could find a lull in his monologue to tell him she was leaving.

"I'm going," she said, at last, when he turned and raised eyebrows in her direction. "Thank you… for this. But I guess I'm just not in a fancy do kind of place."

He shrugged, spread his hands, smiled. "No skin," he said. "You want me to get one of the boys to drive you back to Singh's?"

He couldn't resist letting slip he knew where she was staying. She knew well enough that he didn't mean anything sinister by it, he simply kept tabs on things. That was why she'd come to him, after all. But particularly after Sullivan's comment that Glenn talked about her, it all took on a darker undertone.

"No, no," she said. "I'm fine. Fresh air would be good."

She backed away, turned, made her way to the glass doors through to the lobby area and then outside.

The sun was still bright, and she walked, savoring the freshness of the air. Tried to resist the urge to check over her shoulder every few seconds. Even though she was on her own, she was in the center of town, people and traffic all around. She should feel safe here, not vulnerable, on edge.

A couple of streets away from the anonymous venue of Thom Sullivan's gathering she spotted a familiar building, the Flag and Flowers.

She was tempted to go inside, drawn to the familiarity, to a place that had changed little in the past ten years or more.

She kept walking. Even though Glenn wasn't there right now, it was still Lazenby territory. She needed to break free of all that.

The next pub she came to was the King's Head, another place familiar from her late teens in this town. She used to come here with Rachel and Lila; never with Jimmy, because if they wanted to go to a pub they would always go to one of the family places.

The King's Head had the right mix of comfortable nostalgia and separation from all the crap. It helped that – as she saw when she stepped inside – the pub had been through several refits since she'd last been here, so even the familiar had an air of something new, another step away from the past.

She sat on a tall stool at one end of the bar and ordered a Jack and Coke. She considered moving to one of the tables, then opted to stay where she was, a good vantage point. A place to soak up the atmosphere of normality that surrounded her. It was a bit like sitting on the train and looking out at all the houses, that awareness of all the normal lives going on around her.

It was reassuring. Grounding.

She checked her phone but there were no messages, no missed calls. So much for Jimmy's assurances he'd keep her in the loop.

She'd seen the look in his eye. That great big *Don't call us, we'll call you* in his expression. He couldn't wait to be rid of her, to run away again from the implications of what had happened between them.

Frustrated as she was, though, she felt bad for encouraging Glenn to diss his kid brother, for using it to gain Glenn's confidence again. Through all this, Jimmy was the one person who had stood by her. He'd chosen not to take advantage of her at her most vulnerable. He'd saved her from goodness knows what. He'd had her back.

She'd started to fall, and now she admitted to herself that at least one reason she had just checked her phone was because she'd hoped for at least some kind of contact. To hear his voice, even if it was on voicemail. Even a damned text message. Wanted to know that for at least the time it had taken him to make contact she had been in his thoughts.

She hated to feel so vulnerable, so dependent on the whim of another.

And she hated quite how much she needed to know he understood she was falling, had fallen again.

She remembered lying tangled with him, afterward, only this morning. It felt such a long time ago!

She spotted Suze the moment she entered the pub. Hell, everyone did. She was the kind of woman who got noticed. She wore another short skirt, a skimpy bustier top that couldn't help but draw the eye to the way it pushed her breasts up and together. The first couple of times Mel had encountered the dancer, she'd thought this was how she dressed for work, but now she realized it was probably just normal attire for her. She imagined her doing her weekly supermarket shop dressed like this. Hell, if Mel had a figure like that, she would dress that way all the time, too.

Mel turned in her seat and waited. This wasn't a Lazenby pub so she assumed Suze was here for a reason.

Just then, by cruel quirk of timing, Mel's phone vibrated where she'd left it on the bar. The screen told her it was Jimmy, but she fought the urge to answer. She'd call back in a minute. He could stew for now.

But what if he had news? She fought down the impulse to grab the phone.

Turned, and Suze stood there, statuesque. "Hi," she said, with a little, uncertain, smile. "Do you have a moment?"

Mel nodded. She indicated a vacant bar stool, but the dancer remained standing.

"Mr Lazenby sent me," said Suze. "He's been talking to people. He's made some progress."

Mel felt her heart leap, her throat tighten. Immediately she felt bad for judging Glenn harshly earlier, for feeling so selfishly bad about how he'd abandoned her at Thom Sullivan's do so he could schmooze the room.

"What?" she said. "What progress?"

"Glenn really is a decent guy, you know? A decent guy in a tough world. He really cares. He's been busting a gut for you. You should know that."

"I do." Although she hadn't known that, not really believed it. Not until now. "What is it? Tell me."

She felt sick. Was it bad news? Was that why suddenly Suze was hesitating, stumbling over the words?

Then: "He's found something out," she said. "He knows where your friend is. She's okay. He thinks he can pull strings."

Such a dizzying rush of emotions! Relief, above all. The need to know more, to know everything. Euphoria and excitement. Utter, utter release, of all that had been bottled up.

She clung to the bar, as if she might fall. Felt Suze's hands on her, holding her arm, helping her to stand, to move.

"You have to come," said Suze. "I have a car outside. I can take you there right now."

13. JIMMY

He drove back for the funeral after talking to Penny Rayner, and arrived just in time to take the one remaining space in the crematorium's parking lot.

He sat in the car for a time after cutting the engine, hands tight on the wheel. He was tempted to restart the engine and drive away again. He didn't owe these people anything, and probably none of them wanted him here, or would even notice his absence.

As he sat there, he saw cars pulling up in the long lane leading into the crematorium, parking half on the roadway and partly on the grass, despite the NO PARKING signs. As Glenn had said, there was going to be a good turnout today.

Outside, people milled about, waiting for the signal to go in. He saw familiar faces, family members he vaguely recognized, acquaintances of his father. Also, there were a lot of people Jimmy didn't know. So much time had passed since he'd regularly mixed with the people who formed the backdrop to Trevor Lazenby's life. So much must have changed.

He hated that it got to him like this. That he had even the slightest fragment of interest in what he might have missed in the last ten years.

He should have said no to Doug Conner, that day when he'd led him out of the Section's London offices so they could walk by the river and talk in confidence. The death of his father hadn't so much been the perfect 'in' they'd joked about, but the perfect trap.

He'd been drawn, though, as Conner had known he would be. How could he stay away?

He stepped out of the car, and was instantly aware of eyes on him, conversations stalled, muttered comments.

He was the black sheep of the family, the one who'd turned away, the one who'd disappointed them all by going straight. Sometimes it really sucked to be the good guy.

He saw Uncle Frank standing by the main entrance to the chapel of rest, a cigarette cupped in one hand down by his side, looking uncomfortable in his suit. He stood with a couple of twenty-something guys Jimmy didn't know, and a woman with metal-gray hair who clung to his arm who he didn't know either. Had Frank remarried? It wasn't in the file.

Frank himself looked much older than the sixty or so years he must now be. His face was pitted and gray, his thin silver hair shaved close to the scalp so it was little more than a fuzz. He was still a big man, but he looked smaller than Jimmy recalled. Shrunken.

He nodded toward his uncle and, after a very deliberate pause, Frank gave a brief dip of the head in return.

Jimmy and Frank had been close. The two of them and Glenn. In some ways Frank had been more a father to the boys than Trevor had been.

But now? Frank had turned away already, muttering something into the woman's ear so that immediately her look flitted toward Jimmy before jumping away again.

Jimmy remained standing apart, waiting. Willing the day away.

He should be working the crowd, he knew. He still didn't know how the evidence stacked against his brother in the current investigation. Yes, he'd picked Harriet up and her phone had immediately gone offline, and yes, he'd been evasive about that, but they still didn't really know whether Harriet's disappearance was in any way sinister or simply a well-executed abscondence.

The one way to pin that down was to keep digging, and his father's funeral had brought together pretty much all the people who might, inadvertently, expose any wrongdoing Glenn had been up to, if you knew which buttons to press.

But for some reason Jimmy's mind had frozen.

It felt as if ten years of training and hard-won experience had all been wiped away. He felt like a kid again, not wanting to put a foot wrong. Cowed by the likes of Uncle Frank and Ronnie Bosvelt over there, by Rich Coombes and Emre Denis – more faces he recognized from the files. Ronnie Bosvelt was a Dutch importer/exporter with all kinds of dubious connections; he was talking to David Viera, a Spanish connection, which of course meant drugs; Rich Coombes and Emre Denis, studiously avoiding each other, were here to represent two of the long-standing London outfits.

It was a real Who's Who of the European underworld.

All these people – names attached in the mind-map in his head to terms like extortion, prostitution, trafficking, narcotics.

He felt like a fraud. Not part of this crowd, but equally not worthy of the real reason he was here.

A complete fraud.

§

A low black limo with tinted windows swung into the turning area before the chapel of rest, and stopped so its passengers could alight.

Glenn stepped out first, looking easy in his suit, sunglasses pushed back onto the crown of his head. Clean-shaven today. He stretched, straightened his jacket, looked around. Gave a slight nod to himself, as if approving of the turn-out.

He turned and reached a steadying hand out to the elbow of another man as he climbed out of the car. Tall and slim, with a flop of sandy hair he swept back with one hand. Another name from the files: Thom Sullivan, the software magnate it was alleged Ronnie Bosvelt and Glenn were involved with. The money-man behind various enterprises that hovered over the wavy line between legal and not.

Events like this always highlighted the hierarchies and connections. It was interesting to see who was close, and who hung back on the fringes.

Jimmy caught Glenn's eye then, got a nod, a wry pursing of lips. He tried not to resent the surge of – what? connection? bonding? – he felt at that gesture. An unspoken communication that they shared this, a thing they had to get through; that perhaps there were layers of emotion and history and baggage that only the two Lazenby brothers could fully understand.

Trevor Lazenby may have been a heartless, cruel bastard, but he had still been their father. That should probably count for something, even if Jimmy didn't yet know what that something might be.

Then out of the front passenger seat of the limo another figure emerged. So tall and bulky it was a delicate operation to extract himself, almost an uncoiling of that imposing form as he straightened, turned, met Jimmy's challenging look.

The man was tall, easily six-six, and he carried plenty of excess weight on a body that was powerfully built. He had a silver ring through his nose, a bar through one eyebrow, a thick, dark beard and a shaved head. He wore a black suit that looked about two sizes too small, to the extent that if he squared his shoulders or folded his arms it must surely burst at the seams.

Jimmy took one big stride forward. Another. Buried his fists in the front of Glenn's shirt and drove him back against the limo's closed door.

He'd known. That big bastard sent to scare the shit out of Mel, to damage her so badly she wouldn't dare ask questions about Glenn again… Of course he had been one of Glenn's henchmen.

Jimmy understood that, and Glenn knew he did.

But up to now they'd managed to skirt around it, avoid fully acknowledging it.

So to have his man here, now…

At Trevor Lazenby's damned funeral!

Glenn was rubbing his brother's nose in it. Making sure he knew where he must fit into all this. Making sure he knew Glenn was The Man.

For a moment, Glenn's mask slipped. A grimace of pain as his back impacted on the car, a moment of panicked looking around for options as Jimmy practically lifted him off his feet, forcing him up against hard metal.

Then that sense of arrogant control descended again and his eyes met Jimmy's, his eyebrows arched upwards in a *So what now, bro'?* expression.

The moment briefly froze, the tableau of the two of them up against the car.

Jimmy felt his heart hammering, his breath rasping. Felt the strain of Glenn's weight bearing down on his arms.

He didn't do this. He didn't lose control. He didn't ever do this.

The bastard. Glenn had got under his skin, quite deliberately.

And all around, a sea of faces gathered. A sudden silence.

Then the moment unfroze.

Strong hands closed on Jimmy's arms, another hooked into the neck of his shirt and jacket at the back. A hefty blow landed in his back – to one side just below the shoulder blades, a professional blow landing in just the right place to force his diaphragm to spasm, driving the air from his lungs.

Winded, he sagged, unable to resist the hands dragging him back, throwing him to the ground.

He landed on his back, his skull smashing dizzyingly against hard ground so that blackness briefly swept across his vision.

Even as he gasped for breath, he instinctively drew his arms in to shield his body, his knees up, either to add further protection or so he could flip back up to his feet the moment his empty lungs allowed.

At any moment he expected more blows, boots to the body, the head.

Instead, he saw Glenn looking down at him, shaking his head.

"Not now, bro'," he said in that soft voice of his.

Then Glenn stooped, reached out a hand, and waited for Jimmy to take it and allow himself to be hauled to his feet.

Jimmy stood at the back. That old thing that was so ingrained it was like breathing to him: cover your back, have a clear view, always know the way out. It wasn't as if he expected anything to kick off, it's just how it was. How *he* was.

The place was packed, which at least made it natural to stand at the rear with the others who'd filed in too late to secure seating.

As he stood waiting, he continued his analysis of the mourners. Identifying family members and, by association, the people with them, who must either be partners or family members added to the fold at some point in the ten years since Jimmy had left. Faces he knew from old, business partners and rivals – categories that were always shifting. Yet more he knew from the files.

Among the mourners, he knew there would almost certainly be undercover operatives – from the UK police at least, if not also the security services and Interpol. A gathering like this, drawing known villains and their associates, was too good an opportunity to miss, even if there were not any on-going cases against those attending.

Drone footage of his scuffle with Glenn was almost certainly being analyzed right now in an office deep in the bowels of New Scotland Yard, faces being matched, conclusions being reached: the return of the younger Lazenby, and what that might mean.

The mourners fell falteringly silent as music started up, Louis Armstrong reminding them what a wonderful world it was. Jimmy didn't know who'd selected the music, but back in the day it had been a regular on the playlist at the Flag and Flowers. He suspected his father would have wanted a say in things, when he knew the end was near, but couldn't help being suspicious about the irony of the choice of such a celebratory song.

Movement in the doorway, then the coffin entered, carried on the shoulders of Glenn, Uncle Frank, Thom Sullivan, and three men Jimmy didn't recognize.

He didn't know what he should feel, or what he actually *did* feel.

He knew there should probably be some kind of perceived slight at not even being invited to be one of the pall-bearers, but he felt nothing. It made sense; after all, until a couple of days ago nobody had even known he would be here.

There were tears already at the front, from the woman who'd been standing with Frank outside. Maybe he'd got that wrong: rather than being with Frank, had she been connected to the old man? A lover? There was nothing on the file to say he'd remarried, or was in any kind of relationship.

He didn't know. All these people, apparently so close to his father and yet strangers to Jimmy.

He didn't feel the kind of emotion that woman had on display. Tears, or anything close.

There was an emptiness, though. A space.

It was something, at least. More than he would have anticipated.

He still didn't understand how his father's death had affected him, messing with his thought processes and judgment. This was unfamiliar territory.

They reached the front, and eased the wooden casket onto a bier, then moved to seats saved for them at the front.

Just as he stooped to sit, Glenn paused, suddenly searching the crowd. When his eyes came to rest on Jimmy he arched his eyebrows again in that *So what now, bro'?* expression.

He nodded at the seats, at a space that had either been saved or created as people shuffled along.

Jimmy shook his head, but Glenn just repeated the expression, an impasse.

Everyone was looking now, and so Jimmy relented, threading his way across to the central aisle and down to the front.

He sat with his brother, felt a hand briefly squeezing his shoulder. Very publicly welcomed back into the fold for a time, at least.

The ceremony was brief, at least. A few words of introduction from the non-denominational celebrant, who seemed cowed by the reputations of those in attendance. There was a tribute from Uncle Frank, which was brief and to the point. Not much more than, "Trev, my brother. Meanest bastard you could ever know. And the meanest thing he ever did was go out the way he did, you know what I mean? He hated it. Almost as much as we hated seeing it."

He told a couple of stories of how Trevor had been as a young man, full of life, always one for the ladies, how he was a proper gent in a world where that was rarer and rarer. He finished with, "I tell you, I don't know where he is now, but there's one thing I know for sure: the bastard'll be shaking it up, good and proper."

The crying woman – introduced as Auntie Cyn, so presumably she was with Frank after all – read a rambling poem. Finally Glenn stood up and read something from the Bible, the only religious touch – a hedging of his bets from a man without a religious bone in his body, assuming Jimmy's father had helped plan this.

A short time later, they filed out into bright sunshine, and stood together, the four of them forming a family line: Glenn, Jimmy, Frank and the newly discovered Auntie Cyn.

Platitudes and condolences, smiles fake and genuine, suspicious looks at Jimmy as hands were shaken, cheeks kissed. Glenn was good with those platitudes, at thanking people for their kind wishes, at looking almost like he meant it, easy in this company, this patriarchal role.

"Come on," he muttered to Jimmy at one point, "at least look as if you give a shit, would you?"

He did, though. That was the thing.

He could easily have missed the funeral altogether, and never known what it would stir. That would have been so much easier.

Because now he did know, and it unsettled him more than anything he could recall.

Afterward, as the last few cars pulled away from the cemetery, Glenn turned to face Jimmy. "Come back to the Flag and Flowers, Jimbo. Last respects and all that."

Jimmy shook his head. He had things to do, and his father's wake wasn't one of them. He'd let things slip too far already.

And he couldn't allow himself to be drawn any farther back into this world.

"That thing the other night," he said, "sending your boy after Mel. That was out of order."

And bringing your boy here to make sure Jimmy knew had been, too, but he didn't say that. They both knew that point had been made.

Glenn spread his hands. "In this world you have to deal with the shit," he said. "You have to stake out the territory and see off anyone who threatens it. Whoever they are. You should know that, Jimbo, whichever side of the fence you convince yourself you're on these days."

And the thing was, Jimmy got that, entirely. He'd grown up in this world, understood how it worked. Understood that when you're the king of your domain you have to keep stamping down anything that might threaten that, and if he'd learned one thing today it was that Glenn had very much stepped into their father's shoes.

So yes, he understood. He'd known exactly why Glenn had sent his boy after Mel that night. Hell, ten years ago, Jimmy himself might have been the boy sent on a job like that.

And he hated it.

"Come back, bro'."

He squinted at his brother, tried to read his expression. Tried to convince himself this was just another wind-up.

"You've had your little walkabout. It's time to come home."

"Ten years."

Glenn laughed. "Okay. You've had your *big* walkabout. Whatever. It's not too late, is what I'm saying."

Just then, Jimmy had a flash of insight. He'd been so thrown by his own reactions to their father's death, he hadn't given a thought to what Glenn must be going through. His older brother had been here, dealing with it all every day. The illness, the decline. The old man had been difficult at the best of times; Jimmy could only imagine how he'd got as illness took hold and he'd become ever less capable of being the ruthless old bastard they all knew him to be. As he'd come to rely more and more on others.

And now…

Glenn had taken it all on. He had Uncle Frank, but… well… "Lonely at the top?" Jimmy asked now.

"Fuck off." Said with a smile, followed by a short laugh.

They still stood facing each other, as if this exchange was a fight, or at least a stand-off. Now, Glenn turned, put a hand on Jimmy's shoulder, took a step, and they were walking side by side toward the remaining cars, Glenn's hand still on his brother's shoulder.

"I could use someone like you," said Glenn. Again, by implication, he was telling Jimmy he knew who he was, what he was capable of, even though they'd rarely ever come close to saying such things out loud. Then, more explicit, he said, "Someone with your experience, your inside knowledge. It's always handy to have someone working the other side, if you know what I mean?"

Not coming back into the fold, then, but an inside source in the security service, protection. He should have known: the family dabbled in all kinds of things, but it always came back to protection. And this time, what Glenn wanted was someone in law enforcement to feed his organization inside information, offer that protection.

Jimmy shook his head. Was pleased he hadn't even hesitated before doing so.

"I'm not like that," he said. "I've made my choices."

They'd stopped by the limo. "Really?" Glenn said. "I thought you understood how the world worked."

Glenn had mastered the same air of disappointment in Jimmy their father had. He did it well.

"I'm not like that. I can't work like that." And why was he even trying to justify his choices to Glenn? That strange family thing that had crept up on him this week, the need to be seen by people he'd rejected so long ago.

Glenn still had that easy smile on his face, that tilt of the head, but a hardness had crept in.

"Everyone's like that," he said. "You just haven't realized yet. You should look take a look around yourself."

This was it. Glenn always had a sucker punch. He'd wind you up, wind you in, and then deliver. Ever since they were kids.

"What?" said Jimmy.

He waited.

Slowly, Glenn straightened, looked away, looked back, smiled a little wider.

"All I'm saying is look at those around you," he said. "Those closest to you. Everyone has their price."

There *was* no-one close to him. He'd made sure of that. He never let anyone in. Never let anyone close. That had been one of his earliest lessons. One he'd learned from...

Glenn nodded, must have seen it in his eyes, the slow processing, the plodding journey to that conclusion.

"The guy's close to retirement. He has a career's worth of vulnerabilities, no matter how hard he's tried not to. Everyone plays both sides at one time or another, don't they, bro'?"

He couldn't believe it, even as his brain raced to do so.

Doug Conner.

The straightest of the straight. A Section Eight man, through and through.

Jimmy had always done as Conner had asked. Followed orders without question. That was how they worked. But how much did he really know about his controller? What if things were not as black and white as he had always believed?

He saw the look on Glenn's face. The smile.

Shook his head, turned away, all he could do not to lay into him again.

His brother was winding him up. Toying with him. Sowing those seeds of doubt to undermine him, just as he'd done before.

And he must know that no matter how clearly Jimmy understood this, no matter how much he would choose Conner's word over Glenn's every single time… those seeds had been sown. The doubt planted.

What if Conner had sent him in, kept this whole thing as an off-the-books case, because he couldn't have an official investigation digging around any connections he might have with the Lazenby family's activities? What if he'd found himself stuck between trying to find his daughter's best friend and covering his own back?

Jimmy turned, went back to his car, knowing that for the entire journey back into London his mind would be leaping from possibility to possibility, doubt to doubt.

And Glenn had known he'd be doing exactly that.

More than anyone, Glenn Lazenby knew how to play his kid brother.

The bastard.

14. JIMMY

Sure enough, as he drove back into London Jimmy's mind raced, leaping from thought to thought, speculation to suspicion. He tried to slow himself down, concentrating on what he knew.

He knew Glenn was both a liar and a wind-up merchant, always trying to unsettle those around him.

He knew that his brother liked to dodge around the truth, dressing it up and distorting it, and that perhaps this was why his dig at Doug Conner had rung true, tapping into doubts already there – particularly the unease Jimmy felt about this whole off-the-books investigation into the disappearance of Harriet Rayner.

No. *No.* He didn't know anything. Doubts weren't *knowing*. He was allowing his mind to race again. Hunches weren't to be trusted, particularly when they'd been planted in your head by an arch manipulator.

Conner had recruited Jimmy. He'd hand-picked him ten years ago, and mentored him before becoming his controller when he started to go out into the field.

He still remembered that first conversation, the one that had changed everything. Until then, Conner had been a blank canvas – and only later did Jimmy realize how carefully cultivated that image was: a man who left little impression, made few waves. It was a skill, and one Jimmy had subsequently worked hard to acquire for himself.

Until then, Conner had simply been the cold, distant father of the woman Jimmy loved. Slightly menacing for that aloofness, but Jimmy had put that down to simple disapproval. Jimmy was a Lazenby, after all: he was familiar with that reaction from people. The difference with Conner was that the disapproval wasn't cut through with fear.

"So what now?" Conner had said to him, in a pub in north London where he'd tracked him down, a couple of weeks after things with Mel had imploded.

Jimmy didn't understand. He'd been minding his own business when Conner appeared, and now was starting to see that maybe the man's aloofness hid a core of steel, something to be wary of. Had he come after him on Mel's behalf? Finally free to tell Jimmy what he thought of him, and make sure he never went near his daughter again?

"May I?" Conner had indicated a vacant stool next to Jimmy, and sat. Then: "You've got something," he said. "I saw it straight away. You could have been something so much worse than your old man if you'd wanted to."

What a strange thing to say...

He didn't want this. Didn't want to be talking about his family with the father of the girl he'd lost. But something about the look in Doug Conner's eye had held him.

"Mel tells me you want to be one of the good guys."

"That what she says?" Yes, he'd said that to her, on more than one occasion. Said he didn't have to be like the rest of his family. Trying to impress her. Trying to convince himself. Right now, he didn't know what he wanted any more, only what he'd rejected, and what he'd lost.

"I can help you do that," said Conner.

"How? What do you mean?"

"I can help you, because I'm one of the good guys, too."

He'd believed him, back then. Something in the way he said it, the unlikeliness of the man's choice of phrase.

He still did.

Because if you don't believe you're one of the good guys, then what's the point?

He slapped a hand on the steering wheel in frustration, swerving partway into the next lane to a blaring of horns. Drifting back into his own lane again, he ignored another driver who pulled up level, gesturing. If only that guy knew who he was pointing his finger at.

He breathed deep.

He was one of the good guys, even if he had to remind himself every so often.

He pressed the hand-free button on the steering wheel, told the car to make a call to Patil.

"Hey, Mamta," he said. "Harriet Rayner. Any developments?"

A tap of keys, then: "Not much since we last spoke, sir. No phone activity. Nothing from her on social media, just posts from friends asking where she is. Police investigation is still almost non-existent, although it's flagged for review this afternoon."

That seemed pretty standard. Covering themselves in case a disappearance initially treated as non-suspicious needed to be escalated for any reason.

"Anything on Glenn Lazenby or anyone from the funeral?"

A pause, a reminder that this was family. He knew they'd have a roster of anyone interesting who'd shown up at the crematorium.

"Nothing out of the ordinary," said Patil. "Reports of a fight outside the chapel of rest, but then you'd know about that."

It hadn't been a fight. If it had been a fight, Glenn would have known about it.

"No other leads?"

"Nothing I can see, sir. The police have drawn a blank. The mother's been making a nuisance of herself, which probably hasn't helped change their minds any."

The girl had simply vanished.

Even now, though, he reminded himself that one very valid line of investigation was the possibility this had all been blown out of proportion. Mel getting alarmed, pressing her father into over-reacting, Jimmy wading in and stirring things up with the family; each step an escalation when it was still entirely possible Harriet was just sulking at a friend's place, sleeping off a binge, or simply avoiding an overbearing mother.

He reminded himself again: he should concentrate on knowns, not let his mind race with speculations.

And what he knew was a seventeen-year-old girl had been missing for almost a week and very few people – at least those who could make a difference – appeared to give a shit about it.

Apart from Mel. She cared. She and Penny Rayner were perhaps the only ones who really did.

He told the car to call Mel. Listened to it ring once, twice, four times and then cut to voicemail.

She was blanking him, he knew. He still couldn't work out whether she was pissed with him for pushing her back onto the sidelines, for sleeping with her, or for the barriers he always put up around himself.

Probably all of that, and more.

What might be in Mel Conner's head was the kind of puzzle he had long since given up on.

"Hey," he said. "Just checking in. No news, I'm afraid. We're still digging. Call me if you hear anything."

He ended the call, cursing himself. Not 'if you hear anything', just call me, was what he'd meant, what he should have said.

He wanted to hear her voice – more than just a recording at the other end of a line.

He shook his head, must look like a madman driving along like that.

How had she done it?

How had she made him feel this way? How had she made him fall in love with her all over again?

He recalled what he'd told her, the words that had just popped into his head. *Fall? I have nowhere left to fall. I fell ten years ago and I never climbed out.*

Where had that come from?

Fall… falling.

Whatever.

It made no difference.

All he knew was he felt like this right now, and it was messing with his head. Affecting his judgment.

He needed to stop.

Stop falling. Stop having fallen. Whatever it was.

For now, at least.

Doug Conner hadn't expected to see him.

Jimmy could tell by the momentary look of surprise that flashed across his features before the blank mask descended again.

He'd tracked his controller down to a gentlemen's club in Westminster, across the river from the anonymous buildings where Section Eight had offices, and a short walk from the Houses of Parliament, and Whitehall. A place where senior civil servants, politicians, and other high-ranking officials could take a break from the public eye. A place where connections were made, deals struck, impasses bypassed. A place where ridiculously expensive single malts and clarets oiled the wheels of government.

It was, quite literally, an old boys' club, where the ruling elite could ensure democracy did whatever they wanted.

Jimmy stood in the doorway of one of the private lounges, casually waiting to catch Conner's eye. His controller was seated in a small circle of high-backed armchairs, deep in conversation with men Jimmy recognized as a high-profile banker, a government minister and someone so anonymous he could only be a member of the security services. The walls were lined all the way up to the high ceilings with books, and the place smelled of leather, cigar smoke and something just a little musty.

Conner saw him, and his eyes briefly widened, his jaw twitched. He turned back to his companions, said something, and stood, smoothing down his jacket before walking slowly across to join Jimmy.

"How did you get in?" he asked.

"You should know, you trained me." Jimmy could talk his way into just about anything or anywhere, and out of most things too.

For a moment Conner was going to press, then he gave a slight shake of the head, put a hand to Jimmy's arm to steer him back out of the room, and said, "I assume it's important."

"I don't like working in the dark," said Jimmy. "I don't like surprises. Like going on a job and finding your daughter in the thick of it. I don't like being forced to mix family and business. This job… it doesn't add up. There are too many blanks."

They came to a doorway that opened onto a mezzanine area that looked out over the main entrance lobby.

"That's how we work, Jimmy," said Conner, indicating a pair of chairs by the balustrade, a low table between them. "Blanks all around us. We know what we need to know, and all that."

As usual, Conner was deflecting, repeating what Jimmy had already told him in a way that implied he was actually adding something new to the exchange.

"I need to know," said Jimmy simply. "And all that."

Conner nodded. "What do you need to know?"

"Why is this case off the books? Why are we investigating at all? It's hardly our normal territory."

"That's why it's off the books," said Conner. "It's personal. For both of us."

Personal and messy. Two things Jimmy had successfully avoided for the last ten years.

"How personal?"

Conner paused. He must already have known something was up for Jimmy to track him down here, but now he seemed to sense there was more going on.

"A family friend. Melissa throwing herself into the thick of it. The Lazenby family connection. What more do you want?"

The Lazenby family connection. That's what had brought Jimmy here.

Look at those around you. Those closest to you. Everyone has their price.

That's what Glenn had said.

"Glenn thinks he has influence," he said carefully. "Over you."

Conner didn't falter. He gave that familiar little nod again, and said, simply, "Good."

Jimmy stared. Again, he felt as if he were several steps behind, things slowly slotting into place. Things he should have seen before now.

"Glenn's one of ours," said Conner. "Only he doesn't know it. And if possible, I hope we can keep it that way."

"Tell me," said Jimmy. "Now's one of those times when I need to know."

Conner sat back in his chair, studying Jimmy carefully over steepled fingers.

Finally, he nodded again, and said, "You were right when you said the Harriet Rayner case isn't normally the kind of thing that falls into our remit. But Glenn Lazenby is. Or rather, the people he does business with. Arms dealers. International syndicates. Other malicious influences. I've been cultivating your brother for some time now. He was useful when he was your father's righthand man, and promises to be even more useful now he's taken over. He thinks I give him protection, and he's right. Where he's mistaken is that he thinks that protection is bought by regular payments into my retirement fund and not that he has protection simply because he provides access to far bigger fish."

Jimmy held his controller's look. Conner's story was smooth. So smooth it could be well-rehearsed bullshit prepared by a man who'd been in the family's pocket for years. Or it could be smooth because it was true.

But even if it was true, Jimmy understood that it would only be a skimming of the surface – enough truth to satisfy him. There was always far more going on, and Conner's reference to the people Glenn worked for and with made it clear the Lazenby empire was only a tiny part of something far bigger.

As if to confirm this, Conner continued: "You're right not to trust me. I wouldn't. As you say, I trained you, and I trained you to be smart. What I can tell you is that I'm in a very precarious position. I'm part of the Establishment."

He paused to wave a hand, indicating the grandeur of the building that housed this exclusive gentlemen's club.

"Government is corrupt. Business is corrupt. My beloved Establishment is corrupt. But it works, mostly. Money buys influence, buys power. People like you and me just make the best of it. We work on the fringes, in the interstices. We challenge power, where we have to, but the people your brother is involved with are part of those power structures, too – they make sure of that. They have that kind of control. It's how the world works.

"This is why we have units like Section Eight. We exist outside the normal structures. Our role is to smooth things over, minimize the damage. That sounds abstract, but you know what we do. We stop things before they happen. We intervene where other agencies are held back."

Jimmy knew. He'd lost count of the number of terror attacks they'd prevented, the number of major crime networks they'd disrupted and turned against each other.

"We save lives, Jimmy. That's got to be worth it, however we do it."

Jimmy didn't like to think how many compromises Conner must have made over the years, how many times he'd turned a blind eye for the greater good, how many painful deals had been struck. How many Glenn's he'd sucked up to and let loose, as he pursued the bigger picture.

All to save lives.

It was messy, and Jimmy struggled to get his head around the implications of what Conner had told him, but it came down to the same judgment call Jimmy had made for himself: they saved lives. That was what mattered. They had to do some seriously bad things to achieve that sometimes, but the goal, at least, was worthy of something, surely?

"So what's with Glenn?" Jimmy said now. "He thinks he owns you, which is fine – you say you're aware of that, and encourage it. But… he seems to have a thing about you."

"What kind of thing?"

"Twice now, he's tried to turn me against you," said Jimmy. "He tried to convince me you'd sent that heavy after Mel to scare her away. I didn't believe him, of course, but–"

"Seeds of doubt."

"Seeds of doubt. And then today he tells me he's got you in his pocket. Which, of course, he thinks he has."

"He hasn't."

"I know." He didn't, but Conner's version of things was far more credible than Glenn's sly little digs and suggestions. The odds, at least, suggested to Jimmy that Conner was telling more of the truth than Glenn.

"Well," Jimmy went on. "Maybe we can use that. You seem to matter to him. Maybe you're his vulnerability, in some way?" He didn't know quite what he was getting at, but whatever Glenn was up to, he suspected Conner might be a route in.

Then he stopped, saw the smile on Conner's face, a slight shake of the head. Felt several steps behind yet again.

"Oh no," Conner said. "No. That's not it at all. Don't you see? It's you, Jimmy. You're Glenn's vulnerability. You always have been."

He stared, tried to work out where Conner was heading, what he had missed. He didn't swallow it. He wasn't Glenn's weak spot – his older brother had his measure. He always had. If Jimmy was being honest with himself, that's one reason why he would never have been able to stay: Glenn was the one person who could get under his skin.

Until Mel had come along, of course, and she'd got under his skin in a very different way.

"You're the kid brother," said Conner. "The golden boy. In your father's eyes, Glenn was the one who set the benchmarks but you were the one who surpassed them. Classic sibling rivalry. Youngest child is forgiven everything, and acknowledged for all the triumphs, while the oldest child just soldiers on. And yes, I'm an older child."

Jimmy was surprised at the slight chink in Conner's armor, a glimpse of something personal.

Conner went on: "Glenn's always been in your shadow, and all he's wanted is your respect, your acknowledgment."

"Is that how you were?" asked Jimmy. He was trying to deflect, he knew. Not wanting to acknowledge there may be some truth in the profile Conner was giving.

"And then there was Melissa."

He didn't want to go here. Not with Conner. Not with all the shit that had been stirred in his head regarding Melissa Conner. Not now, not ever.

"There was rivalry, wasn't there? You and Glenn."

Over Mel, yes. Rivalry that had slipped into jokey, heavy-handed flirting and innuendo on Glenn's part when he knew he'd lost that one. A teasing that Mel played along with, without ever understanding the bitter undertow of Glenn's jibes.

Even now, Glenn did it. That proprietorial arm trailed along the back of the seats in Ryders, almost, but not quite, draped across her shoulders, and making damned sure Jimmy could see. The looks that said *She's come to me, bro'.*

"He lost that one, didn't he?" said Conner. "Lost it to you." Almost as if he was talking about anything but his own daughter.

"Not only that, though," Conner continued. "He didn't just lose the girl to you, he lost *you* to her, didn't he? She drew you away, from him, from the family. She made you see alternatives."

She had. She still did. If Glenn had been the first person who could really get under Jimmy's skin, Mel had been the last, would always be the last.

Sure, Glenn had lost the girl. Maybe lost the attention of the kid brother. But then that kid brother had blown it, hadn't he?

"It didn't exactly last, did it?" said Jimmy. "He didn't have to nurse his wounds for long before I fucked it all up."

Conner was shaking his head, making it clear that Jimmy still didn't get it. "Oh, but he did," he said. "Of course he did. Once he'd lost you, he never got you back, did he? After he lost you to Melissa, he lost you to me. I recruited you. I offered you an alternative path. I took you in. He hates us. The Conners. Think of it as a good old-fashioned family feud. First Melissa, then me. We're the ones who tore his family apart. And right now, he's lost his father, too."

Jimmy recalled the look on Glenn's face at the crematorium this morning. The gesture at the empty space at the front. The impasse, until Jimmy had inwardly shrugged and moved forward to take up his slot on the family pew.

Come back, bro'.

"So what is this?" asked Jimmy. "You think he's going to go after you somehow? Now my father's gone, you think he's somehow going rogue? Were you just using this case to get me back in there, close to my brother?"

Was that what he'd been missing? That the investigation itself didn't matter, was simply a vehicle to maneuver Jimmy back into the thick of the family's activities?

"Glenn's flexing his muscles. Getting into new things. Getting carried away. He's becoming an unknown quantity."

Jimmy nodded. He understood how uncomfortable that would make Conner feel, someone he'd been able to control slipping out of his grasp…

"I'm in a difficult position," said Conner, with almost the air of confession. "I've been protecting Glenn, yes, because we had bigger fish to fry. But if he goes rogue now he's been liberated by the loss of his father, that could come back and bite me. Bite us, the Section. And my hands are tied: those shady influences in the corridors of power. Other on-going investigations with other agencies, other interests to protect. It's a messy, messy web of ties, which is why I've tried to keep things contained. But I had to do something…"

"There's more, though, isn't there?" Jimmy said.

Conner looked away, as if noticing their grand surroundings for the first time.

"Penny Rayner came to me," he said. "And then Melissa did, too, almost as if they'd coordinated it between them. I dug a little, didn't think anything of it. And then your brother's name came up. There had already been warning signs about Glenn getting reckless, dangerous, since taking control of the family's activities. Revenge. Old debts being repaid, if you know what I mean."

Jimmy could believe it. Glenn never forgot a thing.

"I reached out to him. Warned him the authorities were taking an interest. He took that as me giving him protection, looking out for him. He loved the idea he had me in his pocket. But then when Harriet went missing, her last trace being when she climbed into Glenn's car..."

A look away again. Jimmy had never seen his superior so visibly rattled.

"Glenn was making it personal. Getting to me through Harriet."

Jimmy started to see it. The relationship between Harriet and Mel – Mel had said the two of them were like sisters. Glenn would like that. Getting at both Doug Conner and Mel through someone close.

But... was Conner really saying Glenn had abducted the girl?

Jimmy still wasn't sure his brother would do anything like that.

"I tried to steer the police investigation," said Conner. "But like I say, Glenn and the people he's involved with have protection, either other investigations that don't want to be rocked, or good old-fashioned corruption in high places. The police only gave Harriet's disappearance lip service. And the Section doesn't take on this kind of thing..."

"But there's always a way."

Conner nodded. "It's personal."

Jimmy saw it, finally. "It's not just Mel he's getting at you through, is it?" he said.

Conner looked down. "My daughter," he said. "Harriet Rayner is my daughter."

The sibling thing. The older child who set the benchmarks, the youngest always surpassing them. The golden child.

"I always steered Melissa to look out for Harriet, you know? To help her. That's what you do, isn't it, if you're a decent human being? You steer others to help those you can't help yourself. I do. That's why I'm relying on you, Jimmy. Don't let me down."

§

He'd rarely been at such a loss on a case. A missing girl, but no trail after her phone went dead. Glenn's involvement, and Douglas Conner's conviction that Glenn was pursuing some kind of vendetta against him, and that he would do so through Harriet.

They had nothing.

He considered calling Mel, trying to pick her brains about her friend's character, see if that might suggest anything they'd missed. But he'd virtually ordered Mel to step away – because of the potential danger to her, and because Jimmy didn't like the idea of a clumsy amateur being involved.

If he asked her for help now, he'd be admitting defeat, admitting he'd been wrong…

He was honest enough with himself to recognize stubborn pride when he encountered it, but that didn't make him any less proudly stubborn.

Maybe if she ever answered his messages, he'd find a tangential way to raise the subject. Maybe they could meet for a drink, even though he'd vowed to step back until this mess was sorted out.

He'd parked in the street, and now he paused before the converted garage Penny Rayner called home.

He couldn't quite work Harriet's mother out. At least a part of it was something familiar from other times he'd had to deal with addicts, that easy facility they tended to have for concealment and deflection. A sharpness that underlay everything else. Penny Rayner came across as absent-minded, confused, and yet he knew she had always kept tabs on her daughter, always knew what Harriet was up to in her life.

Penny Rayner may have lost many of her faculties, but she was not stupid.

"Mrs Rayner."

She smiled, and he wasn't sure if she remembered who he was, then she focused, and said, "Mr Lazenby. You have news?"

He shook his head, and her entire frame visibly slumped.

"I'm sorry," he said. "I just called in case you'd heard anything?"

A slight shake of the head. "She never calls," she said.

He knew that, but he was sure Penny would know if her daughter had reappeared.

"I've been asking around," he said. "I spoke to Douglas Conner. He's very concerned for… your daughter."

Had that been why he'd come here? To dig? To test for reactions?

If so, then he should have known it would get him nowhere.

Now, Penny Rayner smiled fondly, and said, "Doug? Oh yes. Such a nice man. A good friend to Geoffrey, before…"

Either she was so accustomed to covering up her past relationship with Doug Conner that it had become automatic, or she didn't even remember the relationship at all. Now, Jimmy recalled something Mel had said about how Penny's memory was so ruined by her addictions she had almost no recollection of her past life.

Had he hoped she would slip? That she would inadvertently confirm Conner's account? He wasn't entirely sure what that would have achieved, other than to shore up his trust in the man who had steered his life for the past ten years.

It was stupid, though. Penny Rayner was no kind of witness to anything, even her own past.

But then she fixed Jimmy with a look again, and said, "His daughter is such a lovely thing, isn't she? Melissa. Do you know her?"

He turned away. He didn't know what the correct answer to that would be. Yes, he knew Mel, but what, exactly, was their relationship?

"She said she'd keep me informed, though," said Penny. "But… well, nothing. She doesn't answer my calls. So unlike her. I asked her to try to find where Harriet is, but maybe I shouldn't have done that. Do you think she's angry with me for being so presumptuous? I know I can be a nuisance, but she's always answered my calls before."

There's a thing that happens. A pivotal moment where things step up a gear. Until now, Jimmy might have felt as if he was treading water, but all of a sudden…

"When did you last speak to her?" He kept his voice calm, casual. Was careful not to let his body language shift. Careful not to step forward, grip the woman by the arms and shake an answer out of her.

He smiled, waited while Penny tipped her head to one side, thinking.

"I don't know," she said. "I'm sorry, I… You know how it can be."

"You called her yesterday," Jimmy said patiently. "In the morning. She asked how you were. You asked if she had any news. You apologized for calling her." He remembered it clearly. Breakfast in that greasy diner, the stilted conversation with Mel after they'd spent the night together. Mel's phone going, and then sitting there, listening to one end of a conversation.

Penny didn't ask how he knew, just smiled and said, "Yes, yes, I did, didn't I? She said it was fine for me to call. Which is why I worry so, now... now that she doesn't answer."

"Have you spoken to her since then?"

"No. As I say, she's not answering. I think I frustrate her, sometimes. Do you think that's likely?"

He started to back away. Turned, and strode up the driveway, calling back to Harriet's mother that everything was fine, he was just in a hurry. He didn't want to alarm her, but then if he did, she'd probably have forgotten it soon anyway.

Mel hadn't answered any of his messages. He'd put that down to frustration on her part, the voicemail equivalent of a frosty silence.

And that's exactly what Penny had thought, too: that Mel wasn't answering because Mel was pissed with *her*.

He climbed into his car and pulled away, told his hands-free phone to call Mel.

Voicemail.

"Call me, Mel," he said. "I need to know you're okay, so just… call me?"

He jumped a red light, to a blast of car horns. He didn't care. It was a Section car, and if any penalty notices came through they'd be canceled automatically. If the police stopped him for reckless driving, he had a number they would call and he'd be on his way again within minutes.

Then he forced himself to slow down, reassess.

This whole thing was off the books. Yes, Conner had assured him he had the usual protections, but was that really true? His controller was playing hard and fast with the rules.

He couldn't trust anything, and right now the last thing he wanted was to be caught up in the complications of trying to extract himself from the clutches of the traffic police.

He opened his mouth to put in a call to Mamta Patil, then stopped himself. The conversation with Conner had unsettled him. His controller's paranoia about the corruption of those around and above him.

Until now, Jimmy hadn't acknowledged quite how much he relied on the familiar infrastructure and back-up of the Section, but now… for now at least, he was on his own.

"Call Mel Conner." One ring, two, three… voicemail, again.

He hit the red button on his steering wheel column. End call.

Call me, Mel Conner. Just call me.

Early evening, and he was banging at the door of the house where Mel had been staying. An Airbnb thing, a room in a stranger's house. It was cheap and easy, he knew, but he could never do that. Jimmy needed anonymity, wherever he stayed.

He remembered the owner, Singh. The look on his face when he took in the blood on Jimmy's clothes that morning, when Jimmy had stripped down to the waist, laying his gun and shoulder holster on the kitchen table.

He still had the guy's t-shirt.

He didn't know what Singh did, whether he would even be in at this time.

The door opened, and the guy did a double take, clearly debating the merits of simply shutting the door again. Then he probably remembered the gun, and hesitated.

"Mr Singh," said Jimmy. "I'm sorry to disturb you. My friend's staying with you again, isn't she? I'm looking for her. I just wondered…"

He paused. Singh clearly wanted to say something, but was holding back.

"Please," said Jimmy. "What's happened?"

"Your friend has paid for two nights," said Singh. "So tell me, what do I do with her things if she doesn't come back then, too? I have other bookings."

"What do you mean, 'too'? When did you last see her?" It had only been a guess that Mel had come back and stayed here again, but it had been all he had. Singh's confirmation chilled him to the bone.

"I'm calling the police," said Singh, holding his hands up, and shaking his head. "I've had enough of all this."

"Please do," said Jimmy, keeping his voice calm and steady. "But tell me first. Everything."

He didn't need to threaten, didn't need to do anything to remind Singh about the holster under his jacket. Sometimes tone of voice is enough.

"Thursday," said the man. "She took the room for two nights. Went out that afternoon, came back and got all dressed up, and then went out once more. She didn't come back after that. I assumed she'd just returned late, after I'd gone to bed. Then this morning when there was no sign of her still, I just assumed… well, all dressed up like that."

"You assumed she got lucky?"

A brief nod, clearly wary of Jimmy's reaction.

"Do you have any idea where she was going?"

Singh shrugged. "A man, I assumed. She seemed... nervous. Taking a lot of trouble, you know?"

"Thank you," said Jimmy, backing away. "You've been very helpful."

"What about her things?"

"She'll be back," said Jimmy, wishing he believed his own words. "She'll take care of them."

Turning away, he started to walk fast.

The look in her eye when he'd told her to back off and leave all this to him. Frustration, he'd thought – at having to accept her own powerlessness.

He should have recognized it.

Not frustration, but determination.

She hadn't backed off at all.

She'd just waited until he'd gone and then carried on, regardless.

He should have known she would never back down.

She would never let go, or at least, not while she had a breath left in her body.

15. MEL

Mr Lazenby sent me. He's been talking to people. He's made some progress... He's found something out. He knows where your friend is. She's okay. He thinks he can pull strings.

That dizzying rush, like the bursting of a dam. Standing up from her bar stool, clutching at the bar for fear her legs would go from under her.

Suze... The tall, glamorous dancer grabbing at her arm to steady her. The look of compassion in her eyes. The understanding of what a huge moment this was.

You have to come. I have a car outside. I can take you there right now.

Walking unsteadily, her lope like that of a drunk, or of someone who had been at sea for weeks and hadn't yet learned how to walk on stable land again.

The sick lump in her throat, making it difficult to swallow, to breathe.

And all the time, Suze at her side, one hand holding her upper arm, the other looped around her waist. Steadying her with the contact as much as the physical support.

Outside, the evening sun was still harshly bright as her eyes slowly adjusted from the gloom of the King's Head's interior.

A dark car waited at the roadside, engine idling softly.

"Where?" asked Mel, finally finding her voice again. "Where is she?"

"A safe place. She's okay. Come on, we'll take you there."

Suze reached for the door, pulled it open, and gently guided Mel into the back seat.

Harriet. She was going to see Harriet.

Not just that, but Suze had said Harriet was okay. Those simple words both conjured up all the fears Mel had tried so hard to suppress over the past week and immediately dismissed them.

Fears for what her friend might have been enduring. For what she might find if she ever saw Harriet again.

She was okay.

The car rushed through the center of town, then cut down a suburban road Mel vaguely remembered. Across a narrow railway bridge. Past a school, an arcade of neighborhood shops, more anonymous housing.

She realized she was still clutching Suze's hand, and she smiled awkwardly, extricating her fingers.

"Thank you," said Mel.

Suze smiled, shrugged, said, "Just doin' my job, you know?"

She considered calling Jimmy, but held back. Better to wait until she was with Harriet, until she understood the situation.

Her mind rushed with possibilities. Had Glenn rescued Harriet from somewhere, or negotiated her release via one of his shady contacts? Had Thom Sullivan, perhaps, relented and made a reward available – but would that have worked so quickly, though? She'd only spoken to the man a couple of hours ago, at most. Perhaps, though: Sullivan was a man who made things happen, who got what he wanted, to use Glenn's preferred term of praise for those he admired.

Or perhaps it was more prosaic than that. Maybe simply putting word around had finally turned something up, found Harriet holed up in some dealer's house, or maybe even at a friend's place, and Glenn's or Sullivan's people had located her and brought her to some safe location to dry out.

Had Glenn known earlier? At the party? Had that smug smile been concealing the knowledge that Harriet was safe?

She wouldn't put it past him. He liked theater, and would love the idea that he might be the one to orchestrate the end of this drama, with his kid brother floundering some way behind.

If so, she would hate him forever for drawing out her pain, but still always be in his debt for this… which was just about how he would want it, she knew.

The car slowed, a couple of miles along a narrow lane, rolling green fields on one side and dense deciduous woodland on the other. The trees parted at a turning, a long wooden gate blocking the way.

They stopped and the driver got out to swing the gate open.

Mel hadn't seen much of the driver until now, just the back of his head. Now she saw he was a shortish Mediterranean-looking guy, dark hair, thickset features, latte skin tones. Was he one of Glenn's people, or part of some other group? Or just a driver, no connections…?

He climbed back in, drove a short distance, stopped, and climbed out to close the gate again.

"Nearly there," said Suze, with a flicker of a smile. She wasn't just doing her job, despite what she said. The look in her eye told Mel she got it, the significance of this.

They pulled up a short time later in front of an upright redbrick building with white marble columns either side of a double front door. It looked like a rather grand farmhouse that was trying to look more like a modest country manor house. The gardens surrounding the graveled stopping area at the front had seen better days, kept roughly in order now but not actively gardened. Outhouses lay to the side and rear, barns and a low-roofed building that might have been a stable.

The driver opened Mel's door and stepped back. When she caught his eye he gave a little sympathetic smile, too. He was part of this; he knew they were doing something good.

"Come on," said Suze, pausing on the first of two wide steps that led up to the entrance. "It's okay." There was something bizarre about seeing Suze in her short skirt and bustier top standing on the steps of a country house, like a glamour shoot for a men's magazine. Her words and smile were reassuring, though.

Mel swallowed, tried to calm her thumping heart, and followed the dancer into the building.

§

"Not long now, I promise." Suze smiled around the half-open door, then stepped back, out of the room, and let the door swing softly shut under its own weight.

Mel was in a bright, airy room, mostly shades of cream and white with a couple of darker pieces of furniture. Again, it reminded her of a photo-shoot, and she wondered what kind of property this was, the shabby chicness of it seeming more carefully cultivated the more she saw of the place.

She went to the window just as their car pulled away. Leaving? Or simply moving to park in the yard at the side of the building, where she'd seen a couple of other cars?

She wanted this over. Wanted to see the look in Harriet's eyes, to get reassurance in that look. Wanted her friend in her arms, so she might never let her go again.

She remembered Jimmy's call from earlier, when she'd been in the King's Head and Suze had shown up.

Did he know something too? Were he and his people, as he'd called them, converging on this place at this moment?

She reached into her purse, rummaged among make-up, tissues, keys, pen, money. In a moment of panic, she remembered glancing at her phone as it lay on the bar, buzzing with Jimmy's call.

Had she picked it up from there? She'd been distracted, first wondering what Suze was doing there and then by the dancer's words, by the promise that Harriet was safe.

Surely she hadn't left her phone.

She tried hard to remember.

Had there been a moment when she'd reached for the phone as she stood to leave? When she'd realized the phone was no longer there and she assumed she must already have tucked it into her bag? Or was she just imagining that, her memory filling in blanks, trying to construct a plausible narrative?

She must have left it on the bar. She'd probably never see it again – despite its refits, the King's Head was not the most salubrious of establishments.

She cursed her stupidity. Folded her arms across her chest and hugged herself, telling herself the simple loss of a phone shouldn't suddenly make her feel so exposed.

Where was she?

What were they doing?

Why the delay, when Suze had told her she was taking her to Harriet?

She moved across to the heavy wooden door, took the handle and paused, telling herself she really was being paranoid now.

Twisted the knob and pulled.

The door wouldn't budge.

She was locked in.

He made her wait.

Glenn.

Of course it was Glenn.

She watched the shadows grow long outside, the sky take on shades of gold and bronze, and then steadily darken.

She didn't switch on the room's light, instead leaving her eyes to adjust to the fading light. It was the one element of control she had left.

She'd been so stupid.

How had she walked into this?

She knew Glenn had been just about the only suspect in Harriet's disappearance. Not only had she worked that out, but Jimmy had come after his brother, and she didn't doubt he had evidence he hadn't revealed to her.

And yet still she had thought she was being clever, thought she was outsmarting them both.

Glenn must be laughing now. Must have been laughing at her all along.

Her phone… Had Suze simply seen it lying on the bar and swiped it while Mel was distracted by news of Mel? Or had she slipped it from her purse as they sat in the car?

Bitch.

All those little smiles, the squeezes of the hand, the comforting words.

Bitch.

The door opened. She turned, and he stood there. He'd changed out of the suit he'd worn at the party into jeans, a white shirt, a brown leather jacket – he hadn't even come directly here. Drawing it out. Making sure she knew she wasn't a priority.

"Where is she?"

He did that annoying hands-spread gesture of his.

"Safe," he said simply.

"That's what your stripper said."

"She had no reason to lie."

He reached for the light switch, flicked it on, and they both squinted for a second or two, adjusting to the flood of light.

There was something different about Glenn tonight. Less front. That's what it was. He didn't need to impress anyone, didn't need to project an image.

And that was the most scary thing of all.

Glenn Lazenby had won.

"So what now?" Mel said, trying not to let her voice reflect the other side of that coin: that she must therefore have lost.

He smiled, and Mel tried not to feel sick.

"Now?" he said. "Now, darling, I get to take whatever I want."

She held his look, still fighting, but that only made him smile again.

She was right: he'd been laughing at her all along, always at least one step ahead.

"Let Harriet go," she said. "Please. Just do that one thing. She's only a child."

"That doesn't exactly make her less valuable."

She'd never known him like this. Relaxed. Not having to pretend. She realized she'd never really known him at all.

Valuable. That chilled her.

There was always a price.

She recalled now, talking with Thom Sullivan at that party only earlier this evening, the moment when she'd pretty much begged him for help and he'd paused, turned to her, and reminded her of his 'offer' to stay with him at his place in Monaco. Extracting his price. Then, she'd thought she knew her own limits, knew she didn't have a price. She'd thought she could turn him down.

How naïve.

How damned naïve!

She had a price. Everyone did.

"What do you want?" she said, her voice barely more than a whisper.

Glenn had always had a thing for her. She couldn't remember if he'd even been aware of her much before Jimmy was, but a definite rivalry had developed between the two Lazenby brothers for her attentions.

Was that what this was about?

Was that why he'd tricked her into coming here, trapped her in this room?

He took a step toward her, and she did her best to hold his look before finally turning away, looking down at the floor.

Another step, another, and he stood before her. Reached out, used the lightest touch of a finger to tilt her chin up again, make her look at him.

"That all depends, darling," he said. "Depends on what it is you're offering."

"Let Harriet go."

"No, no. That's not what I meant. That's what you're asking for, not what's on offer. You see what I mean, Mels?"

"I… I'll do whatever you want. Just let her go."

Closer still, his finger still pressing lightly beneath her chin. She felt his breath on her face. Breathed his cologne mixed with the scent of leather.

Slowly, he trailed that finger down, under her chin, down the front of her neck and along one collarbone. Down until it came to rest lightly in her cleavage.

She wanted to punch him. Wanted to be sick. Wanted, desperately to run.

She stood there, his fingertip resting delicately between her breasts.

"Do you mean what I think you mean?" he said, raising his eyebrows in mock surprise.

He knew what she meant. She didn't answer. Tried not to breathe, because the rise and fall of her chest only reminded her of where that finger lay.

"You might have to spell it out for me, darling. Make sure I've got it right, you know?"

She couldn't. Couldn't open her mouth, couldn't find the words.

He drew his finger away, pressed the tip to his lips.

"You want to fuck me, is that what you mean?"

She ground her teeth. Wouldn't meet his look, even though she knew that was exactly what he wanted. He wanted her cowed, beaten. He was getting off on it. This wasn't a sex thing – it was beating his brother, beating *her*. Righting past wrongs. That's what turned him on: it was a power thing.

"No," she finally said. "I don't want to fuck you, and you know it. But that's what you want, isn't it? So I'll give it to you, if that's what it takes. Just let Harriet go."

For a moment she thought he was going to. He reached for her again, and she thought he was reaching for the thin strap of her dress, to ease it down over her shoulder.

Instead, though, he pressed his hand to her cheek, cupping her face before withdrawing.

"Nah," he said, that smile on his face, telling her he'd won again, got her to stoop so low, broken her. *That* was what he'd really wanted, to break her.

"Nah," he repeated. "Not that I'm not tempted, of course. I always thought there was a spark between us. Am I wrong? No, I didn't think so. I can tell."

He took a step back, shaking his head slowly. "No," he said. "Tempted as I am, I'm not going to take you up on your very kind offer. Don't want to spoil the goods, know what I mean?"

He laughed one more time, then turned and left the room.

16. MEL

Next time the door opened it was the bearded guy with the shaved head and piercings.

The one who'd attacked her that night in Jubilee Park. The one Glenn had called Wayne.

She still had the bruises on her neck and across the bridge of her nose, the aches in the ribs. The nightmares.

He pushed the door open and stood there, his expression giving nothing away.

Then he smiled, which was worse than anything.

Don't want to spoil the goods, know what I mean?

Was this what Glenn had been referring to? Was he handing her over to this mountainous bastard of a man, to finish whatever it was he'd started that night?

Maybe there was a perverse logic to it, in Glenn's mind. He'd set this guy on her once, only to be interrupted by Jimmy. Was letting this guy finish off some kind of payback on Jimmy? Something to use to hurt his kid brother?

She took a deep breath, trying to calm her racing thoughts.

Told herself this was madness. That whatever 'spoiling the goods' had referred to, it couldn't possibly be this. That thought didn't really help, though.

"Allow me to show you to your room." Wayne's voice twisted the knife in her guts, reminded her of his face up close to hers, his gently phrased threats – all the more chilling for how calmly reasoned they were, for the way he patiently made sure she had known he understood exactly how scared she must be.

As she squeezed past him into a hallway, she considered making a dash for the front door. He was big, bulky – how fast could he be?

The door must surely be locked, though. He would catch her easily.

He gestured at a staircase that ran up one side of the hallway, and Mel did as she was expected to do. Looked away, went to the stairs, climbed, with her guard following too closely behind.

She'd almost thrown up, when she'd brushed against him. He deliberately hadn't stepped back, had forced her to squeeze through a gap too small.

She'd never been so scared. Had never even had any concept of fear like this.

Not even that night in Jubilee Park, although that came closest.

"Left."

She turned left, and walked until they reached the end of a corridor. Three doors: one either side of the corridor and one at the end.

She waited, gritting her teeth.

Felt a meaty hand on the curve of her hip. Did nothing, just stood there, as her guard reached around her, twisted the doorknob, pushed it open.

"Your room, ma'am."

She stepped inside, and felt a powerful surge of relief when the bastard didn't follow.

She turned and looked at him, his bulky frame filling the open doorway.

Now he smiled, and said, "I would, in case you're wondering. Believe me, I would."

She didn't dare ask him to explain. Didn't dare anything.

"All that's stopping me is orders. Do you understand that? One thing... just one thing you do that makes Mr Lazenby or his friends unhappy, and you're mine. So be good, do you hear?"

He waited until she nodded before closing the door, and Mel waited until the door was closed before rushing to the basin in the en suite that opened off the small boxroom and throwing up the contents of her stomach.

Glenn was dressed for his father's funeral when he came to see her the next morning.

Mel had spent most of the night curled up on the room's narrow bed, still in the little black dress she'd bought the day before. At any moment she'd expected the door to open, for something awful to happen and her mind had raced with scenarios, strategies.

She'd dozed intermittently, lain awake for long periods. A couple of times she'd got up and paced the small room, used the bathroom and sat there for so long her legs went to sleep.

The room had a small window. No need to smash the glass, because she could open it, but there were no handholds and the drop too great. Even if she somehow lowered herself to hang from the frame first, she'd break an ankle if she tried to jump from this high up.

The window gave a view from the back of the house over a yard where several cars were parked. There were horses in the stables, and the barns were closed. Was this a working farm, then? Or just somebody's country home trying to look the part?

Where *was* she?

She washed, sometime in the morning, but still she felt unclean.

And then she heard the sound of voices outside her room, the clunk of the lock, and the door swung open.

Glenn came in, straightening his dark suit.

"I hope Wayne's been taking care of you," he said.

She didn't answer, and Glenn didn't seem to care.

Instead, she said, "Do you even have Harriet, or was that just a ruse to get me here?"

Glenn laughed at that. "Nice," he said. "That one's a lot more cooperative than you, believe me."

Again, Mel felt sick. She hated to think what he might mean by that.

"You'd better not lay a finger on her," she said in a low voice.

"You look out for yourself," he said. "Don't worry about Harriet. She's a smart one. She's older and wiser than she looks."

"Yes, but that's not what it is you like, is it? Not that she's older than she looks. It's that she looks younger than she is. Is that what you really like?"

She didn't know what she'd hoped to achieve. To get under his skin, perhaps.

It didn't work.

He just shrugged, smiled, spread his hands, and said, "Doesn't really matter, does it? She's legal."

She swung, taking even herself by surprise, but not Glenn: he caught her wrist easily, his grip painfully tight.

He held on as she tried to pull free, still smiling. "Sleep well?" he said, then barked a short laugh and let go.

Mel stumbled away, caught her legs on the edge of the bed and almost sprawled back onto it, steadying herself just in time.

"What's happened to you, Glenn?" she said. "Why all this?"

She'd always thought he wanted to be an old-school villain like his father. That had been why she'd despaired over Jimmy, ten years ago. She'd seen him drawn to the dark glamour of it all, the naïve belief that you could somehow do all the things the Lazenby family did and still hang onto values of some kind.

Glenn paused, as if considering his answer.

"Why?" he asked softly. "Because I can, I suppose. At last, I can."

A glance down at the dark suit. The funeral. The whole dead dad thing. The meaning was clear.

"Now I'm free," he went on. "The old man was stuck in his ways. But me? I'm open to new adventures. Isn't that exciting?" The softness of his voice gave an added chill to the words.

He was trying to wind her up, trying to unsettle her. And succeeding, of course, but she tried not to show it. This side of Glenn, now that the mask had slipped, was truly disturbing.

"Harriet?" he said, finally coming back to her original question. "She was so easy. You should have seen it! The whole thing could have been choreographed, know what I mean? After that night when I 'bumped into' you–" he made the quotation marks in the air with his fingers "–I gave her my card, we got to chatting online. Exchanging text messages and all that. Very touching. Poor kid was desperate to prove how grown up she was. Didn't even realize she was chatting to Suze half the time and not me.

Suze is so much better at that kind of thing than me. I get bored too easily."

Mel looked away. Reminded herself how Glenn would always embellish things for his audience, always trying to press their buttons.

"It was the anniversary of her old man's death coming up. I gave her a sob story about all this..." He tugged at his dark suit again. "My old man, how heartbroken I was, alone in the world. She told me she'd made that journey of loss – those were her words, I think, the self-important bitch. Told me she could help me." He was laughing now, enjoying this far too much. "We arranged to meet, she climbed into my car, and the rest is history, as they say."

"And now?"

"She's here. She's a valuable one, with looks like that. Remember I told you I had contacts? That I knew all the people to ask about your missing friend? Well I do. For good reason. They're the ones who make the highest bids."

"Where is she?"

"She's here, for now. These things take time to set up. But I tell you one thing: a funeral is a hell of a good way to get people together. They come from all over and it looks legit, and now they're here they get a chance to eye up the goods – in the flesh, so to speak."

"What kind of monster are you?"

He laughed, not even bothering to answer, and her mind filled in the gaps, just as he must surely know it would.

The kind of monster who had the keys.

The kind that held all the cards.

The kind that had been outsmarting her – and everyone else – every step of the way.

The kind in control.

"Let me see Harriet."

"So many demands," Glenn said. "And so very little to offer."

He was enjoying this. That scared her more than anything.

"What now?" Was he really going to sell Harriet off to the highest bidder? And what of Mel? What would he do with her after he'd offloaded Harriet? She knew too much now, and he didn't seem to be making any effort to limit how much he told her.

"Now?" said Glenn. He walked in a small semicircle around her, looking her up and down as she stood there in last night's disheveled dress.

"You should never have said 'no' to Thom Sullivan," he said.

Last night at the party. Sullivan's 'offer' that she should join him in Monaco.

"Mr Sullivan's the kind of man who's used to getting whatever he wants," Glenn went on. "People never say 'no' to him. Not in the end, at least. And sometimes, for a man like Mr Sullivan, the only excitement left is whatever's forbidden to him. The ones that are too young. The ones who say 'no'. Do you realize just how much you turned him on with that one little word?"

The party... the people there. Were they the people Glenn had referred to? The ones here ostensibly for the funeral, but in reality to 'eye up the goods'? And Thom Sullivan... was that what he'd been doing with Mel?

She remembered him letting slip that Glenn had told him about her, and now she understood why.

She'd stepped right into this, just as Harriet had.

Maybe she'd messed up his plans a little, at least, walking out of that party early, before any of the other 'guests' had been given the opportunity to eye her up. But maybe that had simply added to her appeal – the girl who says 'no', the girl who thinks she can walk out on them all.

Glenn had rounded her up easily enough later on, after all.

"Why are you doing this? Why Harriet? Why me?"

That smile. She felt the muscles tensing in her arm, her fingers flexing, talon-like. In her head she saw herself dragging long scratches down the side of his face, marking him. But she remembered how fast he was, how easily he had caught her by the wrist before.

"Oh, so many reasons," he said. "So many, many reasons."

"Such as?"

"Because I can."

As he spoke, he counted the reasons off on his fingers.

"Because I've waited ten years to wipe that smug smile off your face."

He was just how he'd described Sullivan, she realized. The thing he wanted most, was what he could never have. Her. And if he couldn't have her, then he would have his revenge, at least.

"Because Jimmy," he went on. "Oh yes! Because Jimmy, and all that entails! Let's see… there's more. Oh yes, there's more. Here's another reason: because these people matter to me – yes, it's good business to keep my powerful friends happy. It's what I do, what the old man did before me. We facilitate. We supply whatever they want."

She made to speak but he held a hand up, silencing her.

"Because you're you. Did I mention that? Yes? Not just that it's you, though: but also because you're Dougie Conner's daughter. That's a sweet one. Right up there among the very best of the reasons. Dougie Conner's daughter. He's always had it in for me. But now I've got him running."

There was so much hatred in his torrent of words. So much bile.

"And I'll tell you something else," he said. "That really adds to your value. Forbidden fruit. The girl who says 'no'. *And* the daughter of a top secret agent."

She shook her head. "He's nothing of the sort. He's a civil servant. A pen pusher. That's all he is."

Glenn laughed again. "You don't even believe that," he said. "Trust me: your father has some serious enemies. They're lining up for you. Just how much do you think they'd be willing to pay to have Dougie Conner's daughter? To really *have* her? Thom Sullivan. Ronnie Bosvelt. David Viera. They can't wait to get their hands on you. You're going to make me rich, Mel. How cool is that? *And* I get to put one over on your old man. He thinks he's so clever. Thinks he's been running rings around me for years, but I've just been biding my time. Waiting for this. Let him feel what it's like to see his daughters fall into the hands of his most bitter enemies."

He was a monster. And she was totally at his mercy.

His comment about 'spoiling the goods' made perfect sense now. All of it did.

And then…

"Daughters? What do you mean, 'daughters'?"

The sucker punch. The baited trap. He'd been standing there, just waiting for her to pick up on what he'd said.

"Daughters," he repeated. "Hadn't you worked that bit out? Why your old man gave even the slightest shit about Harriet Rayner?"

Daughters.

All the times her father had innocently asked about the time she spent with Harriet. The excuses he'd made, how he was just looking out for an old friend's family. All the bullshit.

Daughters.

That smile on Glenn's face. Her fist bunched again. He might not be fast enough to stop her now. Or strong enough.

"Just think," he said. "A job lot, the two of you. Sisters. The one who says 'no' and the one who looks like a child and is only too desperate to say 'yes'. Both of them, daughters of the hated Douglas Conner. You're going to make me a lot of money. Both of you."

He was still fast enough, and strong enough.

He caught her by the wrist again as she swung, gripping her so tightly she thought the bones might be crushed.

And instead of wiping that smile off his face, she only made it broaden.

Rather than letting go, he twisted his grip, forcing her elbow to turn inwards, awkward and painful.

"You still have fight," he said. "That's good. My friends like fight, and resistance. They like having something to break."

He released her, stepped back, brushing down his suit.

Smiled again, just to rub it all in.

"Must dash, darling," he said. "Got to make an appearance at a funeral. Wouldn't do to miss it, now, would it? It's one of those important things. A rite of passage, if you would. I think of it not so much as a funeral, as a coronation."

And then he turned and left the room, and as Mel stared at the door she heard the clunk of the lock.

17. JIMMY

Mel Conner's trail went cold sometime on Thursday evening.

Before that, in the afternoon, she'd gone back to her room at Mr Singh's, having rebooked it for a further two nights. After depositing her bag she'd gone straight out again, returning a couple of hours later to get dressed up.

A man, I assumed. She seemed... nervous. Taking a lot of trouble, you know?

That's what Singh had said. The landlord had clearly assumed a date, and that she hadn't returned because she'd got lucky.

Jimmy had to step back from this, had to be objective.

Singh's explanation was plausible enough, on the face of it.

Jimmy knew nothing about Mel's private life. Yes, he'd spent some time with her this week. Spent the night with her. But how much did he really know?

They'd talked about her room in north London. Her studies at UCL. She'd mentioned some friends, a few names, the fact she'd had failed relationships. There didn't appear to be anyone significant in her life right now, but that could easily be because she was being diplomatic about how much she gave away.

Perhaps the simplest explanation was that last night she'd got dressed up to meet a current boyfriend, and simply hadn't returned to her rented room.

But that look in her eye… The defiance. The determination not to be swept aside.

She hadn't come back here by chance.

Jimmy didn't believe she had ever let go of the investigation into Harriet Rayner's absence. And if that was the case, then returning and renting that room again, getting dressed up – taking so much trouble, as Singh had put it – were all connected to the investigation into her friend's disappearance.

So who would she get dressed up for?

Who had she been trying to catch off guard?

Glenn.

Frustrating as this investigation had been, the one common thread was that everything kept returning to Glenn Lazenby.

Without even thinking about it, Jimmy had already set off walking from Mr Singh's house. Down to the end of the street, across a couple of junctions, until he came to the iron railing that marked the boundary of Jubilee Park.

He remembered that night, seeing Mel sprawled face down on the ground, raising herself, blood smeared across her face. Staggering to her feet as the guy called Wayne closed in, forcing her up against a tree, even as Jimmy stole up silently behind him, his SIG Sauer raised, the safety eased off, his forefinger resting against the trigger guard.

Was he jumping to conclusions?

What would he do if this was any other case, one that did not involve Mel and his brother?

Would he plunge right in, or step back, reassess and reevaluate?

He was already heading along the path that cut through the park.

This *wasn't* any other case.

It *did* involve Mel and Glenn.

And he was going to get to the bottom of it.

"Hey, Jimbo! Over here. Come on and join us. Here, shuffle up, Cass, make the kid some room, know what I mean? Hey, Jimbo, I didn't think you were coming.

Thought you'd done your bit at the crem. Shows how wrong I can be, eh? I should know never to underestimate you."

Glenn had stood, a near-empty pint glass in one hand. He leaned in to Jimmy, chest-bumping, looping his free arm around his brother and clapping him firmly on the back. He stank of booze and cheap scent.

"Drink?" said Glenn. Then, louder, toward the bar: "Hey, darling. Pint of Pride for the kid, would you? And another for me."

The Flag and Flowers was heaving. When Jimmy had pushed in through the front doors a moment ago he'd been hit by a wall of sound. Voices and music, for once, drowning out the sounds of the games machines.

He'd paused, giving the place the usual automatic once-over, taking in the people, the layout, the entrances and exits. Paying special attention to the people who glanced at him and whose gazes lingered. Their expressions either blank or, as his Gran had always called it, giving him the evils.

Uncle Frank and the woman they'd referred to as Auntie Cyn were sitting in the window table with a couple of the other old-timers. Gordon Walker and Maxine Macrae. Maxine had often looked after Jimmy and Glenn when they were kids, but now there was no fondness in her look.

Jimmy had made his choices when he walked out ten years ago, and it would take more than showing up at a funeral to change people's minds about him.

Funny to think that in these people's eyes Jimmy was the one who'd never made the grade. The family disappointment. If his ten years away had been for a stretch in Pentonville or Wandsworth for armed robbery things would have been so different.

He was glad he'd walked out.

No regrets.

He turned away from Frank and his group, threaded a way through the crowd, knowing Glenn would be holding court at the family table at the rear of the back bar.

More faces, turned to him. Hard stares. This was hostile territory, intensified by a combination of the people present, the emotions of the occasion, and the fact the wake had been underway all through the afternoon and a lot of alcohol had been consumed.

Jimmy had been well trained in avoiding confrontation and going unnoticed, and now he used all the tricks. The quick nod and smile to disarm a hostile glare, because even the meanest bastard would at least acknowledge friendliness before remembering why he's being such a mean bastard. A quickly averted look – let them think he was ducking a challenge. A gaze that slid and moved without ever settling, leaving nothing to latch onto, to confront. Keep moving. Play deaf to any muttered comments.

Just like a wedding, Jimmy knew from experience it wouldn't be a proper wake without a fight, but there was no reason it had to be him.

And so he'd come to the back bar, the atmosphere a little more subdued and quiet here, Glenn and his cronies sitting at the family table with a few of the dancers from Ryders.

Glenn knew how to throw a classy wake.

Glenn's bellowed welcome made sure everyone knew Jimmy was present, which was almost certainly what he'd intended.

The group shuffled around, and Jimmy squeezed into the space made for him, his thigh hard up against the bare leg of Glenn's favorite dancer, the one called Suze. A redhead with tatts and one side of her head shaved down to a fine, velvety stubble pressed in from the other side, resting her hand on Jimmy's thigh as if they were old lovers.

Others at the table included Ronnie Bosvelt, the Dutch gangster whose name cropped up frequently in the Section's Lazenby files, Rich Coombes, the downy-faced representative of one of the old London families, and David Viera, one of the key operators in the South American coke gateway in Galicia, northwest Spain.

"So you couldn't stay away, then? Hey, everyone, this is my kid brother, Jimmy. Dark sheep. Come back to pay his respects to the old man, and all that. Say 'hello', girls."

From either side, Suze and the redhead pressed in, kissing him on the cheeks, the hand on his thigh squeezing way too intimately, another hand squeezing his arm – Suze's knuckles must have pressed against the holster under his jacket, a move far too slick to be accidental.

"Can I have a word?" Jimmy said to his brother. "Just a couple of minutes." Maybe he could get Glenn outside, or at least into the back office, away from the noise and press of people.

Glenn just smiled, though, and said, "Sure, Jimbo, what is it? I'm all ears."

Everything Glenn did right now was exaggerated, a bit too loud, a bit too deliberate. Jimmy couldn't work out if he was drunk or just enjoying being the center of attention. Probably both.

Glenn turned, sweeping his gaze around the group at the table. "My little bro's here on a case," he said. "He's a – what are you, Jimbo? Secret agent? Do they call them that? Security services. Whatever. Hey, bro', I'm really sorry I wasn't able to help you with that thing." A glance around the table again. "That missing girl case. Tragic. I really wish I could have done more."

He should leave. Should never have come here this evening.

He knew what Glenn was like.

He hadn't thought it through though. This wasn't any other case. This was Mel.

"Where is she, Glenn? Where's Mel Conner?"

Glenn looked genuinely confused. "Mel?" he said. "What d'you mean, Mel? I thought… Hang on, bro', what's going on here?"

"Can we talk, Glenn? It's important."

He seemed to have cut through Glenn's bluster, sobered him. Glenn nodded, shrugged himself free of Suze's arm across his back, stood.

"Come on, bro'. Let's get us some fresh air, eh?"

He stepped out, joining Jimmy as he stood, draping an arm across his brother's shoulders.

"Let's go out back. Have you seen the beer garden? It's lovely, and real easy to clear every other fucker out of there so we can talk in peace, okay?"

They sat either side of a slatted wooden table.

True to his word, a couple of gestures from Glenn had been enough to encourage the few people out here to gather their drinks and cigarettes and head back into the pub or round to the front where other smokers had gathered.

"Mel, you said? What the fuck's happened now, bro'?" All of a sudden Glenn was sober, straight. He'd dropped the matey leeriness he'd put on for his friends inside.

"Probably nothing," said Jimmy, trying to read the situation, work out where his brother's head was. "Yesterday evening," he went on. "Where were you? What were you up to?"

Glenn spread his hands, rolling his head back into his shoulders. "What, I'm a suspect now? What's going on, Jimbo?"

"Mel's gone quiet. I just want to make sure she's okay. Hasn't done anything stupid." If his brother knew anything, he was doing a good job of playing innocent and confused.

"I had a little gathering at the Barn," said Glenn. "Thom Sullivan's over. We got together with a bunch of the old man's other acquaintances and relived old times, you know what I mean? We had canapés and posh glasses, would you believe it?" He made a show of raising his pint glass with his little finger cocked out daintily, and laughed.

Jimmy didn't laugh, and Glenn checked himself, put his glass down, more serious now. "She was there, yeah," he said. "I invited her. Mel. She's been very friendly lately, you know? She showed up and I thought I was in with a shout. There's always been a bit of a spark between us, a bit of banter. Sorry, sorry – old sensitivities and all that, but you can't blame me, can you? She still scrubs up well."

Jimmy had been right. The show, the taking trouble over her appearance... Mel had come after Glenn again. Did she have any idea what a dangerous game she was playing?

"So what happened?" asked Jimmy. "Were you right? Were you in with a shout?"

Glenn shrugged. "Nah," he said. "Said she wasn't in 'a fancy do kind of place'. That's how she put it. I offered to get one of the boys to give her a lift back to wherever she was staying, but she said no, said she'd rather walk. Get some fresh air. Not sure what she was implying by that."

He laughed again. "Oh man. Do you really think something's happened? This is some strange shit: first that girl, and now Mel. Maybe you need to bring the heavy guns in, you know?"

Even now, Glenn couldn't resist a dig at his younger brother, the implication he was out of his depth.

Jimmy shut it out. Glenn's ego wasn't his concern right now, except where it had impact on the case.

"So tell me, then," said Glenn. "Are you here because you're just following threads and you think I might be able to contribute something, or do you really think I might be the bad guy here? I'm curious."

Jimmy let the silence draw out as he studied his brother's expression. Finally, he said, "So she came to your party, and left early, alone?"

Glenn nodded. "Mid-evening. I don't know, eightish? She said she just wasn't in the mood. Listen, is there anything I can do? Other than show you to the place where I keep all my kidnap victims, of course."

Glenn laughed. He was the only one. He shrugged then, said, "Sorry. Bad taste. I'm a dick, I know. Tough day, and all that." For a moment, he let his shoulders slump and his expression slide, dropping the false bonhomie. "Do you ever get tired?" he said. "I don't know how the old man did it. How he kept the front up, kept going under all the pressure."

"Sucks to be you," said Jimmy, the first attempt at humor he'd made in… well, days.

Glenn laughed.

"Do you have any idea where she went?" Jimmy asked.

A shake of the head. "She refused the offer of a lift, like I say. I don't know. You have to worry, though, don't you? Dressed like that, out on her own in what's now, to her, an unfamiliar town. I know we're not allowed to say women are asking for it when they dress like that, but…" Another shrug.

Jimmy stood. He couldn't work out if that last comment was Glenn trying to get under his skin again, or simply his brother being a dick. Sometimes it was hard to tell.

Glenn remained seated. He looked up at Jimmy, gave a small nod, and said, "If there's anything I can do."

Jimmy nodded back. He couldn't put a name to the feeling he felt then, the mix of frustration and resentment, but also… a weird kind of connection. Family, he guessed. Was that an actual feeling?

"You're always welcome here," said Glenn. He gestured toward the pub with a nod of the head, a slight roll of the shoulders. "Ignore them. You'll always be a part of this. It's in your blood. You can't shake it all off that easily."

Jimmy made to leave, took a step to go, then paused. "If you're lying to me, you know I'll fucking kill you, right? Family or not."

Glenn nodded. "I'd expect no less from a brother of mine," he said, and raised his glass. "To the old man," he said, "and family," and took a long drink.

Jimmy nodded, turned, and walked away.

It was after eight now. So more than twenty-four hours since Mel had walked out of Glenn's party. Since she'd left her last mark on the world.

Or at least, the last Jimmy had been able to find.

Jimmy got into his car and drove. Nowhere in particular. Country lanes, as darkness descended. Twilight. A couple of deer paused to watch him from the edge of a patch of woodland.

Nature. He'd never really got it, but he knew if Mel were here she'd have been so thrilled to see those deer. She'd have made him get it.

That's what she did. Made him see everything in a new way. What was that? Love? Some other kind of connection, that brought out aspects of you that you didn't even know were there?

He parked in a gateway, tipped his seat back, tried to think.

Checked his phone again, but there was nothing.

He should call Conner, at least. Let him know Mel was missing. He wasn't sure what that would achieve right now, though, other than save himself from a hard time when Conner found out he'd been kept in the dark at some future point.

He didn't like to admit to himself that his reluctance had anything to do with those seeds of doubt Glenn had so successfully scattered. To his decision that he couldn't rely on any of the usual back-up and infrastructure for now.

Glenn's comment about the need to call in the big guns still stung, too. Was he choosing to remain solo on this out of some kind of stubborn pride, or was it the correct, pragmatic analysis?

Patil.

Surely he could still rely on Mamta Patil, at least? She'd always been there for him, a constant in the Section's back-office; one of the smartest people he knew, and one of the few who'd never shown any kind of frustration with Jimmy's pig-headed ways.

"Hey, Mamta," he said, when she answered on two. Did she ever go home, even? "Any updates?"

"Nothing to report, sir. What can I do for you?"

"Melissa Conner," he said. "C-O-N-N-E-R, that's right. I need to trace her movements and present location. Top priority."

"On it. I'll send through details asap." There had been no hesitation at the surname, other than to confirm the spelling. Patil would know it was Doug Conner's daughter Jimmy was trying to trace. Would she pass that on to Doug? Maybe, although Jimmy thought not: Patil was solid, and she had always trusted Jimmy to be out there doing the right thing.

"Thanks, Mamta," he said. "This one matters, okay?"

"Sir."

The line went dead. Patil was, as she'd said, on it.

A few minutes later, his phone went, Patil returning his call. "Sir? No mobile phone activity – or signal – since Thursday, 8.15pm. Last call received was from your number, unanswered, at 8.12pm. No other online activity of any sort since that time."

This was sounding starkly like Harriet Rayner's disappearance, everything going offline around the time she was last seen.

"Movements?"

"She was with you Thursday morning, sir."

Breakfast. Patil had diplomatically chosen to start the report from that point, rather than the fact he'd spent the night at the same location as Mel.

"Then?"

"Train to King's Cross. Underground to Dollis Hill. Then... she retraced the journey almost immediately. She headed back."

Jimmy already knew she'd come back. He could imagine the process: reluctantly accepting she had to step back, going home to London, and then throughout the train journey her head going round and round until she'd convinced herself she couldn't let go.

"I've just sent you GPS coordinates of her last known location before the signal went dead, along with a log of all her activity in the previous twenty-four. Do you need anything else?"

She was asking if she should tell Doug.

"No. Thanks, Mamta. Just... any updates, okay? Get them to me asap."

"Sir."

He drove back into town and parked on a side road just off the High Street.

He had the map on his phone's small screen, showing the triangulation of Mel's signals as they pinged off surrounding masts. It was enough to narrow it down to a section of the High Street, and one street that ran parallel that was mostly residential. He walked along there first, eyeing the backs of commercial premises on the High Street on his right, and a row of shabby terraced houses on his left.

He couldn't help flashing back to Glenn's words, the suggestion she was 'asking for it' by being out on her own, dressed as she was. If she'd come back here at this time of night for any reason, she would have been vulnerable. The yards and garages behind the High Street premises presented numerous shady corners. It was easy to imagine any number of unpleasant events taking place here, an easy place to slip away to for anyone who wanted to be out of sight from the town's main road. Drug dealers, gangs of teenagers hanging out, illicit knee-tremblers up against a wall – she could have stumbled across almost anything here if she'd passed through, perhaps on a shortcut to somewhere else.

This was the kind of place where a chance encounter could easily go tragically wrong.

He studied the houses to his left. Anonymous, run down, neglected. Could she possibly have had any reason to be here?

He was doing little better than trying to second-guess her, he knew. He didn't know what had been in her head.

He went back out to the High Street. Friday night, and perhaps typically for the center of a small town on a Friday night there were clusters of activity: groups gathered outside pubs and fast food places, the occasional roar and squealing wheels of cars being raced, music spilling out from anywhere still open.

He studied the map on his phone again, narrowing his search down to a section of the street. Most places here were closed – shops and hairdressers, a couple of estate agents' offices, a bank branch.

What remained were a kebab shop, an Indian restaurant and a pub, the King's Head.

He tried to think it through. She'd emerged from the Barn, told Glenn she would walk. Her route back to Singh's bed and breakfast place would bring her to the High Street, right along here. She might well have been hungry, probably wouldn't have stopped in a pub, though, if what Glenn had said about her not being in the mood for his party had been true.

He went up to the counter in the kebab shop, ignoring the glares of the three people in the queue he had just bypassed. A guy with a stubbly gray beard and a white *taqiyah* skullcap nodded toward the waiting customers, and said, "Wait your turn, eh, friend? Won't be long."

Jimmy shrugged, turned his phone so the guy could see the screen, and said, "Sorry. Really, I just… I'm worried about my friend. She's been missing since around this time yesterday. Last seen on this stretch of High Street. She wasn't in here by any chance, was she? Or maybe you saw her outside, maybe getting into someone's car?"

The guy squinted, then shook his head. "Sorry, friend, but no. I don't recognize her. I hope she okay, you know?"

Jimmy left. He tried the restaurant next door, but with the same result. Checked the map again. The only other place she might have stopped off was the King's Head.

He was clutching at straws, he knew. Assuming she'd either stopped somewhere on her way back to Singh's or at least that someone might have seen her passing here.

He went into the King's Head, a dark and dingy place that, much like the row of houses on the street behind here, had seen far better days.

At the bar he caught the attention of a woman with a blonde perm straight out of the early 1980s, and went through the questions again. She stared at the screen, but then shook her head.

It was pointless. Mel hadn't stopped anywhere. If this sector of the High Street was, indeed, where something had happened, it had happened in the street, and from inside this pub they'd have seen nothing.

Again, he questioned his judgment, his willingness to leap in. Mel had been rushing about all over the place over the last few days. Had she put her phone on to charge that night he'd stayed with her? Almost certainly not. In which case it was a miracle the charge had lasted through until the following evening. Her phone must have run out of charge after she left Glenn's party, and she hadn't bothered charging it again, perhaps finding she enjoyed a bit of peace.

He was over-reacting. Following his fears instead of the logic of the evidence.

The barmaid with the big hair was talking to an old guy sitting half-slumped over the bar, nursing a near-empty pint, both of them squinting sidelong in Jimmy's direction.

"'nother look?" said the barmaid now.

Jimmy held the phone so they both could see, watching as the guy squinted, then slowly nodded, and then tipped his glass to make sure they could see how empty it was.

Jimmy reached into his pocket, found a few coins and dropped them on the bar, and the barmaid took the glass to refill it.

"Much obliged," said the guy. "Yeah, she was here. Last night. I wasn't watching her or anything. Nothing creepy. I just notice what's around me, you know?"

Jimmy nodded, and waited for him to go on.

"Noticed she didn't look too happy, you know? All dressed up and on her own, staring at her phone. Someone stood her up, I reckon." That last was said in an accusatory tone, as if it was all Jimmy's fault.

"How long was she here for?"

"I was getting to that," the man said with the air of someone who didn't like to be hurried, even though everyone who ever spoke with him must surely wish he would hurry the fuck up. He paused, took a long sup of his replenished beer, smacked his lips, and finally continued. "Then her friend come in, sat with her, and a couple of minutes later they left, got into a car that someone else was driving."

"Friend?" asked Jimmy. Had Glenn come after her? "What did he look like, this friend?"

The guy laughed. "He? I ain't never seen a bloke with legs like that! Mind, it takes all sorts these days, I suppose."

"Legs?"

"Girl, she was. Colored thing. Tiny little skirt and a top that wasn't much more'n a bra, you know what I mean? A real looker. Had her down as a tart or a dancer."

The dancer.

The one called Suze who always seemed to be in Glenn's lap or hanging off his arm.

The one who had so deftly checked out Jimmy's shoulder holster when she'd pressed her tits and pretty much everything else against him at the wake earlier.

No, Glenn hadn't come after Mel here at the King's Head last night. He'd sent one of his people to do the dirty work.

18. MEL

Sometime later, Mel heard someone at the door again. She shuffled back on the bed, her knees drawn up, arms wrapped around her legs protectively.

It would be the big guard again. Wayne.

She couldn't work out now whether Wayne was truly the most terrifying person she'd ever encountered, or if Glenn had stolen that title with the chilling look in his eye when he'd explained the situation to her…

Wayne had brought food earlier. Bread, a plastic bottle of Coke. She was starving. Hadn't eaten anything but a couple of canapés since a sandwich for lunch the previous day.

But she didn't touch the food. She didn't trust it, although she knew if they wanted to drug her they could just grab her and force her to swallow whatever they wanted. It was more that she didn't want to acknowledge that she needed them in any way. Accepting their food and drink felt, in some strange way, like accepting the situation.

She'd drunk water from the bathroom in the night. She'd wait for food. Wait until she was free to get her own, or until she was so starved and wasted she had to give in.

She'd had time since Glenn had left to go over and over what he'd said. So much to take in.

The bitterness in his words had shocked her, the revenge he'd been bottling up for years – on Jimmy, on her father, and on her, too. She'd never realized he resented her personally, so intensely. The girl he couldn't have. The one who'd chosen his brother.

There was real anger in Glenn's eyes. Anger, but also desire – for she saw that, too. How fucked up must his mind be right now, to want someone so badly, and hate them even more, at the same time? To want to destroy them?

She knew well that Glenn Lazenby was not a man you would ever want to come up against.

She tried hard not to dwell on her fate... The fact that Glenn had brought in these powerful men who would buy a woman – a girl – as a plaything to use, break, discard. A perverse kind of auction.

Would Sullivan win her? Would that be a better fate than any of the other, unknown, bidders? Yesterday evening at the party, she'd seen something in Sullivan's eye. Something that had disturbed her.

And Harriet. What kind of a mind-fuck was that?

Her father's other daughter.

They'd known the Rayners for years. Mel's mother had always been the one who stuck closest to Penny when things got tough. The one who picked up the pieces, who helped her pull things back together every time she tried to return to normal life.

Mel's mother had died the year before Harriet's father had... She automatically thought of Geoffrey Rayner in that way: Harriet's father. The remains of the two families had drawn closer together, and at the time Mel had thought it just a natural thing: shared grief, old friends helping each other. She hadn't realized there had been something deeper, a connection and a responsibility that went back years.

She knew nothing of her father's relationship with Penny Rayner. Had there been an affair – what, close to eighteen years ago? Or just a one-off thing. A drunken fumble at a party. A moment of madness when partners were away?

Had the partners known? Had it been something the two couples had struggled through, or something Penny and Doug had concealed?

Did Harriet know?

Harriet. They'd always been like sisters. That's what everyone said. That's what *they* had said, how they'd described their own friendship. *We're the sisters that never were.*

Only, they were.

Sisters.

And now… The door. The clunk of the lock. The rush of fear, as memories came rushing back. That night in Jubilee Park when the man she now knew as Wayne had attacked her, threatened her… And then last night, Wayne telling her he *would*, that it was only orders that kept his hands off her.

She didn't trust him at all. The only reassurance she could find to cling to was that he clearly wasn't keen on the consequences of disobeying orders, and his job was to keep her here, undamaged.

She pulled at her clothes, wishing she'd chosen a longer dress, only now realizing that the way she sat with her legs pulled up could only draw the eye to curves, exposed flesh.

Whatever she did, she couldn't just sit here looking so vulnerable.

She made to move, but it was too late. The door was swinging open.

She stayed where she was, biting down on her lower lip, the pain giving her at least something to hold on to.

A girl stood there in the open doorway, not Wayne.

"Harriet?"

Mel didn't move. Couldn't work out what was quite so surreal about this situation.

All week she'd anticipated this moment, finding Harriet, dragging her into her embrace, and yet now…

"Mels." Harriet's voice was a monotone, as flat as her expression.

She still stood there, as if she didn't know what came next. She looked okay. No bruises or marks. Clean, as if she'd been able to look after herself. Outwardly, the same old Harriet.

But… what had they done to her?

Mel scrambled to her feet, took three steps across the room and threw her arms around her friend.

Harriet's frame was stiff, stayed that way for a second, two, and then, slowly, slumped, melding into Mel's embrace.

"Mels. Oh, Mels."

"It's okay, Harriet. I'm going to get you out of here. I'm going to get you safe."

And as she spoke, she hated the lie, but it was all she could think to say.

Harriet disentangled herself, pulled away, turned. "We have the whole wing," she said, stepping back out into the narrow corridor.

Mel followed her, trying to recall the layout of this floor, the doors opening off this corridor. What she hadn't noticed last night when Wayne had brought her up here, was the heavy door, now closed across the far end of the corridor, sealing this area off from the rest of the building.

They were still locked in, still prisoners, just with more space than the small room Mel had been in overnight.

Then she realized something else.

Harriet had been able to unlock the door to Mel's room. She either had a key, or had already had access to this area and had found the key in the door.

In some strange way, this was Harriet's domain, and she was like some kind of hostess, showing her new guest around.

And she'd waited until now to open Mel's door, had left her to stew in that small room until well into the day. It must be late morning by now, Mel worked out: Glenn had been dressed up for the funeral when he came to see her earlier, all ready to go.

Had Harriet been putting off this moment, for some reason? Or had she only just realized Mel was here?

"Harriet." Mel put a hand on the girl's arm, forcing her to turn and meet her look. "What is it? What have they done to you?"

Harriet opened her mouth to speak, then stopped herself. Started again: "Nothing, Mels. *They've* done nothing. Glenn's been good to me. Given me everything I need."

She pulled away, stepped into the next room, a kind of living room with sofas, a chaise, a big TV suspended from one wall.

"There are clothes," said Harriet, gesturing to a doorway that led through to another bedroom. "You might want to freshen up."

Again, Mel felt like some weird kind of guest, Harriet her hostess.

"We need to get out of here," said Mel. "Right now, while they're away at the funeral."

She didn't like the way Harriet had said *Glenn*. He wasn't just a guy called Glenn, he was their abductor. He'd kept Harriet imprisoned for almost a week, was promising to sell them both off to the highest bidder… to men out for revenge.

She wondered if Harriet knew about their father. Wondered how to raise the subject. Whether she even should.

Harriet was staring at her. As if she could read what was on Mel's mind, she said, "It doesn't change anything. He's not my dad. He never was. Geoffrey will always be my real father."

Of course Glenn would have told her! He'd never miss an opportunity like that. A chance to twist the knife, to screw with people's perceptions of their world.

Did this explain Harriet's strange mood now? The distance. The awkwardness between them.

Mel reached for her, but Harriet stepped back.

"Nobody says it should change anything," Mel said. "Maybe it explains a few things, but that's all. Don't let whatever Glenn's told you get under your skin. Real sisters, or the sisters that never were, we're still the same *us*."

"I'm not your sister," snapped Harriet. "I never was."

Mel was shocked by the anger in Harriet's voice. What had Glenn been saying? What tricks had he used to get into her head?

"It's okay, Harriet," she said. "We'll get through this."

§

She changed into jeans and a sweatshirt, because that was what Harriet seemed to want.

Maybe the girl was clutching at anything vaguely normal, like the need to see Mel in normal daytime clothes instead of a dress you would only ever put on for an evening out.

She wondered if anyone would be looking for her by now.

She hadn't answered Jimmy's calls. Surely he'd realize something was up? This was what he did, and he'd told her he was good at it, one of the best. He'd called her yesterday evening, and while he'd said he would do that to keep her informed, she was sure it was at least partly in order to check up on her – make sure she was okay, and yes, to make sure she was keeping her promise to back off.

If he was as good as he claimed, he must know something was wrong by now.

And her father... *their* father. Glenn had said he was some kind of spy. She'd always known he was more than simply the pen-pusher he claimed – that was why she'd asked him for help when Harriet had first gone missing, after all.

Did he monitor Mel? If not regularly, then now, when he'd known she was putting herself in danger? He must have some way of tracking her down when he wanted to. If so, then surely he would be close on her tail, too, by now.

That was the best she could do: two flimsy straws to cling onto. A father who'd never paid her much attention, and a – what? lover? friend? there wasn't a word for what Jimmy Lazenby was to her right now... – who might just be starting to wonder why she'd ignored his call last night.

She went back out into the main room, spread her arms and did a little curtsy, a twirl, as if she'd just put on some glamorous new outfit and not some hand-me-down casuals left out by her abductors.

Harriet still had that slightly blank look on her face, and suddenly Mel understood. She went to Harriet, took hold of her arms, made her look her in the eyes.

"What have they filled you with?" she said in a tight voice.

Harriet was high. Stoned. It was obvious now she'd worked it out.

The girl looked away, shrugged, trying to shake her arms free. "Nothing I didn't ask for," she said. "A bit of blow, a bit of weed. Glenn's been good to me, like I told you."

Mel remembered Glenn telling her Harriet had been using. One of the few true things he'd told her, as it turned out, although he hadn't mentioned the fact he was the one pushing it on her.

She squeezed Harriet's arms again, said, "I'm going to get you out of here, do you understand?"

Harriet pulled clear, walked across to the chaise and threw herself down.

"Will you stop *saying* that?" she said. "I'm not a child anymore!"

Mel didn't know what to say, or think. Harriet's manner was very much like that of a petulant child right now, and Mel struggled to see why she was acting this way. What was in her head?

"You're sixteen," she said. "You've been abducted. Imprisoned. Given god knows what drugs to keep you docile. So no, I won't stop saying any of that. I'm here to get you out of all this."

But Harriet was shaking her head, her arms folded tightly across her chest.

"I'm not sixteen," she said. "I'm seventeen. I'm old enough to make my own choices."

They'd brainwashed her. With drugs, with whatever lies Glenn had been feeding her. Mel had seen a documentary once about how a sympathetic bond can develop between kidnapper and victim – the Stockholm Syndrome – could that explain Harriet's bizarre faith in Glenn now?

Mel dropped to a squatting position, matching Harriet's eye level. Said, gently, "They're not interested in you because you've just turned seventeen, babe. They want you because you look like you're about twelve."

It was harsh, but true, something Harriet had always hated, that her looks were so stubbornly pre-pubescent. In Glenn's brutal terms that added value, added a level of the forbidden, which he said was exactly what these people were drawn to.

Mel didn't add that they also wanted her because of who her biological father was.

"What's he told you?" she asked. "What promises has he made?"

Harriet wouldn't meet her look.

"Do you even know why you're here? Has he told you what's happening?"

"I came here of my own free will," said Harriet, finally. "I've made my choices, and I've chosen to reject my old life. You don't get to take that away from me."

"Free will?" said Mel. "Is that why you're cut off from the world – nothing, not even a phone. Is that why that door at the end of the corridor is locked? When was the last time you even set foot outside?"

"Locked doors only exist in the mind," said Harriet. She sounded as if she were quoting from a teenagers' magazine, or an inspirational website.

Mel wanted to slap her. She had to remind herself that this wasn't Harriet, this was what had been done to her. Somehow Glenn had managed to convince her she actually wanted all this.

"There's a group of men out there," Mel said, patiently. "Rich men who can have whatever they want. And what they want is a girl who looks illegal, who they can have whether she wants it or not. And one of the reasons they want to indulge in the fantasy of raping a child – because that's what this is... one of the reasons is that they want revenge against that girl's biological father. Whatever Glenn's told you, that's the reality of it."

"I know about the men," Harriet said, her voice calm, silencing Mel. "It's not like that. He said you'd say all kinds of horrible things. Your father's daughter, trying to control me, as always."

This was seriously screwed up. How had Glenn managed to twist Harriet's perception of the entire world in so short a time?

It was like telling a lie, she realized. The best lies are couched in truth.

And these lies Glenn had planted in Harriet's head – he'd taken the truth that Mel had always looked out for Harriet and twisted it into the idea that she had controlled her. He'd taken the truth that Doug Conner had always felt some kind of responsibility toward his secret child, and twisted it into the idea that Harriet's life, rather than being as remarkably free and liberated as it had been, was somehow constrained and manipulated.

He'd taken the knowledge that Mel would try to convince Harriet of all this, and built it into those fantasies of control and manipulation, so that whatever Mel might say would always work against her.

Again, she was reminded of how Glenn had always been at least one step ahead.

She couldn't let it go, though. "These men want to destroy you," she said softly. "And they'll have fun doing so. That's what they're paying for. That's what they're buying. You're not going to end up as some millionaire's girlfriend, living in the south of France."

One last try… "And what about me? If Glenn's offering you a path to some kind of freedom, then why am

I here? Why has he locked me up? Why is he going to sell me off to the highest bidder, too?"

For a moment she thought the simple logic of that observation had chipped through Harriet's cold veneer, then the girl shrugged, still hugging herself. Said, "He told me you'd say that. You're just one of them. You always have been."

Mel looked away.

"We'll get through this, Harriet. I promise you, we'll get through."

19. JIMMY

The crowd at the Flag and Flowers had thinned. Fewer people in black, in suits and somber dresses, and more in casual clothing or dressed up for Friday night out, as mourners had left and normal customers replaced them.

Young guys in hoodies and joggers clustered around the games machines, their voices loud, their movements exaggerated. A mixed group in their teens and early twenties now occupied the window seat where Frank had been earlier. Orange skin and hair gel, piercings, lots of exposed flesh. It made Jimmy feel old.

He pushed through to the back bar, unconcerned by the raised voices left in his wake.

Let anyone try to stop him right now. Just let them.

He saw a few more familiar faces here in the back bar. Family, friends of the old man, business acquaintances.

There was no sign of Glenn and his big-hitting friends, though. Now Frank was holding court at the family table at the back, one arm draped across the shoulders of Auntie Cyn, who looked as if she'd been crying again. Jimmy was struck again by the oddness of being a stranger in his own family.

Then the red haze descended once more and he strode over to stand before Frank.

Everyone at the table turned to stare. Frank, Cyn, the lad Tyler who was some kind of cousin; Billy Macrae and Kieran Lee; the redheaded dancer he'd sat next to earlier.

"Where is he?" Jimmy demanded, glaring at Frank.

His uncle didn't react, other than matching that glare with one of his own. Jimmy knew of at least two men for whom that glare had been the last thing they'd seen.

"Leave now, Jimmy," said Frank calmly. "I don't want to have to make you."

Only now did the rational, trained part of Jimmy's mind kick in. He'd come here with no plan, had barely given a thought to how this might play out. If he had, he'd have known an approach like this would never work.

He hadn't thought it through, though. He'd just burst in, hoping Glenn would still be here.

"Just tell me where he is, Frank," he said, forcing his frame to slump, a visible signal to his uncle that the moment of confrontation was past.

Frank shook his head. "I genuinely don't know," he said. "I'm not his babysitter. Your old man made that clear: Glenn's The Man now. Me? I've retired from all that crap. And good riddance."

Frank had been drinking all day. His words, although not slurred, were slow and enunciated, his every movement careful.

"I need to find him," said Jimmy. "Before he does something stupid."

Frank laughed at that, shaking his head. Then – slowly, deliberately – he stood.

He was still an imposing man, taller and broader than Jimmy, his boxer's nose reinforcing an impression of casual menace.

"I *said* I don't know where your brother is, and I asked you very politely to fuck off. Now which part of that didn't you understand?"

Jimmy's mind rushed through the kind of calculations he'd had to make many times before now. Assessing the risk, not just from Frank but from all the other drunken mourners who were following this escalating confrontation. Assessing the consequences of rising to Frank's challenge or making good his escape. Separating out the elements of pride, the testosterone haze, the potential humiliation of either losing or backing off.

He could take Frank, he knew. He was younger, stronger, faster, and trained. He could probably take on most of the other drunks in this room, too.

But it was a distraction. None of this mattered – the testosterone haze, the thoughts of what they would think of him, whatever. He didn't need any of this.

He turned, and walked out through the bar.

For a moment silence descended as drunken brains struggled to catch up. Then a jeer, a burst of laughter, a rising babble of voices.

And then the pub doors were swinging shut behind Jimmy and he stood outside, pausing to let his brain catch up, to try to focus, and work out what the hell to do next.

He sat on the bed in Mel's room. A space to think.

He'd come here on the pretext that there might, conceivably, be some kind of clue. Something to indicate her thinking. An insight into the woman she had become. Anything that might somehow make sense of the story of the past 48 hours.

He knew that was bollocks, though.

He'd come here because it was the most tangible connection he had with her. The few things she'd deposited in this room before heading out for the evening – the make-up, the wash bag, the clothes. Pieces of Mel Conner.

The air she'd breathed. One small space she'd considered, even temporarily, her own.

He'd spent the night here with her, and the morning after.

That was all he had.

When he'd knocked on the door, Mr Singh had clearly wanted to turn him away. But then he seemed to read something in Jimmy's expression. In the time Mel had been here, she'd shown up with bruises on her nose and neck, she'd brought Jimmy in his blood-soaked shirt, she'd gone missing.

"Is Ms Conner in trouble?" Singh said, stepping back to let Jimmy in.

"I hope not."

"I only started having people stay here last month," said Singh. "Is it always like this?"

"I won't be long," Jimmy told him. "I just need to check her things."

And so now he sat here, legs twisted so his shoes were clear of the bed covers, Mel's bag beside him, its contents tipped out.

Again, he came close to calling Doug Conner. Mel's father should at least be made aware of what was happening.

He didn't even reach for his phone.

He had to think this through.

So what did he know?

Glenn had been lying. Playing games with Jimmy. He'd sent the dancer, Suze, after Mel at the King's Head the previous evening, and the two of them had left sometime after eight in a car that had been waiting outside for them – clearly a planned maneuver and not a spontaneous thing. Around that time, Mel's phone had gone offline, so either she had handed it over for some reason or it had been removed from her possession.

Had Glenn made some kind of deal with her, and handing her phone over had been part of that? Or had she been duped, and the phone taken from her either by force or stealth, a hand slipped into her bag when her attention was distracted?

And if Glenn had Mel, then that must surely mean he had Harriet, too.

What kind of game was his brother playing?

Jimmy hated to think of his family in their own preferred terms, as old-school villains with principles, but that was what they had always been. The Lazenby family had been responsible for some serious crime, but kidnapping had never been part of the portfolio.

Revenge had been, though. The idea of 'face': that you never let anyone get the better of you.

Doug Conner had said this was all about revenge. That was why Glenn had taken Harriet, and now it must be why he'd taken Mel, too.

Revenge against Conner, but also a chance to come out on top over Jimmy – that 'face' thing, again.

So what was his end game?

Murder? Let the bodies turn up somewhere, so Conner and Jimmy would know they'd been bettered? In that case, Harriet was almost certainly dead already. Mel, too, in all probability.

Or would Glenn draw out their suffering first, so Conner and Jimmy would have to live with the knowledge of what had happened to them?

He knew that by far the most likely scenario was that Harriet and Mel were dead already.

The other scenarios – that they were being kept alive in order to maximize suffering, that they might be handed over in exchange for something even more important to Glenn, that there was some kind of vaguely innocent explanation still – were highly unlikely.

But they were all he had.

He couldn't give up now.

"Hey, Mamta, don't you have a life?"

"No, sir. My husband has left me for his twenty-two-year-old mistress, and I comfort eat when I'm on my own at home, so this job is my safe haven. What can I do for you?"

Mamta Patil was happily married and skinny as a stick, last time he'd checked.

"Glenn Lazenby. I need details of any properties in which he has an interest – places he owns or has leases to, places he visits, places he's looked at lingeringly. I need a phone trace on him, too. A record of where his phone's been over the last forty-eight hours. The same for Ronnie Bosvelt, Emre Denis, Thom Sullivan, David Viera, Frank Lazenby. Cross-references between their movements. Anything you can find."

"And you want all that asap, right?"

"Afraid so."

"I'll have details with you as soon as possible, sir."

The line went dead.

Idly, he flicked through the things lying beside him on the bed. A top, a pair of linen trousers that had been neatly rolled until he tipped the bag out, toiletries, a pen, a notebook – which had snagged his attention until he opened it and found it blank, unused.

This was stupid. It's not as if Mel had known in advance she was going to be abducted. There were no clues here.

He went to the window and looked out over a neat array of urban gardens. Bird tables, shrubs, trampolines surrounded by safety netting, patios, and barbecues.

He went down to his car, came back in with a laptop.

Back in Mel's room, he sat at the dressing table, scrolling through reports, intelligence chatter, social media, news reports on anything involving Glenn and his cohort.

Close to eleven, Patil messaged him, said there was a report waiting for him on the Section Eight system.

She'd been thorough, as she always was. Logs of phone activities for the people he'd named. Details of properties owned and leased, of hotels stayed at, flights taken. All these details were layered onto a heat map of their activities in the area. Clusters around the town, and down in London. Other hotspots across the Home Counties – country homes, industrial units, commercial premises.

In the last 48 hours, Glenn had remained within a few miles of his home town. Or, at least, his phone had – Patil's trace was on the phone records, not the person.

There were gaps, too, though. Periods of an hour or two when his phone had been turned off.

Why would he do that, other than to conceal his activities?

Jimmy stared at the reports and maps until his head hurt, trying to extrapolate from those gaps, from the last known locations before phone silence, to the locations where the phone was reactivated.

It was no good, though. All he could determine was that, if Glenn had kept his silenced phone on him, at least, then he'd probably not strayed more than twenty miles or so from the center of town. That still left a vast area where he might have been.

He didn't even know that Glenn would have gone anywhere near where Mel and Harriet were being held.

Jimmy was sure he would though… Glenn would not miss a chance to gloat and witness the suffering he was causing.

Jimmy looked again at the list of properties. Ryders, the Flag and Flowers, half a dozen more commercial addresses in the center of town. The old family home on the south side of town, a modest Victorian townhouse that had been in the family for years before the old man started to bring in serious money. The farmhouse their father had bought to the north of town, where Jimmy had lived with his family for a few years before leaving for good.

He pictured the place, the sprawl of outbuildings. Of all the properties Patil had found, this was the most likely, perhaps. Familiar territory. But would Glenn be stupid enough to hold them at the family home? Some anonymous industrial unit would make far more sense. He started to scan through the details of commercial properties around the town where the family had at least a tentative interest. So many!

He closed his eyes, took a deep breath and held it. He needed to think like Glenn, like a Lazenby.

Yes, Glenn would make sure to minimize the risk. But he was an egotistical bastard, too. Playing host to his 'guests' at the family home would appeal to something in him.

Jimmy's head was spinning by now, jumping from one likely conclusion to the opposite and back again. But he had to start somewhere.

Jimmy closed the laptop, let himself out of the house, and went back to his car, trying hard to convince himself he wasn't clutching at the flimsiest of straws.

They could be anywhere, and here he was, doing little better than guessing.

Frustrated, he stabbed a finger at the ignition button, kicking the car into life, and set off along roads far too familiar.

The farm brought back memories long buried.

Jimmy's mother had been the stabilizing influence, the rock of the family. When she became ill they'd stayed on in their modest townhouse even though they could have afforded somewhere far more comfortable – stayed there right until the end, when cancer took her, with Jimmy still only in his teens.

After that his father had said he couldn't stay in the same house, but to Jimmy it was as if the old man had been liberated. Now he could spend the money he'd accumulated, could live the life he'd earned, as he put it one drunken night with Frank and the boys.

The farm had already been a base of operations for years – the outhouses cover for lorries that came and went in the dead of night, the house itself a base away from the prying eyes in town. After the death of his wife, Trevor Lazenby had moved to the farm, taking his two sons, and an ever-changing entourage of minders, hookers, business associates, and lovers.

In Jimmy's memory, the farm was the place where his father's inner monster, previously constrained, had finally emerged.

He wished he'd burned the place down when he left ten years before.

He approached along the farm's private track from the public road with lights off, relying on night vision and memory. He parked on an area of hard-standing where a barn had once been, still a couple of hundred meters from the farm.

Glenn still lived here, at least occasionally, according to the files, and the address was flagged up repeatedly in the dossier Conner had given Jimmy, still a base for Lazenby family operations.

The place was in darkness, though, which could not be a good sign. If Glenn had Harriet and Mel here, there would be guards and others. People would be awake, and that meant lights on at least somewhere in the building.

Unless they were trying to give the impression of abandonment.

He approached on foot, the way lit by stars and a half moon.

Somewhere an owl screeched.

From what he could see, the property looked well-maintained. The hedge neatly trimmed, the paintwork around doors and windows fresh.

There were no cars in the yard at the front, and as he circled the main building, there was nothing but a tractor and an old van with a wheel missing at the rear.

A white box truck occupied one barn, but that was it.

He worked his way from outbuilding to outbuilding. Again, there were plenty of signs that this place was in regular use, but nothing to indicate it was currently occupied.

He was putting off checking main farmhouse, he knew.

There was a door at the back that led into a half-basement – the point of entry least likely to draw attention if he had to force it. It took him seconds to work the lock, and then he was down the half-dozen steps into a wide basement stacked with boxes.

He climbed a flight of stairs and paused at the door that opened onto a hallway on the main floor, listening for long seconds. Nothing.

In the hallway, again, nothing.

He hated the way this place transported him back. The feeling that at any moment he'd hear his father's voice, that he'd know a shit-storm was about to descend.

Glenn had taken beatings for him, and, as many times in return, Jimmy had taken them for his brother. They'd had each other's backs for the longest time.

He worked through the ground floor, lingering in a room Glenn had made into an office.

He was getting nowhere.

He went upstairs, and checked through the bedrooms and dressing rooms and god knows what, but still found nothing. No sign that Mel or Harriet were here, or had ever been here.

There were clear signs that Glenn lived here, though. This was his place – his clothes and shoes; a games room; photos of Glenn and their parents, and even one or two where Jimmy featured.

This, at least, was a minor result. If this was Glenn's home and he was not here, even though he had been in town until late, where was he now?

Did he stay at one of the other places he had around the town with one of the dancers, or was there somewhere more important for him to be?

He drove around. He should sleep, he knew, but he wouldn't, and anyway, night was the best time to observe atypical activity on many kinds of premises. A farmhouse with lights burning in the early hours; an industrial unit with cars parked overnight.

He stopped for a time at a block of warehouses leased by a company indirectly owned by the family, drawn to the burning lights coming from within. Then an articulated lorry pulled up, reversed into a loading bay and metal doors rolled up to reveal one unit's cavernous interior. Night deliveries of some sort. Just normal activity.

The story was the same elsewhere. The old family home in town, in darkness now. The Flag and Flowers and two other pubs, closed up for the night. Ryders still open, but then that was normal for the kind of place it was. Another industrial unit, this time in darkness, and revealing nothing suspicious when Jimmy let himself in.

He parked up in a picnic area in the woods to the north of town, tipped his seat back and was asleep in seconds.

Woke to sunlight, the sound of birds. Checked his phone, but nothing.

He drove back into town.

He'd call Conner when he got there. He'd run out of options, run out of time.

He'd never failed on a case before. Never run out of ideas.

But this time he'd got so much wrong, every step of the way.

Was too involved, too close.

Conner had got it wrong, too, sending Jimmy in. He should have sent someone who didn't give a shit, and who wouldn't have got lost in it all.

The main reason Jimmy had got it so wrong was the illusion that he understood his own brother. They'd grown up together, had each other's backs. Competed with each other and stood by each other at the same time. They had history. Each knew how the other worked, how he thought.

But ten years was a long time.

Glenn was someone very different now, a man twisted by resentment and simultaneously liberated by the death of their father.

And despite all the aura around the family, the illusion of being villains with principles, old-school gangsters, Glenn had become something else entirely. Ruthless and cruel. Relentless.

He was not their father – he was something far worse, and it shocked Jimmy to see this.

He stopped outside Uncle Frank's house on the edge of town, an anonymous suburban redbrick surrounded by neat shrubberies and flower beds, immaculate bowling-green lawns. Frank had learned to garden when he was in jail, the growing cycles of his crops giving him a sense of scale, and time passing. It wasn't something you'd necessarily associate with a man like Frank Lazenby, but was clearly something he'd stuck with in his retirement.

It was still early, but from his vantage point in the back garden Jimmy spotted movement in the kitchen window. Frank, filling a kettle, scratching his jaw, stretching.

Jimmy had been over-complicating things. Relying on technology, on other people, on protocol and established approaches.

He needed to be more direct.

He went over to the back door, and stood where Frank would see his shape through the frosted glass.

Waited for the door to open.

Frank came out, and eyed him up and down. Said, "I thought you were fucking off, like you were told?" He didn't seem surprised, though. He nodded toward a set of black wrought-iron chairs and they sat.

"He's out of control, isn't he?" said Jimmy. He remembered Frank's wry laugh when Jimmy had said he needed to find Glenn before he did something stupid. He knew.

"Glenn was never *in* control," said Frank. "He just knew how to create the illusion. I was the only one who ever understood that. I'm retired now, Jimmy. I'm not a part of it anymore. We all have to know when to walk away, don't we?"

Like in the Flag and Flowers last night, Jimmy turning away from the challenge, the jeers. Sometimes 'face' had to be put aside.

"Where is he?"

Still, Frank shook his head. He shrugged, then, and said, "Not my business, is it?"

"Is kidnap your business? That and whatever else he's got into? Help me, Frank. Do the right thing."

Silence, still. Frank sat with his gaze averted, as if studying his immaculate lawn.

"What would the old man have made of all this?" said Jimmy. That moment of realization as he drove, the understanding that all the old bullshit about villains with principles might actually have meant something. His father was a bastard. Frank was a bastard. But neither one of them was what Glenn had become.

Frank laughed, short and sharp, shaking his head.

"You could have been something, you know?" he said, obliquely. "If you'd stuck around."

"I am," said Jimmy. "I'm someone who stops shit like this. And you know what? I reckon that somewhere in his heart the old man would have got that."

"Maybe he did."

Jimmy looked away, took his own turn at studying the lawn, the evenly trimmed blades briefly blurring.

"You checked the farm?"

Jimmy nodded. "Where else?"

"He's been spending time with Ronnie Bosvelt and Thom Sullivan," said Frank, the distaste clear in his tone. "Sullivan has an old farmhouse on the edge of Hatherly Forest. Used to be the Slater place."

Jimmy knew the farm. Terry Slater had been a friend of Trevor Lazenby, had ended up owing him for getting him out of some big gambling debts and had done occasional jobs for the family ever since. No doubt Sullivan had got hold of the place through Lazenby connections. Jimmy wouldn't be surprised if his brother had called in Slater's debts once their father had lost his grip, seeing an opportunity to use the property to ingratiate him with his new friend.

"That's where they are?" he asked.

Frank shrugged. "I don't know. Like I say, I'm well out of it all now. Your brother gives me the creeps, and not many people have ever done that." He paused, then went on, "But he's been out there a lot recently. Even before Sullivan was back in the country. Has to have a reason, doesn't he?"

Jimmy stood, and his uncle followed suit, the two coming to stand awkwardly, facing each other.

Finally, Jimmy nodded, started to turn, then paused as Frank came to him, took him into a brief hug, stepped back.

"You're right," Frank told him. "Your brother's out of control. Look out for yourself, you hear?"

"I will."

He made the call from where he'd parked, deep in the shade of the trees, a hundred meters past the turning to the old Slater Farm.

A quick reconnoiter had been enough to confirm that the place was in use, with four cars parked to the rear, including Glenn's black Range Rover.

"Sir."

"Jimmy." His controller's voice gave nothing away.

"I'm making progress. You were right, it's Glenn. I don't know quite what his game is, but…" The crunch. He braced himself for Doug Conner's reaction as he went on, "He has both of them. Harriet and Mel."

Nothing. Seconds passed.

Then: "I know. You have it in hand?"

Of course Conner knew. Even though he'd stepped back from direct involvement, it was inevitable he'd be monitoring things.

"I think so. I… I don't know what I'm going to find."

"We rarely do."

And so Jimmy brought his controller up to speed, told him about Glenn, and what Frank had told him. Told him where he was and what he was going to do.

And then he climbed out of the car, closed the door gently, and set off through the trees.

20. MEL

What could she possibly do?

She explored the wing of the farmhouse they'd been allocated, searching for any way out, anything that could be used as a weapon.

But seriously… a weapon against a man-mountain like Wayne, who was just looking for any excuse to beat the crap out of her, rape her, punish her…?

And escape… They were only one floor up, but it was an old building, the ceilings high. The drop from any of the windows she could actually open was high enough, and the ground beneath so uneven, that she was sure she would break an ankle if she jumped. There were bed sheets they could use as ropes, but how did that really work? How did you tie a sheet so securely to something it would hold and take your weight? Even if you could trust the person still in the room above you to neither untie the sheet nor give the alarm to their captors.

She was tempted to try, even so. Would Harriet really go against her? Even if the girl somehow believed this bizarre situation was her own choice, surely she must see that it wasn't Mel's?

"We could get out of here," Mel said from her vantage point by the window. "Let ourselves down from one of the windows. Get to the woods, the road."

Harriet didn't even bother answering.

How much must she have hated her former life, that she now clung so stubbornly to whatever fantasy Glenn had offered her?

Mel didn't say any more. Every time she tried, the pattern was the same: the sullen silence until… breaking point, and an outburst against Mel, Penny, Doug Conner, the world. At times like that it was hard to tell if this was something Glenn had done to her, or if at least some of this was the true Harriet Rayner, her inner bitch finally set free.

They watched films of Harriet's choosing. Mel didn't care what was on – it was all distraction, and if Harriet felt in control maybe that was a good thing.

Mel prowled their wing, unable to stay still for long.

Time seemed to have slowed, and she'd never felt so powerless.

She knew Glenn was away at the funeral, so this should be the ideal opportunity to get out of here, but there didn't seem a way that wouldn't land them in a worse position than they were already in.

She tried to occupy her mind. Stop herself thinking about what might come next.

She absolutely refused to allow herself even the slightest fantasy of hope.

Jimmy might be looking for her by now. Her father. The police. But all these things were beyond her influence, no more than guesses about what might be happening in the wider world.

All that could concern her right now was this. The few rooms she could roam. Harriet. The mindless stupid movies playing on that big screen on the wall.

The day passed. The evening.

Someone brought food, but she didn't see who. One minute she was sitting with Harriet, and the next the girl was coming back in with a tray bearing pizza, drinks.

She gave in and ate, unable to hold out any longer.

Was this how it happened? At first you resist, but then after a day or so you buckle, and once you've accepted food and drink, you've started to accept what's happening to you, until finally, a week later, you end up like Harriet?

The lights of several cars sweeping up the farm lane outside marked the return of Glenn and his friends, late that evening.

She watched the lights approach from her vantage point, watched them swing round to the other side of the farm, out of sight.

Minutes later she heard distant voices, laughter, from somewhere downstairs.

She saw the change in Harriet. The sudden anticipation. The alertness. The way her eyes kept flicking toward the door. The change in her posture, even.

Then the disappointment, as the voices fell silent.

Mel wanted to reach for her, draw her into a hug. Make some kind of connection. But every time she'd tried to do so it had been thrown back in her face. Why would it be any different now?

They went to bed a short time later, Harriet in one of the bedrooms here, and Mel retreating to the small boxroom where she'd spent the previous night. Odd how there should be comfort in even a trace of familiarity, when your whole world had been snatched away.

Surely Jimmy was looking for her by now?

How many times would he try calling her before concluding her silence was sinister?

She clung to that hope, lay with her arms wrapped tight around herself, her knees drawn up.

She'd never dreaded what the next day would bring as much as she did right now.

Glenn came the next morning. The moment they heard sounds from the corridor Harriet perked up, leaped from her chair and paused, smoothing down her clothes, her hair.

When the door opened, she went to him, paused by him, like a dog craving attention but not quite sure what response it would get.

"Babes," said Glenn unctuously, putting his hands on the girl's arms, drawing her in, kissing her on the cheek, and all the time his eyes on Mel.

"It's all good, babe," he said to the girl. "It'll all be different once we're out of the country, you wait and see."

The worshipping look on Harriet's face was chilling. Glenn really had brainwashed her. Blinded her to what was happening, what he really was.

"Oh please," said Mel.

Harriet pulled away, her gaze flitting up, down, sideways, down again, her skin actually blushing pink.

"Really?" said Mel now, squaring up to her friend, finally letting the anger and frustration boil to the surface. "Can't you see how pathetic you look?"

Now Harriet's shy flush deepened, her gaze hardening and fixing on Mel, surprised perhaps at the animosity in Mel's voice.

"Okay," said Mel, "I've had enough of all this… this *bullshit.* Just spare me, okay?" She glared at Harriet, and went on: "And you, you spoilt, ungrateful little bitch… Well, I hope you enjoy the fate you claim you've so freely chosen, I really do. But right now you can just clear off. Glenn and I have some grown-up business to discuss."

Harriet stared at her. Her lip trembled, then the muscles in her face tightened, tears and anger vying with each other. She opened her mouth to say something, but Glenn cut her off with a hand sharply raised, and said, "Give us five, would you, babes? I think your friend has something she wants to say to me in private."

Harriet looked from Glenn to Mel, outflanked, angry, uncertain. Then with a toss of the head she turned and marched from the room, and moments later her bedroom door slammed resoundingly shut.

Mel turned her glare on Glenn, but he didn't flinch, just stood there, that smug, superior grin on his face.

"Feeling the strain, darling?"

She wanted to punch him. Instead, she forced herself to slow down, to breathe. She couldn't lose control now. Couldn't give that to him.

"Please," she said. "Let Harriet go. She's an innocent. She's never done anything to you."

He shrugged, spread his hands, palms out. "You see?" he said. "You keep using words like 'innocent'. You should know by now that's part of the appeal."

He laughed, and Mel breathed long and deep. Slow.

"You've lied to her," she said. "I don't know how you've made her believe the lies, but you have."

"She came with me freely," said Glenn. "I offered her the world and she said 'yes'. Tell me what crime I've committed."

"You're selling her off to the highest bidder. To men who only want to use her and hurt her in some perverted kind of revenge against the man she doesn't even recognize as her father."

"Ah, but Doug Conner recognizes *her*, doesn't he? That's the bit that matters. Nobody gives a shit what

Harriet fucking Rayner thinks, do they? The stupid little tart."

He shrugged again. "And anyway," he said, "It's not an auction. This isn't modern day slavery. Don't think of it as a bidding process – think of it as a job interview for a role she's uniquely qualified for. One culminating in a legally binding contract, which she'll enter into voluntarily."

"She's only just turned seventeen."

"As I say, uniquely qualified."

"She looks like a child!"

"And that makes her worth more. What's your problem, Mels?"

"Pedophilia, for starters."

"The kid has daddy issues. My friends like it rough and barely legal. She's their dream, their fantasy, and I'm handing her to them on a plate."

"Selling her to them."

"I facilitate. It's what we Lazenbies do."

"She'll see through you, eventually."

He shook his head. "You think?" he said. "She's blind. And fucking stupid. And anyway, this time tomorrow I'll be shot of her. Shot of both of you. Believe me, darling, I don't give a flying fuck whether she sees through me or not because within a few hours you'll both be out of my life for good."

"You won't get away with this."

He laughed. "No? Just watch, darling, Just you watch."

And with that he went to the door, before pausing, turning, and saying, "Scrub yourself up, you hear? I want you to look your best for your suitors. And you never know your luck: I might just let them sample the goods before they commit to bidding. It's only polite. Just you, though – not Harriet. I want to at least preserve the illusion that little slut is pure and untouched."

Then he turned again and left. Seconds later, Mel heard the thud of the door at the end of the corridor.

She let go the breath she'd been holding.

How had she never really seen just how bad a person Glenn Lazenby was? Oh, she'd hated him, of course. Despised him. But still... She'd never seen the true evil in him.

She heard a door, turned, and saw Harriet standing in the doorway of her bedroom.

"You heard all that?" Mel asked, and Harriet nodded.

Of course she had. Banishing her from the room so 'the grown-ups' could talk had pressed all the right buttons. The girl had been physically unable to do anything *but* stand at the door eavesdropping.

"Do you believe me now?"

And again, Harriet slowly nodded.

"He said it'd be different. Once we were out of the country."

"He got into your head."

Mel had never known anyone like Glenn Lazenby for getting inside people's heads. He'd done it to Jimmy all their lives, he did it to her, he'd done it to Harriet. Oh, how he'd done it to Harriet!

"He wanted to destroy you," Mel went on, "and screwing with your head is how he does that to people."

"So," said Harriet, "what now?"

"The food," said Mel. "Last night: how did you know the food was here? You went out to get it."

"There's a telecom," said Harriet. "By the door at the end of the hallway. It buzzed, and I heard it – you must have missed it."

Mel thought back, but couldn't recall hearing anything in the moment before Harriet jumped to her feet. Maybe she had, but had thought it was something on the movie's soundtrack.

"Can you use it to call out?"

Harriet nodded.

A short time later, they stood by the telecom, looking at each other.

Mel nodded, and Harriet pressed Call.

"Yeah?"

"Hey, Suze, that you?"

A bored grunt of acknowledgment.

"Any chance of some breakfast? Some coffee at least?"

Ten minutes later, the door swung open, and Suze stepped into the corridor. She looked odd in jeans and a hoodie, and not her usual fishnets, mini-skirt and bustier outfit, although obviously she wouldn't dress like a stripper all the time. In one hand she had a cafetière of coffee, and in the other two cups.

From the doorway of the main living room, Harriet smiled, and said, "Hey." Then the girl hugged herself, looking vulnerable, maybe coming down from a high. A shrug, then, a smile. "I don't suppose there's any chance of–"

Mel stepped out from behind the door, and threw herself forward, barging into Suze from the side. The dancer grunted, swore, twisted, fighting for balance. Hot coffee sprayed through the air and the cups clattered against the wall.

Suze staggered sideways, through the open doorway of the boxroom where Mel had been locked on her first night here. Mel caught herself on the frame, reached for the door and slammed it shut, twisting the key in the lock just as Suze tugged at the door from the other side.

The lock clunked home.

From within the room, Suze's voice was angry, screeching, but thankfully, muffled.

"Quick," said Mel. "Stick with me."

They emerged onto the landing. Would they post a guard here, as well as keeping that heavy door locked?

There was no-one.

"Do you know the layout?" Mel asked.

Harriet shook her head. "Only our rooms," she said.

Mel tried to remember. The stairs down to an entrance lobby, the rooms opening off it, that one room where she'd waited when she first got here, when she'd actually thought Suze was on her side.

She heard voices downstairs.

They couldn't just head down and leave by the front door. They'd be too exposed.

But equally, they couldn't delay. Suze's absence would be noticed, or her muffled shouting heard.

Two more corridors led off this landing area, and more stairs led up to another floor. Glenn had described the rooms where they'd been imprisoned as a wing, so presumably the corridor opposite led to the building's other wing.

Mel took Harriet's hand and led her to the other corridor, heading straight back. If the other wing mirrored theirs, then there was no way out in that direction, but there might be something along here.

This other corridor led to the back of the building – maybe there would be another staircase. Servants' stairs, perhaps? The building was old enough, and large enough for there to be more than one staircase.

The two proceeded cautiously, Mel fearful that at any moment a door might burst open and they'd be confronted by their captors.

They had to keep moving. Had to get out of here.

Already, her thoughts were racing ahead, visualizing the layout of the farm buildings, pieced together from what she'd been able to see from their windows and what she'd seen from Suze's car as they approached the farm on Thursday evening.

If they could only get outside, it should just be a matter of finding the shortest, most out of sight, route to the trees, and then they would be hidden in the woods.

Did Glenn have dogs?

She stopped that line of thought. She'd gain nothing by making herself panic right now.

One step at a time.

This corridor, doors to either side closed.

They reached the end, but there was no staircase.

Perhaps the closed doors concealed it. But should they really try each door? What if someone was in one of the rooms?

Tentatively, she tried the nearest door, but it was locked.

Harriet was staring at her, so she smiled, hoping it was reassuring and not a mask of fear.

She looked around, and then she saw it.

At the end of the corridor was a sash window, like the ones in their rooms.

And beyond the window, a metal grid that formed a platform, surrounded by railings.

A fire escape! Outside the window was a fire escape!

She reached for the window, heart thumping.

Open, damn you!

The latch slid free easily, but the window itself wouldn't move. She heaved again, and the frame jerked up with a groan, then stuck.

Together, they pulled at the window, managing to work it up a little farther.

She eyed the gap. Was it enough?

She swung a leg through, resting her butt on the sill. Slipped her other leg through, and felt the window frame bearing down across her hips.

She wriggled, managed to get a little farther through. Twisted, and felt the frame give a little more, edge up another fraction.

Somehow, she squeezed through as far as her ribcage.

She was starting to panic now. She felt so damned vulnerable like this.

She tried not to think about getting stuck. Pulled and pushed and twisted, a fraction at a time. Breathed out to flatten her ribcage, and couldn't breathe fully back in, adding to the feeling of panic welling inside.

Then she felt something give, something shift, a painful dragging across her breasts as the weight of her body pulled on her.

The frame gave again, suddenly allowing her to breathe, and then she wriggled, pulled, and was tumbling free, down onto the hard metal platform of the fire escape.

She wanted to cry, she hurt so much.

But she couldn't.

On her knees, she peered back, suddenly fearful for Harriet.

The girl was eyeing the gap, her mouth open, her eyes wide. She was scared, maybe having second thoughts. What if someone came now?

"Come on," said Mel, beckoning. "Quick. I've got you."

She didn't know what she meant by that, but it seemed to work. Harriet swung one leg and then the other through the gap, and slithered through far more easily than Mel had – a combination of her skinny frame, and the gap having been forced wider by Mel's passage.

Mel caught her, realized she *had* got her. Held on for a moment, and then stepped back, turned.

Metal steps led down from the platform to the yard where the cars were parked.

If only they'd been able to get hold of keys to one of them, but she knew that had never been a possibility.

Simply to be out here, breathing fresh air, stepping cautiously down the steps, was miracle enough.

They were doing this!

They paused on solid ground, Mel getting her bearings.

There was a gap between the outbuildings across to the side of the main building. Maybe a hundred meters across rough grazing land to the first of the trees, with the outbuildings giving them some kind of cover most of the way.

She took Harriet's hand, and said, "Come on. This way."

When they reached the corner of the farmhouse, they paused again, and that was when Mel heard a dull thud, an impact of something on the ground behind them.

She looked back, looked up, looked down again.

Suze had jumped from a window, landed in a low squat to take the impact, and now was slowly uncoiling her tall frame, her eyes fixed on the two fugitives.

"Quick, run!" Mel snapped at Harriet. She turned and took a couple of steps, and that was when Wayne stepped out from the shade of an outbuilding, moved toward her and she felt his powerful grip closing on her upper arm, so hard she cried out until the other meaty hand closed on her mouth, smothering her so she feared she was going to suffocate.

She was powerless, could only pray that at least Harriet had been able to evade them.

But then, as Wayne drew her into his embrace, like a spider with its prey, she saw Suze standing over Harriet, the girl flat out on the ground, not moving.

And then Mel felt her feet lift from the ground, felt her body being crushed against Wayne's, his arms around her, his hand still covering her face. Felt swamped by his strength, over-powered by his presence, entirely at his mercy.

"You're mine now," he said softly. "So fucking *mine!*"

21. JIMMY

"You win. Name your price. Tell me what it is you're after. I'll come back. I'll do whatever you want."

He knew what Glenn wanted.

Revenge.

And here, right now, Jimmy was making a down-payment in humiliation.

The two stood in the entrance lobby to Thom Sullivan's farmhouse.

Jimmy knew this place well. Remembered it from parties the two of them had attended when they were teenagers, wild gatherings held by Terry Slater's daughter, who both Glenn and Jimmy had a thing for at one time. Briefly, she'd chosen Jimmy, even though he was the younger brother.

So it had always been.

Had Glenn chosen this place for the memories, some kind of symbol for the life he was avenging? Or was that coincidence, this simply being a convenient holding ground where he could keep the girls out of sight for a time?

Because if Glenn was here, Jimmy was sure Mel and Harriet could not be far away.

"Seriously?" said Glenn. "Now you want a part of it, after all this time?"

He seemed to have forgotten he'd virtually begged Jimmy to come back only the day before. For him, that had never been the prize, though – the prize was forcing his brother to make that mental shift, to give in.

"I can be useful," Jimmy said, breaking away from Glenn's searching eyes.

"And why would you do this now?"

"Let them go. Harriet. Mel. Me for them. There are things I know that could be valuable. Details of investigations. Information about your rivals. Information about the people you think are your friends. Harriet and Mel are nothing set against all that."

"Why would I ever trust a word you said?"

"Because by then I'd have lost everything. Leave me in position and you'd be right not to trust me: I could feed you all kinds of bullshit, and that's exactly what I'd do. But blacken my name and make me a fugitive, and all I'd have to bargain with would be the things in my head."

"What if I can't pay your price?" said Glenn. "What if I don't have them? Would you come back to the family anyway? Share your secrets, be part of it all again. Come back because it's the right thing to do, not because you think you can extract a price from me. There's a place for you, Jimbo. Just say the word."

He was playing mind games. Jimmy knew that.

Testing him.

Teasing him.

Pushing him to the edge.

"Where are they?"

"You're too late, Jimbo. Late to the game, like you always were."

"What do you mean?" He wouldn't allow himself to react, or to speculate. He clamped down on everything, focusing on his brother's face.

"You're right, I'll admit it. They were here. But not any longer. I sold them. Highest bidder. A job lot: two sisters, the sweet innocent one and the one with fight. You're too late, kid. They'll be on their way out of the country by now."

Jimmy didn't respond. He didn't allow his expression to change.

Mind games.

He knew never to believe a thing his brother told him, and never to be drawn into a response.

"Who? Where?"

Glenn laughed. "They're gone," he said. "Leave it at that."

"Why should I believe you?" It was like a dance, the two brothers circling each other. There was no trust. There never had been, never would be – and they both knew it.

Glenn spread his hands. "You want to look around? Be my guest."

It was impossible to tell if it was bluff or not. Glenn was the best liar Jimmy had ever encountered, at least partly because at any one moment he seemed to believe just about any words that came out of his own mouth.

Jimmy turned away, his mind racing through odds, statistics, probabilities.

He walked to the door. Let Glenn think he had won. That didn't matter now.

They had names. They knew who Glenn was dealing with. They were closing in.

They just had to get there before it was too late. Before Mel and Harriet had been smuggled out of the country to whatever fate awaited.

22. MEL

Mel tried to break free, but Wayne's grip was unbreakable.

He held her tight against him, so she felt the power of his body, felt every move, felt his breath on the crown of her head as his big hand clamped her mouth shut, forcing her head back against him. His other arm pressed crushingly against her belly and ribs, reaching across her front to hold her arm.

She couldn't move. Couldn't make any noise more than a pathetic whimper. Could barely even breathe.

What had happened to Harriet? Why was she still not moving?

Suze had hit her, taken her right out in one flowing movement as she rose from that squatting position where she'd landed below the window.

Harriet moved at last, and Suze dropped on top of her, knees either side of the girl's arms, a hand clamped across her face.

Why were they silencing them?

What had she missed?

Two figures, appearing around the front of the farmhouse.

Glenn.

Jimmy.

Talking intently, seen from the back.

Even if they turned, they probably wouldn't see Mel or the others, hidden in the harsh shadows between farmhouse and outbuildings.

She tried to cry out, but Wayne's hand only pressed harder across her face.

Tried to squirm free, but it was no good.

She felt as if she was about to black out, unable to breathe, smothered.

She felt dizzy, her vision darkening at the edges.

Everything started to drift, become not real. Glenn… Jimmy… they might not even have been real. Figments. Mirages.

Then… a slight tensing in Wayne's body, in the way he held her. She struggled to twist, to see, to…

She managed to raise one leg, bring it down sharply, her heel driving into the big man's instep. He wore heavy boots, but still the impact startled him and he flinched, grunted, squeezed harder with that big hand across her face.

He tensed then and she had an instant of absolute fear, knowing this must be the prelude to something new, something worse, and then… a tiny fraction of a second later an explosion ripped through the silence.

Wayne fell, one arm still around Mel's ribcage, and Mel crumpled with him, pulled down on top of him.

She felt a spatter of something hot and wet against her cheek, then the abrupt impact as the two of them hit the ground.

Reflexively, Wayne's fist had clamped around her arm, twisting her as they fell, and only now flopping free.

She gasped, cried out, tumbled away to end up lying on her side on the hard ground of the yard, staring back into the man's lifeless eyes, his mouth part open, and a dark red circle in the middle of his forehead, a red line of blood drawn down from it toward the ground.

She heard footsteps, felt hands on her, turning her, saw Jimmy looking down, so close.

Was this still a fragment, a cruel vision of some kind?

He drew her up to a sitting position, folded his arms around her.

This was no dream, no vision.

He'd found them. She'd thought he was walking away when she'd first spotted him with Glenn but he'd seen them. Maybe he'd heard Wayne's grunt when Mel had stamped on the big man's instep. He'd…

"Jimmy? I love you, Jimmy. I never stopped. You have to know that."

He squeezed. "I know, Mel. I know."

He drew away a little then, and she felt his arm move, saw him pointing his handgun in the direction of Harriet and Suze.

The dancer took one look and backed away, hands half-raised.

Harriet turned, pushed herself up, said, "Guys?" and nodded past them to where Glenn still stood at the front of the farmhouse.

He wasn't alone.

The gunshot must have drawn attention, and now he was flanked by two more men, each with a gun drawn and leveled on the three.

Jimmy was standing already, moving across to form at least a partial shield for Mel and Harriet, as they climbed to their feet.

He had his gun aimed, and Mel felt as if she was standing in the middle of some Wild West shoot-out.

She reached for Harriet, curled an arm around her friend's waist.

"I'll tell you what's going to happen, Glenn. Are you listening?" Jimmy paused, then went on: "Me and my two friends are going to walk away from here, and no-one else is going to get hurt. That's what's going to happen. That's all I want out of this."

"You've got nothing on me, Jimbo," said Glenn, after a long, calculating pause. "Nothing that will stick. By the time you get anyone here the place will be clean as a whistle."

"I know that. I don't care. I've got what I came for. I knew I'd never get to take you down as well, much as I'd like to."

She heard the bitterness in his tone and saw from Glenn's expression that he had too.

"You never had it in you, did you, kid?" Glenn said. Then: "Go on. Run. Tail between your legs. I don't care about you. I've realized that, at last. You don't matter."

Glenn turned, and walked back toward the farmhouse, arms across the shoulders of his two henchmen.

Jimmy turned to Mel, and shrugged. "I guess we walk," he said. "I may be brave, but I'm not stupid. I could never take this lot out alone, and both Glenn and I know that. But I don't care. I've got what I came for."

How tough must it be for him to simply walk away? To swallow his pride.

She went to him, just had to hold him again. "He hasn't won," she said. "He can't just get away with what he's done."

Jimmy smiled. Said, "Oh, I know that. Like I say, I knew I could never take out this lot alone, so I'm leaving that to your old man. See, I called him before I came in here…"

She stared. "But… you just let him–"

"I gave Glenn his moment," said Jimmy. "One little glimmer of triumph, and a bit of space to gloat, where he thinks he's got away with everything, where he might actually believe he's untouchable, before he loses everything. All I've done is give him a greater distance to fall. Mind games. It's exactly what Glenn would have done."

He reached for Mel's hand then, turned, and led her and Harriet down the lane that led away from the farm, and before they'd taken more than a dozen steps Mel saw dark cars approaching them from the main road.

23. MEL & JIMMY

The two lay tangled, spent. Skin pressing against skin, as if both feared ever losing touch again.

They kissed, slow and tender. Memories sparked, recent and very old. Of kisses, of touching, of snatched moments. Of one moment, still fresh, the look exchanged as he pressed, pushed, entered her slowly. The widening of eyes, the sag of jaws, the tensings and easings. The utter, deep connection.

Of starting to move, of savoring every sensation, every moment.

Reclaiming this, reclaiming each other. Reclaiming a future they'd lost.

Of…

"How can this ever work…? Us. This. You, doing whatever it is that you do."

He carried a gun. He did awful things, in the name of good. He would disappear at no notice, for unknown lengths of time. Might never return.

She knew this. They both did.

It was anything but a normal life.

"Ask your father. Your parents found a way."

They'd had anything but a normal life, too: Doug and Yvette Conner. They'd had ups and downs. Challenges, to say the least. Things that must have come close to pulling them apart. But they'd managed somehow, they'd stayed together. They'd made it work.

It must be possible.

They must have a chance.

"I love you."

"I love you, too."

They kissed, slow and tender.

Pressed skin against skin, as if both feared ever losing touch again.

About the author

PJ Adams is a bestselling writer of erotic romance and suspense – love stories with that added heat and adventure. Her most popular titles include *Rebound*, the Bailey Boys trilogy (*Trust*, *Hit Me* and *Ruthless*), and the standalone novels *Winner Takes All*, *Damage*, *Let's Make This Thing Happen*, and *Black Widow*. Writing under other names, PJ is a successful novelist, with several titles published by major publishing houses and optioned for movies.

Mailing list: http://pollyjadams.com/list.php
Web: http://www.pollyjadams.com/
Twitter: @pollyjadams
Facebook: https://www.facebook.com/pollyjadamswriter

PJ Adams
Web and mailing list: http://www.pollyjadams.com/
Twitter: @pollyjadams
Facebook: https://www.facebook.com/pollyjadamswriter